Dedication

This, my third fictional novel, is dedicated to my son, Matthew, and my brother.

Matthew has suffered from Cerebral Palsy since birth. Although confined to a wheelchair, his handsome smiling face lights up all our lives. He has a special affection for my brother, who has helped us both through thick and thin.

David R Dye

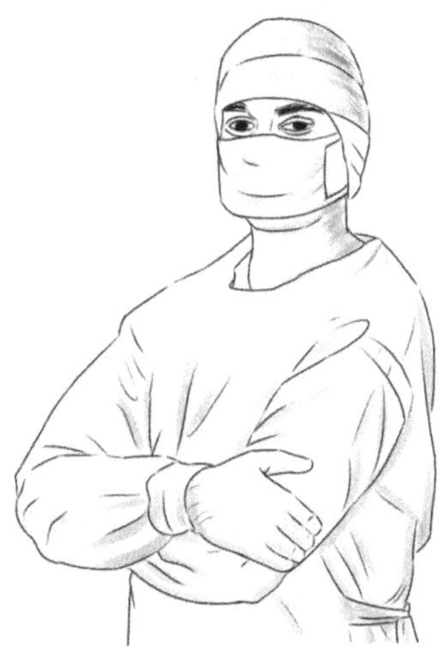

New Havana Syndrome!

Author: David R. Dye

First Published in 2025

ISBN 978-1-83538-571-5 (Paperback)
      978-1-83538-572-2 (Hardback)
      978-1-83538-573-9 (E-Book)

Book cover design and Book layout by:
      White Magic Studios
      www.whitemagicstudios.co.uk

Published by:
      Maple Publishers
      Fairbourne Drive, Atterbury,
      Milton Keynes,
      MK10 9RG, UK
      www.maplepublishers.com

A CIP catalogue record for this title is available from the British Library.

David R Dye

New Havana Syndrome

MAPLE
PUBLISHERS

David R. Dye

Anneliese and the Geezer

(Prequel to the book – Cold War, Hot Pursuit)

ISBN: 978-1-83538-335-3 (Paperback)

978-1-83538-336-0 (Hardback)

978-1-83538-337-7 (E-Book)

Cold War, Hot Pursuit

A Sequal which follows the under-cover career of agent Anneliese

ISBN: 978-1-83538-162-5 (Paperback)

978-1-83538-163-2 (E-Book)

Chapter 1

COBRA Meeting

The Cabinet office gradually quietened. The Prime Minister had called this COBRA meeting to discuss a new threat. In recent times there had been regular COBRA meetings because, politically, this was a very volatile and turbulent time.

The Gulf War had been raging for six months. There were severe security concerns over the continued presence of Sadam Hussein as Iraq's leader. The dissolution of the Soviet Union and Comecon was in full flow. And it seemed that most of the world was in recession and suffering economic pressure.

The cabinet office was full to the brim. Around 40 people in attendance, mostly having whispered conversations.

Now wanting to begin, the Prime Minister tapped his fountain pen on the table a few times. His head moved slowly back and forth, as he searched the faces throughout the room. Once or twice, his eyes back-tracked as he made a mental note of people he knew to be important to the meeting.

His gaze first fixed on Commander Synder Farrell, his Security Chief, seated at the end of the table. The PM nodded to him, but retained a serious expression. Next was the Health Secretary, but the PM's eyes quickly continued to scan. He soon found the two he was looking for. The Director General of GCHQ and the Assistant Director. Both had held their positions for more years than they cared to remember. That vast experience may be essential in tackling today's crisis!

Looking around the room as he spoke, the Prime Minister opened. "In the last week or so, you may have heard rumours, mumblings, about unidentified illnesses, among our Diplomatic Staff."

"The American Staff in various countries have suffered more than we have. It's real, and has been slowly escalating. Then only yesterday, GCHQ and my security advisors came to me with details of a new development. Our NHS Economists and Accountants will tell you that we import almost 50% of our medical equipment, facilities and technology from the United States of America."

"Yesterday, under the cover of darkness, two very important U.S medical companies were compromised. Their scientific laboratories were sabotaged; completely wrecked. In the same attack, their manufacturing facilities were destroyed. Their security personnel were disabled. Indeed, several employees in both facilities were killed. Their security systems were hacked and then obliterated."

"I would explain that these two companies were in totally different locations. Nearly a thousand miles apart. One in Boston, Massachusetts, the other in Wilmington, South Carolina. Both these suppliers are extremely important to the NHS. But, they will now be out of action for several months. This appears to be a coordinated terrorist attack, which may turn into a long-term strategy. We have to stop them or the fabric of our health service, indeed, the preservation of life in this country, may become severely challenged."

"I will now hand over to Commander Farrell to provide any further insights." The Commander raised his eyes from his note pad.

With an anguished expression, he scrolled around the faces before he spoke. "First, I must say that neither we nor the Americans know who is behind this. It's an extremely difficult one. No previous patterns to follow, other than one from many years ago. So we don't, I mean our Intelligence Analysts, don't have much faith in it having any significance. It's just a copy-book scenario from almost 40 years ago."

"Following the Cuban Revolution in 1959, the CIA recruited operatives on the ground in Cuba. They waged a violent campaign of terrorism and sabotage against facilities important to the Cuban economy. A secondary element involved the destruction of manufacturing and health care providers across the country."

"These clandestine operations ceased after the "Bay of Pigs" assault on Cuba in April 1961. This attempted insurrection totally failed because the CIA under-estimated Cuban military strength and popular support for Fidel Castro."

"At this time, all American diplomats were withdrawn, back to America. Almost completely in parallel with this withdrawal, the Russians secretly installed KGB agents and scientists on the Island."

"Most of the American diplomatic staff were recalled to the U.S.A, however, some were relocated to other parts of the world. A small proportion of these personnel subsequently suffered quite serious health issues. Some still exhibit this disabling affliction today!"

"We have a name for this condition, although it's not widely known because it has been so many years without any new cases. Until recently! This scourge was originally named "Sonic Evil". Over time, however, the U.S scientists re-named the condition "Havana Syndrome", as they became convinced that it had originated from Cuba."

Now, everyone had a chance to speak; to ask a question you needed to hold up the green card. The Home Secretary sitting opposite, in the middle of the table, held the card up, then was invited by the PM to speak. She smiled a thank you, then asked if anyone could describe the condition.

The Director General of GCHQ stepped forward. "It is reported that affected individuals suffer an acute onset of neurological symptoms associated with perceived localised loud noise. For example, screeching, chirping, clicking and piercing noises. Two thirds of the people experience visual disturbances such as blurred vision and sensitivity to light. These symptoms may not abate for months or even years! Recent cases have replicated this pattern."

The GCHQ Director scratched his cheek as he leant back against the office wall!

The PM continued. "We must be ready to handle the media on this condition. But you should also be aware that, due to yesterday's sabotage, we may rapidly find the NHS is unable to treat all Cardiac cases, kidney dialysis and ENT conditions. If there are more attacks, shortage of all types of equipment and devices may severely worsen."

"I am calling a halt to this meeting now, as I will convene a task force to work with the Americans on strategy and tactics. Any one of you may be seconded to this action group."

That evening, a small group were called to meet at the Foreign Office. The Health Minister and Chief Medical Officer, GCHQ Directors, the Chief Security Adviser and for good measure, two Neurological Consultants from Kings College Hospital. They would be available on video conferencing, if required.

The Prime Minister led them straight into business. "First, I have an announcement. Our Deputy Director of

GCHQ, Ruth Jepson has requested to retire in three months." All assembled looked toward Ruth. "After tonight, she will step down from this taskforce to work on wrapping up her outstanding assignments. I'm sure most of you know Ruth's worthy replacement, Jerome Janowski. Ruth will be a hard act to follow, Jerome, but I am confident you will do your very best!"

"Moving to our meeting subject, I am sure you all have noticed there are two completely consistent and compatible features with the Cuban scenario outlined earlier. That doesn't prove much or take us much further forward. But, at present, it's the only lead we have."

"Jerome will use his statistical prowess to work on this. He will, along with his Intelligence Analysts, turn over every rock, stone and boulder." The PM stopped and slowly looked down the table. "Commander Farrell, we need the best of your Counter Terrorism people to work with Jerome. I know you can't identify them but have you settled on your personnel to take on this assignment?" "Not quite Sir, they are flying in to meet me tomorrow and I am confident they will accept." "And Sir;" he took a breath as he scanned the faces in the room. He began again. "And Sir, you can all be assured they are the elite. They have worked with the CIA on several occasions and are renowned for their past achievements and expertise."

Chapter 2

Anneliese Arrives

The flight from Canada was on time, arriving mid-morning. Frank, already on an assignment in the UK, had been up at 7am for a teleconference call with the Commander. They had been preparing for their meeting with Anneliese.

Jerome and Frank were waiting by the Arrivals gate. Jerome looked a bit agitated; fidgeting, pulling a comb through his blonde hair, adjusting his man bag, pushing it to his front, then behind. He just couldn't wait to see Anneliese again. His thoughts trickled back over the gloriously happy times in Marbella, and then the finality of the sad ones in Buenos Aires. He thought of Albie and Barry, and the pain made his heart miss a beat.

In contrast, Frank stood looking at the paperbacks in the W.H. Smith racks. Cool, unmoved, nonchalant with that black beret angled down towards his right eye.

A sudden rush of people exiting arrivals got their attention. Frank moved close to Jerome, just as the elegant refined proportions of Anneliese appeared. In a delicate gossamer summer dress, she rushed towards Frank and Jerome. Anneliese flustered Frank with an embrace.

Jerome had matured into a strong, fit fellow with seriously attractive features. As he marshalled her cases, Anneliese clasped his arm, staring all the while at this handsome example of manhood.

The Commander's secretary had reserved a suite for Anneliese in a small boutique hotel close to Admiralty Arch; only a short walk to the Foreign Office for their 3pm meeting!

On the way to the hotel, Anneliese asked in her usual direct manner, "Jerome, how did you get promoted into such an exalted position?" Jerome, with a wide grin replied, "Probably due to all the things you taught me. No really, after I joined CECD, I spent several years studying mathematics, statistics in particular. I gained a degree, then worked hard every single day and, obviously, made a difference!"

After dropping off the cases, they strolled along The Mall, only a few hundred yards to the Foreign Office. As they climbed the steps, adjacent to the Foreign Office, Jerome gave Anneliese her security badge. They stopped for a moment as Jerome pinned it onto her dress. He also gave Frank a document to keep safe. A security pass, signed by the Prime Minister, listing all of them!

Jerome led the way through the massive, sparkling, white Georgian door, and then down a passageway. As they neared the end, Commander Farrell appeared. After a sincere, loving embrace for Anneliese, he vigorously shook Frank's hand. Then, with one arm around Jerome's shoulder, he escorted them into a meeting room.

"Oh, it is so good to see you. It's like deja vous all over again." They sat and exchanged pleasantries for just a few minutes. The Commander pressed on. "Will you please indulge me as I have a full calendar this afternoon?" He continued to detail in the briefest possible way, the events of recent days. "Jerome and Frank will be able to give you more information. However, my part in all this is to persuade you back to work with us. I know you have been away from this scene for a few years but it hasn't changed. You are sorely needed by this country. CECD need you and the CIA are imploring me to gain your acceptance. Frank and Jerome will be in your team and there is nobody else that delivers results the way you three always do. And I'm hoping you realise how much it would mean to me personally."

Anneliese stood, slowly paced across the room to the Commander. Leaning forward, her face lowered gently onto his cheek, as she pursed her lips. "We can never resist a difficult assignment, or indeed, the charming way you invite us to join you. So, yes I will be extremely happy to work with you and CECD once again!"

"Well, to finalise the initial plan, Frank and I would suggest the following. You three should spend some time at the CIA Headquarters in Langley, Virginia. Get more groundwork done and a better understanding of the potential assailants. For the moment, Jerome will remain here to continue in his world of statistical analysis. That may turn up some indicators of who we are dealing with and where they may hit next. In parallel, some work is needed on understanding the Havana Syndrome and the likelihood that it will worsen. The next step would involve identifying the causal factors. As a last resort, this may require a sortie into Cuba! You can all jointly agree when you may need Jerome to join you, perhaps with a few of his Intelligence operatives."

"One more thing. Tomorrow, another CECD agent will be joining you. She is experienced and is transferring to you from another sector team. Her name is Hana!"

The Commander was now in a rush. But so was Jerome. Outside he said to Anneliese and Frank, "Would you please come back to GCHQ with me. There is something important I want to show you. It won't take long."

A few minutes later they were in a taxi, approaching GCHQ. To their surprise, Jerome stood on the pavement, then said, "Follow me." They walked about 10 yards and stood at the bus stop. Jerome, looking at his watch said, "Just a couple more minutes!"

A number 25 Routemaster bus arrived. Standing on the platform, in her smart navy blue uniform, was Joan! Anneliese screeched and clambered on the bus. There was an explosion of emotion. No bell was rung, so the driver, Jess, left his cab and walked to the back of the bus to see what the hold-up was. Now Jess was the target of embraces.

Passengers on the bus were mostly regulars, office workers on their way home. They all realised this was a special time for Joan, and, in unison, stood, clapped and cheered.

But all good things come to an end! The bus had to continue on. Anneliese stepped back off the bus to join Frank and Jerome. As the bus moved away, she shouted "We will visit you soon!" Joan shouted back, "That was Barry's HQ!" Jerome explained to Anneliese! Tears drifted down her cheeks.

Jerome had always been a wonderfully thoughtful friend to them all. The memories of their last Secret Service assignment would remain extremely painful!

Barry and Albie had died in an air crash. Barry had been Anneliese's partner. Albie's partner, Anya, a CECD agent, had died in a CECD operation.

Barry's Mother, Joan, lived with heartache every minute of the day. But that bus stop outside "Barry's HQ" always reminded her of the happy times with her loving son.

Jerome's life had been transformed by these friends. Frank would be forever grateful that his life had been touched by them.

Chapter 3

CIA, HQ, Jackson

Two days later, Anneliese, Hana and Frank drove into the car park by the George Bush Centre for Intelligence. They had flown into Norfolk, Virginia and driven to Langley. It was a rather unimpressive building. The long journey had given them time to get to know Hana a little. She was originally from Czech Republic and spoke several languages. She was very likeable!

The CIA HQ was a very long building with 4 floors and a semi-circular entrance building. To enter the complex, they were required to show their credentials and appointment. They had to wait about 10 minutes whilst these were verified, as only authorised vehicles are granted access to the private road that leads to the complex from the George Washington Memorial Parkway. Once all this had been achieved, they mustered together at the entrance.

Having announced their arrival at reception, two casually dressed gentlemen appeared. Both, couldn't believe their luck and, stood back, open mouthed for a few seconds, admiring the beauty before them.

Frank moved forward to shake hands and present their letter of authority. The two guys managed to pull themselves together and the one in a blue check shirt, stepped forward to do the introductions. They were named Chuck and Denton;

they turned and led the way through the foyer and into the building.

Their next stop was a small conference room on the second floor. The CIA Director was in the chair. He welcomed them, saying his name was William Webster, but they could call him Bill. At the outset, he said he had the utmost respect for the work of CECD and greatly appreciated their help on this assignment. All CIA resources and facilities would be placed at their disposal.

Frank was first to ask if they could have access to all of the statements made by employees of the two companies that had been subject to attack. Also a listing of all medical facilities, suppliers of equipment and medical devices, including addresses and phone numbers.

Anneliese politely began to explain that they would spend the next few days analysing all the paperwork. The Director interjected saying that Chuck and Denton would assist them throughout their stay. Anneliese continued, saying that later they would wish to visit some of the medical suppliers, including possibly, the two that were attacked. Hana, smiling at the Director, said she would be looking after bygone years. Mr Webster, smiling back quipped, "You look far too young to be concerned with bygone years!" Hana replied, "Sir, by that I meant the CIA's records on the events in Cuba, following the revolution. There may be some tiny clue in that history regarding the needle in this haystack."

"Hana", replied the Director. "It is Hana isn't it? I will seek clearance and I'm certain it will get approval. And, for what it's worth, I think this is a good idea. In my previous life as a lawyer, I learned a very important lesson. Looking back often helps when trying to move forward."

"I will leave you now, in the capable hands of Denton and Chuck. They will also take you through some arrangements. If you need me just ask! It has been a joy to meet our cousins from Europe."

After the Director left, Denton said they had reserved rooms for them, only a couple of miles away, at the Staybridge Suites in Tysons-Mclean. Also, a Ford Explorer would be available for their use and they should forget the rental car. Grinning, Denton remarked that the Cadillac De Ville they had arrived in was too much of an attention-getter for Secret Service Agents!

Three days into their stay, most of the groundwork seemed complete. Each day they had conference calls with Jerome. He believed he would get somewhere if he had a longer wheelbase. He craved more data, more information from the research Anneliese had accumulated.

Disruption reared its ugly head on the morning of the fourth day, Thursday. Chuck and Denton were waiting as they arrived at the main entrance. There had been two new attacks on medical facilities. And now a new development. Two trucks with container loads of specialist medical equipment, bound for U.S. hospitals had been hijacked. The medical equipment factories were in different areas of the U.S. but both were also essential to supplies for the U.K.

They all collected coffees from the coffee shop in the lobby then Chuck led them to a meeting room. Denton stood in front of them giving details. The two manufacturing facilities had been attacked by insurgents who had accessed the building's compounds. A well organised and well planned operation! Both installations were in California. One in San Diego and another near Carmel.

The trucks were a different story. They were driving up from near Tallahassee, Florida, to Toledo, Ohio. A drive of over 15 hours! With several pit stops, the trucks were an easy target. They disappeared into "nowhere land" as the drivers stood in the parking lot wondering what to do next!

It was almost 10pm in GCHQ. Jerome was finishing up. He had put in a very long shift, working through many different forms of statistical analysis to determine if there were any strong relationships between all the different variables. He had calculated correlation coefficients, standard deviations and even simple primary statistics; mean, median and mode, for a gigantic collection of data. Nothing extraordinary was showing up!

He was over-tired. His brain just would not stop working on every angle. His blonde hair was tussled and greasy from continually running his fingers through it. But tomorrow was another day. Possibly, the attacks on medical facilities and the growth of Havana Syndrome were completely independent events and totally random. He did not believe this for a moment and would continue in the morning!

Chapter 4

Jerome, Havana and Attacks

Jerome's dreamy sleep would not let go. He woke around 4am, his psyche intent on a different approach. He decided to bring the human element into his scenario. Later he would talk with Frank and Anneliese, and request to be allowed to interview U.S. diplomatic staffs that were afflicted by Havana Syndrome. A tele-conference call with Frank was already scheduled for mid-afternoon.

Anneliese, and then Hana, answered the call. Jerome told Anneliese that his investigations had not come to anything yet. So he wanted to try getting some details on the Havana Syndrome in face-to-face meetings with U.S. staff. Anneliese went away to speak with Frank. Anneliese returned. "Frank thinks you should interview some of the Brits before you come. That may provide some comparisons. He knows there have only been a few U.K. cases, so you may need to visit some European Embassies, as well as British staff."

Jerome said he would get that done, and be over to them in the U.S. by the end of next week. Anneliese would work with Chuck and Denton to arrange meetings with diplomatic personnel, probably in Washington D.C.

Jerome spelled out in the call that the media were getting deep into the U.S. sabotage; concerns were being raised in Parliament and protest groups were beginning to make the news. Hana interjected at this point. "The list of equipment and devices is growing and the NHS will surely be affected soon by lack of supply. Mechanised equipment for liver and kidney transplants, insertion of stents and an array of cancer equipment are all likely to become serious soon. Jerome, I think it would be an idea to get the Health Minister to begin talks with her German counterpart. They may be able to begin expanding their capacity to offset some of the losses."

Over the next 10 days Jerome sat through hours of meetings with individuals from the U.K. civil service diplomatic staff. Twelve in all, mostly suffering badly from Havana Syndrome and, therefore, on sick leave. They all exhibited similar symptoms, but three of the personnel, whilst responding to questions on Jerome's questionnaire, drifted into new elements that had never been mentioned or recorded before. As Jerome eased each of them through intense, but gentle, stimulation of their recollections, the memory trickle began. During the episodes, the loud noises, searing headaches and unsettling weird noises, led them into something similar to a migraine. Except, as their vision blurred and bright colours flashed constantly, the short, sharp flashes contained pictures, some of these were like looking at a one to three second video, with a time in the corner. Almost like those adverts that were designed in the 1960's to subvert one's conscious mind!

Jerome thought he was on to something! Initially, he thought that he should involve the neurologists from Kings College Hospital. After bouncing that around, he changed his mind. He would wait until he had gone through the same exercise with the U.S. diplomatic staff.

The medical instruments and equipment factory in Boston became the focal point for the CECD team. Chuck and Denton would accompany them to investigate the methods used by the terrorists, take statements and search for evidence.

It was an easy journey as arrangements were made to fly out of Langley Air Force Base, just down the road, about 60 miles south of Richmond. The CIA had a Learjet at the base. They were afforded VIP treatment, their two cars being allowed to drive to the hangar alongside the runway.

An hour and a half later, they landed at Boston Logan Airport. It was only mid-morning which allowed them almost 8 hours to plough through the whole site, and seek answers to all their questions. The Company had their own security personnel who had already done a lot of work, examining the terrorists' modus operandi.

Their security people, working with the Boston police, had concluded that they had arrived by boat in Boston Harbour. The Coast Guard had recorded a motor cruiser arriving and mooring close to the Boston Tea Party Tourist Attractions. They had been asked to move further along the harbour to allow a better view of the Mayflower replica ship.

They had driven to the medical facility plant, only five minutes away, east of Boston Park. Then cut their way through the steel fencing to access the factory machinery. The factory only operated a mini-shift at night, so only 12 employees were around. The terrorists' were wearing black ninja type uniforms making them difficult to see.

Semtex was planted, with detonators, at the beginning of a robotic production line. Further down the line were the production operatives. Essentially they worked at the end of gravity roller conveyors, assembling components. The terrorists were commando crawling towards the mini-shift. Two of the security staff were in an office on a mezzanine floor above the production line. As they left the office they spotted the insurgents. Stupidly, one of them shouted! A terrorist stood up, pulled a machine pistol round from his back strap. He took a couple of seconds to move the back strap away, then casually, looking up, pulled the trigger. Bullets sprayed upwards. Both security guards were hit, fell forward, and plummeted down from the mezzanine floor above. The production workers stood silent, as the terrorists approached, screaming for them to move towards the ground floor offices. As they filed, hands on heads, or in the air, a second insurgent group were packing Semtex and detonators along the rest of the line, where the shift had been working.

Four of the operators working in the mini-shift were ladies. They worked on final assemblies requiring dexterity, inserting tiny screws to secure minute flexing equipment into tubing used to install stents into arteries.

One of these ladies was absolutely terrified. As they reached the offices, two of the three were completely empty and darkened. With the rest of the mini-shift, they were told to form a line against the office walls. The poor woman could not take any more! She felt behind her and found a door handle to one of the empty dark offices. Trembling as she watched the terrorists, she dropped to her knees, opened the office door, and crawled in. Hiding herself under a table, she thought she had found safety. But these guys were professionals. One of them had counted the ladies, and as he strolled back along the line, he knew one was missing.

He slowly and quietly opened the office door. With accurately placed, almost silent steps, he edged to the table. Still without light, he just stood, listening to her heavy breathing, getting heavier as each moment passed. She lost control and began to whimper!

He reached down under the table. She was frozen to the spot. He decided he would make an example of her. In a callous rage, he grabbed the table and tossed it backwards. She began to scream as he seized her ponytail and dragged her into the office space. He leant towards the door to turn the light on.

Immediately, with ferocious punches, he pulverised her face. She fell silent, but the torture continued. He kicked her relentlessly. Stomach, chest and head! He stood over her, with a contented smile, as if his evil appetite had been appeased.

One of the male operatives in the line, indeed the foreman, had watched. He couldn't stomach this cruelty. His rage boiled over and consumed him. He broke ranks and flew into the office, wielding a massive spanner. In a split second he knew he had made a terrifying, possibly, terminal error.

The insurgent spun around, and as he did, reached down and pulled a knife out of his boot. In one screaming action, he slashed, from left to right across the employee's throat. The foreman stood completely rigid for ten seconds, as his eyes moved up into their sockets. Blood pumped profusely down his neck and chest, as he sank to his knees; falling forward, he exited this world!

The terrorists herded the employees out to the car park. An insurgent kneeled by the main entrance. Casually checking around, he shouted "clear!" With a small wireless controller in the palm of his hands, he flipped the switch. The first explosion shook the ground and the whole building. As he pushed the joystick left, explosion after explosion reduced the production facility to rubble. Some windows nearest the production line shattered and showered down onto the car park. At that point, the terrorists ran for their vehicles, and disappeared into the night!

The attack on the Wilmington facility followed the same pattern. Another terrorist gang attacked about an hour later than Boston. Their incursion also had used the Eastern Seaboard and its waterways to get close to the factory. This mob used less violence in their offensive. They had worked fast with an objective to be in, do the necessary damage, and be out and away in under an hour. It was an easier attack as there were no late shifts or night shift workers.

Chapter 5

Where are the Risks

Over the next couple of days, news reports through all types of media, began to proliferate across the world. In the U.S. and the U.K. the media speculated on who was responsible and the growing impact on health services. They had also begun to interrogate Government Ministers and White House Spokesmen regarding potential defensive actions, or indeed, offensive measures.

By the time Jerome arrived at the weekend, there was growing unrest; small, but heavily reported, protest marches, with fear building as urgent life-saving operations began to be cancelled. What would the Government's response be?

Saturday evening, Jerome, assisted by Anneliese, called an urgent meeting. Key players were the CECD agents, CIA and the U.S. Coast Guard and U.S. Navy SEALs.

These last two U.S. security organisations had been instructed by the CIA Director. He had figured the attacks were being initiated around the U.S. coast; exactly in line with Jerome's thinking.

Jerome was in the chair! About 20 plus people were in the room. The buzz level was high. Jerome's stature was now gigantic compared to his early life as an airline steward. He had taught himself the methods to get attention. He stared around the room at every face and the buzz diminished. He stood, and taking a deep breath and a couple of seconds adjusting his tie, with a quiet but emphatic voice, said he was sure that everyone in the room realised the dangerous situation they were facing. "If it continues to expand, our countries will be at war with an unknown aggressor." He brushed his jacket straight and thought for a second!

"Every person in this room will, I know, put their heart and soul into finding the answer. And in a moment, I will ask each of you to introduce yourselves. But before I do, I would like to introduce you all to someone that will willingly interface with each and every one of you. She is recognised by both Europe and the U.S.A. as their most accomplished secret service agent, both psycho-analytically and militarily!"

Jerome turned towards Anneliese; holding his arm out in an inviting way. He said, "I wish to introduce our CECD secret service agent, Anneliese." She took it on the chin, just smiling around the room at everyone.

Now he stood and proudly and confidently walked around the room, passing everyone as he touched their shoulders or patted their backs. His voice still complemented his almost female face structure, but now had a presence that was magnetic.

"I've been working on this parallel phenomenon called "Havana Syndrome" which is a debilitating condition affecting diplomatic and now, other Government Personnel. It's too early to say more than I think I am getting somewhere. But the primary issue before us is to prevent the terrorist attacks on U.S. medical manufacturing facilities. If this continues, we will have people all over the U.S.A. and U.K. dying in the streets and suffering horrendous pain and trauma."

"My Director General and the U.K. Prime Minister have directed me to remain here with you to focus on this assignment. I intend doing just that, but I will let you into a little secret." Jerome developed a soft smile as he saw the yearning in peoples' expressions as they expectantly waited for the secret! "In all this mess, there are only two things that I am almost totally convinced of. First, the anomalous Havana Syndrome is linked in some way to the sabotage of our health systems. Second, the attack on U.S medical manufacturing facilities will continue to target facilities close to the coast. The CIA Director agrees with this assumption, and that is why you, the Coast Guard and our colleagues from the SEALs have become part of this assignment." As he spoke, he nodded politely in their direction.

The meeting continued for another hour and a half. Many questions, but few answers. Many reports from Anneliese, Frank, Chuck and Denton. These two CIA agents from Langley HQ gave a very detailed review of the attacks on Boston and Wilmington. They also touched upon the Truck heists, but their conclusion was that this was not important in the scheme of things, and had probably been initiated to confuse the dimension that indicated attacks would come from off-shore!

In summarising, Jerome stipulated that all involved should work together over the next 24 hours to identify high risk medical factories and facilities around the U.S. Coast. The Companies identified would then be put on high security alert. The Coast Guard and SEALs would be required to institute surveillance off the coast areas in close proximity to the identified high risk medical facilities.

Last but by no means least, Anneliese and Hana were required to work with all agencies to sort and sift every possible piece of intelligence that may increase the knowledge base in an attempt to develop indicators that possibly would lead to the Country or terrorist group responsible for the attacks.

Just as Jerome was about to wrap up the meeting, Frank stepped forward from the corner of the room. With his right arm raised half-way, his eyes searched Jerome's face. His expression showed his reluctance to speak to a room full of people and Jerome immediately recognised it. "I'm so sorry Frank, of course, please, say whatever you want to say. I want to emphasise to everyone in this room that Frank has been trained in every possible military discipline. In any sort of war he is the man you want alongside you." Frank dropped his head hearing Jerome's words, but gradually, slowly, lifted his eyes and looked around at his audience. Frank's steely eyes took a few seconds searching the faces around the room. As he began to speak, it was a quiet but confident tone. "I've been in this business for more years than I care to remember. You care about making this world a place without fear. I have a wife sitting at home in Canada worrying about me. Anneliese has a husband and three year old son living just up the road from me in Canada. And I know she is always worrying about them! But she does this sort of job because she wants a safe and secure future, for all of us."

"But, down to business. Once you guys have agreed the high risk list, please give them a priority. A listing of 1 to 10. High risk to lowest risk. I will then take the top 3 and request that all your different Agencies, CIA, CECD, SEALs and maybe the FBI give me their best personnel. We will stake out the high risk facilities until we find success. I have sat and listened to all you wonderful people, here trying to do a very difficult job. You all deserve better than the shit these bastards are trying to serve up to us. And your families deserve much more. A civilised world where love and respect are the by-words!" The room fell quiet for a whole minute.

Jerome stood and began to thank Frank, but the sincerity of Frank's exhilarating speech drew warm applause, followed by handshakes as everybody began to mingle.

Chapter 6

Health Care is Diminishing

That evening in the hotel, Jerome, Frank, Anneliese and Hana sat talking about the whole business. Frank and Anneliese were waiting for the top ten risk list. Both Jerome and Hana sat quietly listening.

Every so often, Hana would study Jerome's face. Intuition told her he was wrestling with something. Frank and Anneliese were in full flow, but it was as if Hana could not hear them. With a strained expression, she turned to Jerome, reached for his arm, saying, "What is it? Something is gnawing at you!" Frank and Anneliese stopped mid-conversation.

Jerome, let his tension release as he smiled at Hana. "Ok, there is no way I want to leave you guys behind. It's this new thing that has emerged regarding those suffering from Havana Syndrome. One of the Foreign Office Civil Servants gradually recalled an unusual sensation whilst experiencing a Havana episode. There were short sharp bursts of flashes that he believed were somewhat like the TV flash advertising, aimed at invading the subconscious, in the 1960's. The Government of the day quickly banned this type of advertising; it was personal invasion that could not be avoided!"

"The more I probed, the more descriptive his memory became. It didn't provide a clear picture of whatever was seen, but he was definite about it being a name, a place, or a time!"

"I re-visited two of the Havana volunteers. Both were feeling poorly, so I couldn't push too hard on them. But one of them began to remember something similar."

"Anyway, I will have to search for the same pattern among the U.S. diplomatic staffs that are experiencing Havana. Chuck and Denton have arranged for us to trip over to Washington two days hence. I will only be away for the day, then we can share updates when I return."

As Jerome relaxed for a few seconds, Frank took the chance to remind them that the first task tomorrow would be to review the critical high risk facilities list and consense the three requiring stakeout surveillance; and organise security protection for the whole list!

Jerome, with his eyes moving back and forth across his colleagues said, "Well we do have one piece of good news. The Germans are aiming to increase their capacity by about 30% over the next few weeks. That should give us a reasonable contingency on supplies to the NHS. However, as expected, it will be financially costly!"

Anneliese had been very quiet as she listened intently to every word and absorbed and analysed every expression. She moved slightly forward in her seat as she uncrossed her legs. Her tongue began to moisten her lips, then she spoke in a gentle tone. "I think there is one thing we all need to be acutely aware of. I received some intelligence reports today that have worsened the dimension we are dealing with. The attacks on San Diego and Carmel in California have resulted in potentially catastrophic impacts on high demand areas of the NHS. Equipment and devices used in cancer operations, specifically bowel, liver and oesophagus cancer, were desperately needed. These Californian factories are the U.K's mainstay. They will be off line for several months. When the impact starts to be felt, people will be dying. The media will become more vociferous, and fear will grip the nation. Where that leads is uncertain, but it's obvious to me it won't be pleasant. We will have to do 100% better than we are doing, and I'm saying this because I know that if you adjust your mindset now, you are capable of it."

Anneliese stood, a trait of hers that always seemed to keep people focused. For a moment, she stared blankly at the wall opposite. Then her words slowly began to flow. "There is another new angle. The Carmel production facility is only one of two the U.K. relies upon for Dentistry equipment and small tooling. This also will be out of action for quite some time. We all know the devastation tooth pain can cause to people, and in the midst of a volcanic explosion of fear in the U.K. we must all be ready to introduce extraordinary measures."

"In this context, I have spoken with Commander Farrell. I have suggested, and he has agreed, that we should begin some preparatory work. As a first step, he will talk with the Canadian CSIS. We may find it necessary, in the near future, to fly U.K. citizens to Canada for urgent operations, dental work or medical procedures to keep them alive. We must not allow it to get to the point where people are dying all around us!"

"The Commander will ensure our request gets to Mr Mulroney, Prime Minister of Canada, as a request for a failsafe against any future deterioration in the U.K. position."

Chapter 7

Call to Arms

The following day, the team concentrated on the continuous flow of intelligence details provided by CIA Intelligence analysts. Locations of key medical factories and facilities all around the U.S. coastline, addresses, contact details and the type of equipment and devices each manufactured. By mid-afternoon the team had sufficient data to review and develop the high risk list.

Anneliese had worked with GCHQ and the NHS to establish a listing of surgical waiting lists prioritised by health issues with the highest death rates. The top ten critical high risk listing based on the amalgamation of these data, with 1 to 10, highest to lowest, was agreed as follows:

1. Brunswick (Georgia)
2. San Francisco (Calif.)
3. Houston (Texas)
4. Baton Rouge (Louisiana)
5. Portland (Oregon)
6. Tampa (Florida)
7. Norfolk (Virginia)
8. Dover (Delaware)
9. Tallahassee (Florida)
10. New York (NY State)

Following a short team meeting, Frank and Jerome assigned themselves to organise a late night conference call with U.S. and U.K Defence Ministry Agencies, to include U.S. representation from the CIA, FBI, SEALs and U.S. Coastguard. European representation, on behalf of the U.K. to include CECD.SAS and Royal Marines presently on manoeuvres in San Francisco, training with the U.S. Navy SEALs special operations force.

The call to arms was a complete success. It was agreed that the CIA and SEALs would jointly take the leadership role. The highest risk, top three, would be subjected to Special Forces surveillance combined with military intervention in the event of attack. The remaining seven facilities would be simply defended to deter any sabotage.

The intention for the top three was to engage any assailants in the event of attack, to apprehend them and, in other words, ascertain who they were and disable their terrorist group! This would be in place for at least the next week. The plan was to prevent a damaging concerted campaign.

After a very late night, Jerome would fly in the morning to Washington to continue his investigations into the Havana Syndrome; hopefully, to get more of an understanding of the cause of this growing debilitating disorder.

Very early next morning, Chuck and Denton arrived at Jerome's hotel. Jerome, in his business suit, strode with confidence to the car. His strength of character, underpinned by his obvious assertive expression, placed him in the forefront of global security intelligence.

So far, Chuck and Denton had both maintained a reserved, almost introverted persona. On the Learjet flight to Washington they began to forge a business relationship with

Jerome. Gradually the secret service tight-lipped approach diluted and by the time they landed at Anderson Air Force base, banter with some chuckles had developed.

Although beginning to take shape, it was a few weeks away from becoming a close working relationship. However, it would eventually happen as these CIA characters began to appreciate the competence of the CECD team.

Denton had a soft, welcoming expression, enhanced by smiling eyes. He was probably in his mid- 50's, and with a heavy, rotund body; he did not appear athletic. But apparently, he was an exceptional thinker, with a reputation as the best CIA intelligence analyst. Today, he was smartly dressed in a dark grey business suit, which must have been difficult to find, in view of his size. He proudly, exhibited a walrus-like moustache that encroached on his mouth and fluttered as he spoke!

The surprise, that Jerome had noticed as Denton crossed his legs, were his socks. With his sombre dark grey suit, he had worn bright orange socks. During the banter, Chuck had mentioned it was a trait that Denton was famous for!

Apparently, these two guys, Chuck and Denton were the best in their business. They say opposites attract and certainly Chuck was the opposite!

Chuck was about 30 years old and an impressive 6foot 2inches tall; a lithe, handsome fit-looking guy. One would think he had just stepped off the Olympics podium, except he was impeccably dressed in a three piece handmade bespoke suit.

Whilst they were talking, Denton mentioned that Chuck's claim to fame was that his body had more bullet hole scars than anyone in the service. Jerome gasped, but thought to himself, I have both a thinker and a do'er on my team!

Jerome was physically attracted to Chuck; not surprising really because he probably would be able to compete with both Michael Jordan and Donovan Bailey, both in terms of looks and athleticism. And yes, like those gentlemen, Chuck was black!

A luxurious Lincoln Continental met the plane on the runway. They were quickly off to the Old Executive Office building, almost opposite the White House at the junction of Pennsylvania Avenue and 17th Street. They were pretty close to the Potomac River, so, almost immediately, Chuck took Jerome to the roof to view the river.

Chapter 8

A Fragile Lead

Holding the fort in Langley, Anneliese and Frank were having an unscheduled get-together. Frank had received some disturbing news from the Commander. "The treatment situation in the NHS is worsening day-by-day." Frank continued that the country was becoming racked with anxiety. "Mechanised equipment and computer programmes required to deliver liver and kidney procedures were not available. Insertion equipment for stents in serious cardiac procedures were not available. And an array of cancer facilities and equipment were in disastrously short supply." The German capacity expansion was still several weeks away so no relief for some while yet!"

Anneliese interjected with a similar story for the USA. Denton had been closely following developments. He had told Anneliese that they were now staring down a barrel that may fire at any minute. "Protest groups, all over the country, were meeting, with Sheriffs and Police reporting serious levels of agitation and anxiety. Individual cases of grandparents, parents and, in a few cases, children, dying due to lack of surgical procedures, were being reported in the media." Anneliese said "the media coverage will worsen anxiety, and behaviour will deteriorate concurrently. Whilst we try to find an answer, all we can do is circle the wagons and put everything into preventing further attacks and sabotage."

Frank was due to fly to San Francisco next morning. Chuck would meet Frank as he would fly directly from Washington. Denton would return to Langley with Jerome, in order to manage the Command Centre for the operation, now named "PRESERVE."

Anneliese would join the joint Agencies force in Houston, Texas, while Hana would be flown from Jackson with two FBI operatives, joining her joint Agencies force in Brunswick, Georgia.

Back in Washington, Jerome was scheduled to meet with eight US Diplomatic and Government personnel. They were all relatively well, but continuing to occasionally experience the malevolent, painful, mind-bending episodes.

A very understanding Jerome picked all his words carefully; an intense, stressful approach for anyone! Denton sat silently recording all the interviews. The excitement level lifted as Jerome interviewed the last three candidates. One after the other recalled seeing a flash of an image or some kind of inexplicable sign, during their painful events. Then, with the last person, Pandora 's Box began to open. This gentleman had been working for diplomatic staffs applying his talents to the Middle East Region, specifically, Iraq and Iran. His brain had collected, and reminded him constantly, of the image he had seen. Indeed, it wasn't a picture or anything explainable. It was simply a name. He was absolutely clear on that and was dogged by the name every waking hour. The name was DAN BIE.

He said it had penetrated so deep into his subconscious that just talking about it made him feel like vomiting. He said it felt that way every time it resurrected itself, so now he was getting psychiatric help to suppress this thought.

Jerome perceived him as a very strong character, and with a caring voice, assured him that, eventually he would recover. This guy, by name Bernie Bowes, was a very solid, intelligent person who had spent his life working for the US Government. He was not the type to roll over and capitulate. At the end of the interview, as Jerome was saying how helpful his information had been, Bernie replied that he intended being back in his job in the next three months and nothing would prevent that. And if Jerome needed any more help just to call him.

As he left the room, both Jerome and Denton turned to one another and expressed how proud they were to have met Bernie!

Now they had a lead. A fragile lead, but it was more than welcome!

Chapter 9

Importance of Dan Bie

Jerome and Denton set off to return to the CIA Langley headquarters. On the Learjet, Jerome was already attempting to find a way to unravel the importance of the name. Denton, similarly, tried to prevent himself constantly returning to the name, but it became such an obsession that by the time the plane landed at Jackson, Denton could not even recall what his flight dinner had been!

By the time Jerome and Denton arrived in the CIA HQ, Anneliese, Frank, Hana and Chuck had left for their surveillance and protection assignment. They had been issued with new micro video and sound recorders that doubled as radio transmitters, and receivers.

Jerome and Denton also received this new, advanced equipment. They would stay in the HQ dormitory overnight, for as long as the assignment. The radio transmitters would lay alongside their pillows as they slept!

Absolutely nothing first night. Jerome and Denton were grateful for a good night's sleep. During daytime, just a few call-ins with nothing to report. Whilst hanging around, all Jerome and Denton were absorbed with was the name.... DAN BIE!

They spent every spare moment delving into the archives, CIA reports, FBI reports, and CECD European libraries. However, nothing was showing up. Even the name was difficult to find on either Continent.

The second night passed without anything unusual occurring. Anneliese, probably weary, phoned Jerome occasionally, to alleviate boredom. She spent some time discussing and outlining the exceptional back-up and support that had been organised. Chinook helicopters were stationed in airfields in close proximity to the Medical Plants; CIA personnel were situated in surrounding areas, their vehicles camouflaged and invisible. Military personnel, particularly the SEALs were anchored off shore, close to tributaries that may provide the terrorists with an escape route.

Jerome tried desperately to maintain his concentration but his mind kept trying to claw its way through the plethora of information and data that he had been sifting to find the meaning of the name....that name that was clearly important.... DAN BIE.

Denton, working independently, had also been fixated. Although his experience was much greater than Jerome's he also felt he was sitting in a desert without an oasis in sight.

He and Jerome were now at the point where they would both relax, lean back in their chairs, stretch and then stare at one another.

On the last occasion this happened, Jerome realised they were both staring into a yawning hole. As he pondered where to go next, the lightning strike hit! To calm himself, he brushed his blonde locks off his face. Took a deep breath then shouted across to Denton "What if it's a code? If so, we have to spend our time trying to break it. Should not be too difficult, its only six digits. The more difficult are eight digits!"

Denton had been caught completely off guard. He stopped what he was doing and slowly developed a wide smile. Pulling on his walrus moustache he responded. "Jerome, you may be correct. We saw a name, and have been searching for a name. But what we think we're seeing may totally change when viewed from a different vantage point!"

As he stood, flexing his legs, he brushed creases out of his trousers. From a semi-bending position he slowly lifted, straightening his back. His face, now in full view, became contorted as he looked at Jerome. His expression soured, as his eyelids and socket skin tightened! Then with a short sighing breath, he uttered, "No Jerome, it doesn't add up!" His mouth led his face into a solid grimace. "A human brain suffering a painful migraine type episode, indeed, an episode similar in intensity to epilepsy, would not go through the rigours necessary to translate a coherent message into coded secrecy!"

With his eyebrows tightening into a frown, Jerome, scratching the back of his hand drifted into a whole minute of thought. "Denton, you are on the money, in the world we are in today! But if we slightly expand our paradigms, things may be different."

"We all learned at school who invented the telephone, the television, because in our early years, technology moved relatively slowly. As it gained speed, computers were invented, mobile phones and amazing things like microwave ovens. I've no idea who invented these more recent pieces of technology. I think that's because technology is moving at the speed of sound and is now entering a new era that is taking it towards the speed of light."

"So that takes me to a what if? What if the human brain has been developing? Learning from all the clever scientists using their brains to create the technology we are seeing. What if the human brain has found a way to take information that is fed into it, and interpret it? Could it be possible that the human brain is becoming able to determine if information it's receiving is good or bad. Maybe discern if it's constructive or destructive."

"Denton, for several decades, this thing called Havana Syndrome has been around, and is still with us. Nobody has ever understood it. Nobody has got to understand it. It may be something that the Russian scientists were working on, but never completed. So, possibly, they have resurrected their work. This is all complete guesswork, and I know it sounds ludicrous, but back in the 1930's, so would the description of a microwave oven!"

"As for coding, maybe, just maybe, the human brain has not developed to the extent that it can give us a simple message in English. It originally was used to input data into computers using coded language. It has probably only lived with binary code input for 30 or 40 years."

Chapter 10

Another Code Clue

Denton had listened to Jerome's monologue for almost a quarter of an hour. "I have listened carefully to everything you have said, and I think it has possibilities. Every syllable you iterated made some form of sense to me. If you have something, it will stretch you and me beyond anything we have ever known before, but, what the hell, let's give it a go! So I think I agree to going hard on trying to decode DAN BIE. I will talk to our specialist Intelligence officers and get all the best people on it."

Another 24 hours passed and still no action on Operation Preserve. Jerome and Denton were beginning to suffer from loneliness and brain ache due to the domination of DAN BIE. Calls from the "Preserve" teams were increasing as boredom began to bite. However, calls from Hana were few and far between; she seemed to be enjoying the attention of the men accompanying her!

A further two days crawled by. None of the dots had been joined by the CIA Intelligence analysts. They reported they had played thousands of tunes on the message, used a myriad of code-breaking systems, but so far all they had were negatives.

That night it was particularly hot and humid. Jerome was having difficulty getting off to sleep. His last thought, before dozing off, was there was only 2 days to go before the "Preserve" teams would return. What was about to happen would bring them back sooner!

At about 2am, first Jerome's micro radio, then Denton's began to bleep loudly. Jerome answered first; it was the CIA Director. Two more facilities had been hit. Nowhere near any of the factories that were staked out. Both these were in Florida, in close proximity. One in Miami and the other in Palm Beach. The Director was waiting on information and his field staff would be in touch soon!

Throughout the rest of the night, phone calls, radio calls, staff milling around, was constant. Although they were still waiting for detailed feedback, the outline information indicated that these attacks had resulted in a severe impact. According to one unconfirmed report, one of the factories had been burned to the ground!

Just as a very weary Jerome and a dishevelled Denton were leaving their office to get coffee and breakfast, the phone rang. Jerome expected it to be a report about the incidents or one of the "Preserve" teams, but to his surprise it was neither. It was Bernie Bowes!

He asked Jerome to excuse him if he didn't seem quite compos mentis, but he had a severe Havana attack about 2 hours ago. "I am continuing to suffer flashing lights and weird sickening sensations. But I had something occur that you may consider important. I knew I had to get it to you fast. Jerome, you are trying to help me so I will do everything in my power to help you." The line went quiet for a few seconds, until Jerome said, "Bernie I think I know you well and trust you implicitly. So what's worrying you? What's happened?"

"Jerome, during the first episode, whilst I was screaming with pain, I clearly saw some discernible details. This time, not alpha's, rather it was numerics. I tried to memorise them, but it was a long set of numerics. But I managed to remember the first four digits....9021. Then another attack struck just as I was planning to call you. This one wasn't as bad and although lights were flashing, I was able to write the whole set of digits down. The whole set of numbers, which flashed twice, but only for about two seconds was, 90216221. I can't guarantee it is totally correct. It was so fast and I can't describe the pain along with changes in background colour and loud screeches distracting me. But that was what I think I saw. 90216221!"

Jerome, with emotional sincerity muffling his vocal chords, slowly responded. Looking across at Denton, Jerome managed to clear his throat. "Bernie, that's the best news we have had for weeks, and I can't imagine the trauma you had to go through to concentrate on writing this long set of numbers down. Your personal professionalism will be applauded by your Government and the American people. I will make sure of that!"

As the call ended, Denton wandered across. "From what I heard, that was Bernie Bowes." "Yes" replied Jerome, "and he was reporting a new mystical message he received during an Havana episode. This one is different from the last. It's a long numeric listing!" Denton raised his eyebrows as his expression showed surprise. Jerome handed a paper to Denton with the numeric data written in large black ink." I'll get this to the intelligence coding specialists right away." As he spoke, Denton appeared excited that this might be the baton handover that secures the Olympic gold medal.

However, as Denton stared at the paper with the long list of numerics, his face transitioned into one that had complication in every crease. He dropped the hand holding that paper down by his side, and faced Jerome. He began to tug on his walrus moustache. As his mouth moved into dismal mode, he got Jerome's attention. "There is some very bad news," Jerome, looked up with a searching peer. "There has been an excruciating increase in Havana Syndrome. Both here and in the UK. If we don't find an answer soon both our Governments will not be able to fulfil the basic duties required by their countries!"

⸙

Chapter 11

More Medical Destruction

Late evening and next morning the pendulum swung back to the destruction of medical facilities at Palm Beach and Miami. The Governor of Florida had made it absolutely clear to the House of Representatives and the President that the Government needed to do much more to protect the Country from these terrorists. Obviously, the repercussions reverberated throughout the Agencies responsible for defence.

The phone rang off the hook constantly. The CIA Director made it clear he wanted the word to go out to all his senior people that they should return to Jackson pronto. Chuck and Denton were charged with this assignment. They should all convene for a meeting at 10pm that very evening.

During the day, Chuck, Denton and Jerome were talking to all the teams out working on Operation "Preserve". Flights were arranged for everyone. CIA aircraft were assigned to airlift as many personnel as possible, back to Jackson. Eventually, a mixture of commercial and CIA aircraft were scheduled to retrieve all personnel and return them to Jackson HQ.

At 10pm, all Agencies chiefs and subordinates were quietly, but expectantly, seated around the Jackson HQ boardroom horseshoe table. The atmosphere in the room was intense. You couldn't cut it with a knife!

The CIA Director's entrance provided no relief. He shoved through the door that was held open for him and bustled round the table to his central chair. He sat for a minute, without looking up, whilst he shuffled the papers he had in a leather bound folder.

The elevation of his face was slow and gradual. He looked around every person in the room; not quickly! Indeed, he hovered at every individual, with deliberate eye contact. The boardroom remained eerily silent.

He was about to speak, but then raised his right hand to his mouth as he coughed. A deep breath and then he began.

"The situation, ladies and gentlemen, that we find ourselves in, is completely and absolutely untenable. Two countries, the USA and Great Britain are being threatened and dictated to by a bunch of terrorists. They are dominating a war that is becoming a war of attrition. The longer they are allowed to hold our feet to the fire, the more we will be burned. We just cannot let our nations, our people, continue to suffer like this. I don't know if you all have this information, but in parallel with these terrorists attacks, our Governments servants, both here and in the UK, are suffering a serious debilitating health issue, and it is spreading exponentially. If we don't find an answer, I will be sitting here having meetings alone!" With that, there were a few stifled chuckles.

The Director smiled, before he continued. "All you guys know me well enough to know that I am not easily rattled. We've taken on lots of adversaries together, but we have always maintained a professional calmness. We need that now! I need you to work to keep me calm. The pressure and stress I am getting from the Government and the President are like I've never seen before. And it is the same in the UK, our ally."

"So the bottom line is, I need you all to work, as a team, to find a breakthrough. There are only two assignments that you should work on. Firstly, we must quickly find a way to prevent these attacks on our medical factories, facilities and equipment. Hopefully, we can find a way to bring the perpetrators to justice! Secondly, we must, urgently, find an answer to Havana Syndrome. If we don't, and I am not joking, the spread amongst Government personnel will stifle our Government such that the country will be left without leadership!"

"I'm going to finish with assignments. The prevention of the attacks on our Medical Manufacturers will be the responsibility of Anneliese, Frank and Chuck. Will you please stand up for a moment so those that need to know you will never forget you. When you crack this, I know they will never forget you!"

"The other assignment is the Havana Syndrome. That is the responsibility of Jerome, Hana and Denton. You probably all know Denton, and possibly Jerome, but Hana is here from Czech. Well it's like this. Jerome has solved many difficult cases, and now has a very strong lead on this one. So I am begging you to give him your utmost support along with our other operatives from Europe." With that the Director smiled and nodded to everyone as he exited the room.

Chapter 12

Hana Steps Up

After an exceptionally long stressful day, everybody slept as if in a coma. As they began to arrive at Jackson HQ, initially, the key requirement was coffee to get the day moving.

Anneliese suggested to Frank that the main players in both teams should meet in the small conference room on the first floor. Frank didn't question her idea as he knew Anneliese would have thought out a strategy and, as always, it would be worth listening to. So, he stood, stretched, and put his half-finished coffee down on the small coffee table. Smiling at Anneliese, he gave a short sharp salute, then strode off to round up the teams.

"As I awoke this morning," said Anneliese, as she gave them a gentle smile, "I immediately started to churn through the two separate assignments we were given last night. But here we all are together. We work well together! If we approach these two issues as one team, rather than two separate teams, we have everything to gain and nothing to lose! I know, you are thinking how does Anneliese get to that conclusion? Well, my logic is pretty simple really. Jerome has a fundamental belief that the sabotage attacks and the Havana Syndrome are linked in some way. I am in total agreement with him on this. And if we approach this as one team, as I said earlier, we have all to gain and nothing to lose. If we are proved wrong, we can move to an independent strategy later."

Her eyes scanned the room as she took a deep breath. Her eyes finally settled on Frank. Speaking to him directly, she said she had a suggestion. "We don't have long to find solutions, and this will be quite tough on us all. I think we should lock ourselves in this conference room for the next 48 hours, with 5 hours permitted sleep. We should review and evaluate every piece of information and evidence we have. Try to answer everyone's questions, listen to theories and do everything possible to make progress." At that point she eyeballed every person, one at a time. Not seeing any clear looks of dissent, she continued. "One more thing, we should start in 2 hours' time, at 2.00pm. During that two hours, all of us should set down on paper clear, concise thoughts, questions, theories for us to consider in our 48 hour sortie."

"Does anyone disagree or have questions or issues to raise?" Nobody moved a muscle, except Anneliese. She jumped up and with a wide smile and glistening eyes said, "Ok, so let's get going!"

They re-convened on the dot at 2pm. There was no messing about from Anneliese. She went straight into "Let's get this started. Hana, you are the newest amongst us so would you get the ball rolling?"

Hana, out of traditional respect, stood. Anneliese politely thanked Hana, but reminded everyone that this 48 hours would be physically demanding. "We will not be standing on ceremony, so Hana, please sit and relax."

Hana, looking around with a gracious smile, opened, "The first thing on my list is to tell you more about me, because my talents may prove to be useful. First, I have been an Agent for two years, working close to the Western Europe border with

Russia. I am fluent in six languages. Czech, my home country. Also Russian, Spanish, French, German and Iranian. My mother was born in Iran. My degree, my specialist subject, is Computer Science. I'm only telling you all this because, if you know it, you may find you reach a point where my attributes may be useful to you."

"The only other question on my page is this. Has anyone reviewed when people began to exhibit Havana Syndrome. Was anything else happening at the time. Was there any change in their home or business life. For example, had they just got a new work computer, because computers are easy to tamper with and just radiation effects can cause illness."

Denton and Anneliese both jumped out of their chairs. That is a fantastic thought! Anneliese, appearing very excited, indicated to Denton he should speak. Denton, beside himself with the possibilities, exclaimed, "I will make it my priority task and report back in the morning." Anneliese, keen to continue thanked Hana and, turning to Jerome, said "You're up next!"

Jerome, just as he was about to commence, was struck by a throat tickle and coughing brought tears to his eyes. A jug of water was passed along the table and he gratefully gulped half a glass. Apologising, he leaned back in his chair, breathing heavily until it subsided.

When he felt comfortable to begin, he took it very slowly. "Most of you know me, but more because of the reports of my successes with CECD and the UK Government. I cannot claim past academic achievements like Hana. I achieved absolutely nothing in my early years, but with significant help from my CECD friends, gained some academic progress in my mid to late twenties. My specialism is in Mathematics and, particularly Statistics. And my intuition has achieved fabulous results!" His cheerful handsome face glanced across at Anneliese and Frank.

Looking across to Hana first, Jerome said, "We are all so glad you explained more about your abilities. Indeed, you, in your first sentences have given us clues." He moved his eyes across to Anneliese. "Yes, and I think your idea of us all working together on this has already been confirmed, with the input from Hana."

Jerome, with some trepidation, quickly covered the interviews he had completed with personnel both in the UK and USA. There had been several that explained how they had seen short sharp images, pictures, numbers and time-clocks. But they could not memorise details. "That was until we met one of the US Government employees, Bernie Bowes."

Keeping it short and brief, Jerome spelled out the name Bowes had seen, DAN BIE. Jerome, looking across the table at Denton detailed every different avenue they had explored to see if the name was recognised. Recently they had concluded it may be a code, rather than a name. They had submitted it to the coding specialists in Central Command, both Europe and USA, but so far nothing.

Jerome was about to move onto the third bullet point written on his page. There was a knock at the door. It opened as a friendly face, a lady pushing a trolley brought in coffee and cakes. It added pleasure to the proceedings, but as they seemed to be making good headway, they all seemed to want to press on. Denton, in particular, had left his chair and was leaning over Jerome. Both of them excited by the progress so far. Denton was whispering to Jerome that all he wanted was to get out and start work on Hana's idea. He thought it would bring significant results. Jerome asked him to be patient. If he wanted he could continue instead of sleeping tonight!

Jerome continued his dissertation. As everyone was sipping coffees and enjoying cake, Jerome explained that there had been a recent development with Bernie Bowes. He had suffered a bad period of Havana Syndrome, but had seen some new images. These were numerics. Initially, he wasn't sure if he had recorded it accurately but it returned in a second episode. He had got it correct, but it was extended. A long numeric....90216221!

Chapter 13

Hana Sees the Light

Thank God, Commander Farrell had re-assigned this lady, Hana, to work with this team. She jumped up out of her chair, laughing all the while. She was a very beautiful, exotic, young woman that never appeared a temptress. However, now everyone, was perceiving her not just as a reserved but attractive female, but also one with extraordinary intelligence.

"Jerome, I have to apologise for interrupting, but this code is easy for me. My sister lived in Istanbul. I phoned her almost every day for over a year. That simply is the phone code for Istanbul. The parts 216 and 221 are just the European or Asian side of the Bosphorus Strait! I recognised it immediately and I am absolutely certain I am correct!"

The enormity of this early, important, discovery engulfed everybody in the room. Astounded expressions, were transformed, as jaw-dropping disbelief became gleeful euphoria.

Everyone looked towards Anneliese who was slowly standing and leaning across the table, hand outstretched to Hana. "I would like to express our gratitude." Anneliese continued as she glanced around everyone. "You have, in the space of the first few hours with us, contributed thoughts that will help get us out of the starting blocks. So, once again, thank you!"

"We have made a rapid beginning to our first day." Anneliese, stroking her hair back from her face, exclaimed, "However, we now must continue our endeavours, hopefully, at the same pace. But first let's have a coffee break!"

Denton couldn't wait for this moment. He rushed out of the conference room to speak to some of his CIA Intelligence Analysts to get them looking for anything that occurred concurrently with the timing of the Havana Syndrome striking down individuals.

They carried on through the afternoon reviewing all questions and theories raised by each individual in attendance. The majority of questions were regarding patterns that the Intelligence Analysts may or may not have considered and reviewed. For example, was there any geographic pattern to the attacks other than them being close to the US coastline? Was any particular Medical Company the main focus of the attacks?

In the early evening break, Anneliese arranged for all her handwritten notes to be typed and a copy provided to each attendee. During the break, Denton and Chuck sat together having an in-depth conversation. And as the meeting got back on track, Chuck asked to be first to speak.

Anneliese, with a mischievous glint in her eye asked "Chuck are you holding the green card?" Chuck raised his eyes to the ceiling then returned to look at Anneliese with a subtle grin. "No mam, sorry but the last I saw of it was when it left with the break food trolley! But I am certain you will see the importance of my request. Denton and I are requesting a short parole from this cell because our staff have been working on Hana's suggestions and have some information.

We also need to review some intelligence, which sounds important. Once Denton and I have looked into this stuff, we will return to give you all some feedback. It shouldn't take much more than an hour!"

"You have parole for a maximum of 2 hours, but you'd better return with something good!" she gave a wry smile as Denton and Chuck left the room.

Two minutes after they went over the wall, the door opened and a CIA operative appeared, lingered then nervously entered. Frank stood and walked to meet him. A few quiet words were exchanged, and as he drifted out of the room, Frank patted him on the back saying, "many thanks." Frank took a paper he had been given, across to Anneliese. The room fell quiet for a few moments while she read the contents. She looked up and her eyes drifted around the room. "It's not great news." she said. "The CIA Director is reporting to us the disastrous impact of the incursions in Palm Beach and Miami. The sabotage will impact surgical operations, mainly intestinal, bowel, liver, and pancreas, and so the list goes on. It will hurt both the US and UK. But don't let this distract you. It has always been my war cry. If you can't control it, if you can't influence it, ignore it. Don't let it crash you off the road you are travelling along."

She searched everyone's faces, looking for acceptance, and she found it. She wanted to finish on a high note. With an expression that said she knew that standing in water, in that stream, they were going to find a large gold nugget soon; she summarised. "We have only been working on this for several hours. We are moving closer to our goal all the time. Your input today has been extraordinary. We will not let negatives outweigh the positives. So let's continue."

Frank, holding up a green card, and with an innocuous expression, laughed as he said, "Yes, I rescued the green card from the food trolley. A thing I wrote on my list was not my favourite. I've never been one for defending, but you may think it's worth some thought. Someone once said the best form of defence is attack. May have been Wellington or Napoleon. I'm not good on history, but that is how I have always lived my life. However, considering what we are dealing with, and the disastrous results, I think it may be worth considering defence rather than attack! And before I explain, I know it will, no doubt, be more than budgets can stand."

"As I understand it, there are over 30 key Medical Manufacturing facilities, supplying all our hospitals. Would it be possible to install the latest technology, protection equipment, cameras and alarms linked to local police and CIA?" Just as Frank was getting into his stride, the door opened. Chuck and Denton quietly took their seats. Both looking like the cat that had got the cream. Anneliese recognised that, smiled and addressed them. That mischievous smile re-emerged. "Frank retrieved the green card that Chuck thought had gone with the food trolley. So he will pass it to you guys if you have something good to tell us." As she finished, Anneliese nodded to Denton.

Chuck stood and rushed outside the conference room. Amazement was on everyone's faces. Just a second, then he was back in, bouncing a basketball as he entered. This was such a relief after the intense day they had experienced. His control and moves were superb. Through his legs, down his back, static on the back of his neck, flipped up in the air and as he caught the ball, with the most gigantic smile, he leaned back and tossed the ball over Jerome and Hana, scoring into a waste paper basket at the end of the room.

With beads of sweat forming on his ebony brow, he walked and sat next to Denton. The room erupted; everyone stood and clapped with a few cheers following. The room gradually settled as Denton began to speak. "What was all that about?" "Well, we Americans enjoy finding answers, especially those that may get us onto the podium. And we both think we are in the winning mode." Denton, with a wide grin, bowed to his audience.

Anneliese, along with everyone, had enjoyed the spectacle. She couldn't resist saying, "Denton, please, take us to the place that you two are camped in." Denton leant forward, tugging on his walrus moustache. Chuck elbowed him, saying, "get on with it, we've had our fun!"

Chapter 14

Another Istanbul Pointer

Denton, looking down at his writing pad said, "Well the first and most important element is that we have received intelligence from our field operatives. They are convinced that Iran is behind this. They have been tailing an Iranian for a while. He has flown to the US several times. And guess where he is based? Istanbul!"

"The second piece of news is somewhat questionable and needs more work. Yes, possibly Hana was correct; a sample of operatives experiencing Havana Syndrome, had recently received a new desk top computer! We selected a 30% sample and that result is both for the USA and UK."

The rest of the night was taken up with the computer subject. Anneliese stepped up to a flip chart and they all set about agreeing and listing every possible task that needed to be done.

After a few minutes, Denton asked Anneliese if he could help her and wished to make a point before they moved on. Anneliese nodded agreement with a somewhat enigmatic expression.

"In view of the urgency, I think we need this at the top of our work list." Denton fumbled in the flip board shelf, then finding a wide felt tip he wrote: 1. AS FAR AS POSSIBLE OUR ACTIONS SHOULD BE IMPLEMENTED SIMULTANEOUSLY!

Denton turned to face everyone. "To get fast results we may all have to take responsibility because some of the tasks may be involved and complex." Then turning to Anneliese he continued, "The first job is wide ranging and should fall to me, Jerome and Chuck. It's the need to validate that computers are the culprit in the Havana Syndrome. From now on it will help if we refer to it as HS."

"The work will involve checking out all HS sufferers to confirm the percentage that have had new computers. The next part of this exercise will be to establish the suppliers of these computers.... The Company Names and Locations. Then, importantly, we need to find the whereabouts of the offending computers. All our CIA Special Investigation Analysts will be involved because it is a very widespread task, here in the USA, the UK and potentially in many rest-of-world countries. Fortunately, we have about 40 of these specialists."

Anneliese walked across to Denton, and put her arm around his shoulder. "Denton, you have already worked this through in your mind, so I am going to join the rest of the group. Please carry on; you are doing a fabulous job."

Denton, smiling as Anneliese sat at the conference table continued, "Someone should collar Purchasing to determine who they have the supply of Desk Top Computers sourced with; which Companies and their locations. I know that their recent strategy has been single sourcing. If that is the case, it will be a day to celebrate. We will only have one Company to interrogate about the computers. If not, we may be into reviewing US and UK suppliers and, possibly other individual companies around the world!"

At each point, Anneliese had left her seat and helped with the flip chart listing. Denton, brushing his grey hair behind his ears, smiled and said, "That's me I'm done" as he began to trundle back to the table. He had only taken two strides when Hana asked "Denton, may I add a couple of things?" "Oh, Hana, of course, I should have asked if anyone had anything more, but tiredness is getting to me! So what do you think should be added?"

Hana stood and said, "I hope I am not going to offend anyone, but I need to walk around as I speak, or rather as I think and speak." Anneliese rushed over to Hana, and embraced her saying, "we are the same; I thought it was just me, but now I've found someone with exactly the same trait. Indeed, I think it's a form of OCD but it works for me, and now I find it works for you." Hana was clearly becoming a very strong presence with everyone, and particularly, Anneliese!

Anneliese, looking back at Hana as she floated back to her chair said, "Hana, please carry on, we can't wait to hear your thoughts."

Hana, as she strolled around the horseshoe table said, "Denton, once we know the suppliers, or the majority supplier, we should ask if any of their product contains components from Turkey. I don't think I need to explain the potential link. A secondary thought is Iran! I know it's unlikely, but based on the information from Denton and Chuck today, it would not hurt to pose the question!"

⸺⋖◈⋗⸺

Chapter 15

Hana Wants Hardware

Anneliese, quick to the flip chart, had this captured in the work list. "This next one is in my domain." Hana straightened her back and with pride in her expression continued. "Once we have a target computer, and I know, that could be almost imminent because Denton has already surveyed 30%. So let's get one stripped down and investigated. All we need is a good look at the hardware internals and if we find the answer we can immediately bury HS."

Denton and Anneliese in unison, totally simultaneously, started to say," Do you really think," but Denton stopped. Smiling as he graciously held his hand out to indicate to Anneliese to continue! She nodded a thank you, then said, "Do you really think that's a possibility Hana? I know you told us your degree is in Computer Science, but does that include knowledge of all the internal hardware components?"

"Yes I do and yes it does," Hana replied. "It would help if I had a hardware engineer to strip it down. He would be quicker than me. But once done, I'm sure I know where to look and would spot any foreign objects!"

"I will try to get things moving with Purchasing" said Jerome. Anneliese said, "Ok, I suggest we break for an hour and spend the time getting these tasks underway. And whilst we wait to get the computer and an engineer, perhaps you Hana, would give Denton and Chuck some help."

Anneliese joined Jerome in an immediate conference call to the Chief Procurement Officer in Washington DC, who called upon two of his Senior Purchasing Officers responsible for sourcing office equipment.

Anneliese and Jerome didn't beat about the bush. Anneliese began by explaining this was an urgent situation and that their assignment had been directly initiated by the President of the United States. That got the necessary level of close attention.

The Chief Procurement Officer had earlier introduced himself as James Blocker. Anneliese thought, not a name to encourage confidence! However, once Jerome explained their operation involved the Havana Syndrome, James became very amenable. He was very aware of the issue having been debriefed on the subject by no less than the US Chief of Staff. He further explained that his awareness had been increased in the last two weeks as HS had arrived close to home. Four of his staff had gone down with the affliction and his organisation was paying the price.

Jerome and Anneliese recognised the door was now wide open for them. They rattled through their questions thick and fast. Essentially, the Procurement roll-out of the new generation of Desk Top Computers had been going on for over a year. The supplier Corporation was based in the USA. They had been assigned complete responsibility for the global programme. They had won a single-sourced bidding competition and were also charged with providing installation, security programmes and devices, maintenance and customer support. The planned roll-out was USA first, followed by the UK. Some other countries' Embassies were early, due to the age and failure of their equipment.

So far, Jerome and Anneliese were delighted with the answers. Single sourcing made everything rapidly possible! So now they pushed on with the last few essential questions.

Jerome went first. "James, I'm sorry to put you under so much pressure, but would you attempt to get one of these computers, together with their best hardware engineer to the CIA HQ in Jackson tomorrow."

James Blocker was silent for twenty seconds, but his response was positive. "Jerome, I will, you have my pledge! I have a million questions rambling around in my head, but I know not to ask now. You will give me the answers eventually."

With appreciation being expressed all around, their call was about to end. Anneliese, apologised saying, "I have a couple more questions." Down the phone, James was heard to breathe deeply. "James, I am so sorry, but these last two are key questions. What is the name of the Company supplying the global Computer Programme?" James replied, "I will fax you all the details shortly!"

"The last question, and I understand that you may not have the answer at your fingertips. But an answer tomorrow by phone or fax will suffice. The question is this, are any of the components in these computers sourced from sub-suppliers in Turkey or Iran?"

James, responded in an understanding way. "I know you guys have a really difficult job on your hands and need to play your cards close to your chest. Maybe one day we will meet for a drink in a more relaxed atmosphere."

Just before he clicked off Anneliese shouted, "James, thank you, your help has been amazing. I would like to help you with one last suggestion. Until we have finished our investigation, keep all your people away from the new computers! Look forward to hearing from you tomorrow."

They had used up the whole hour, but so had everyone. One after the other, on time, they gradually settled back in the conference room. Everybody seemed to be in a good place, with smiles on their faces as they began to chat.

Anneliese, first leaning back in her chair, then tidying the papers in front of her, said, "We only had an hour but looking around you, it looks like it went well. So, who would like to speak first!"

Chapter 16

Terrorists Cheer the PM

Frank, always the unobtrusive one, sitting at the back of the room, stood. Anneliese knew more than anyone that Frank's input, although always appearing introverted, was totally invaluable!

Anneliese's respect for Frank had increased and developed over several years. So much so, that she had named her young 3 year old son after him. As she spoke, her mind glanced back to Frank Junior. But what she was involved in was her way of ensuring he would experience a better world!

Frank edged toward the horseshoe conference table. "I raised a proposal earlier but we never got to finish it. You may recall I thought that, probably, budgets would not accommodate the idea, but possibly we could install the latest technology, cameras and links to law enforcement to protect the top 10 list that we agreed earlier."

Anneliese interrupted Frank. "Oh, I'm sorry Frank, I don't have an excuse other than things are moving so fast, and need to move fast. I know we will be ill-advised to ever ignore your thoughts."

Frank now entered the world that was most important to him. There were a few others, but Anneliese would always be there for him, as he would for her. He blotted out everyone else in the room and strode around to where she sat. Leaning over her, he clasped her cheeks as he kissed her forehead. Then standing straight, he searched the silent faces around the room. He slowly, quietly began to speak. "I have worked with this woman on several difficult assignments. She will never let any of you down. She will handle whatever is thrown at her, and there are many other people in our organisation that feel the same way. This last 48 hours has achieved fabulous results. And I'm sure we are about to hear more. Her thinking, her planning, her execution, will result in complete success!"

Frank now sidled back to his position in the corner of the room. "My report", he uttered, "involves the possible installation of high technology security equipment in the Top 10 Medical manufacturing facilities. Cameras and phones linked directly to law enforcement Agencies. My initial thinking was it would be deemed too expensive. However, I talked with Commander Farrell of CECD who would contribute 50% of the cost. He will discuss the proposal with the CIA Director, so it may have some mileage after all. The thinking is, it may be possible to get the equipment in place within ten days."

It was the beginning of the working day in London. In Number 10 Downing Street, another COBRA meeting had already commenced. The Sixth meeting in only five weeks. The central topic under review was the gradual collapse of NHS services, predominately, surgical and dental. The resultant escalation of waiting lists, death rates and overwhelmed A&E services! And in consequence, originally peaceful protests that had been spreading through Great Britain were becoming less peaceful, and in areas of London, developing into riots!

Subsequently, the Prime Minister and Home Secretary appeared on television to address the Nation, in an attempt to calm peoples' nerves!

Senior Government Ministers were due to convene again early evening. The subject of this meeting would be Havana Syndrome, which also had suffered serious escalation. Internally, Government circles had agreed to not give this public exposure as the NHS crisis was more than enough to cope with!

On the upper floor of a vast building, four hours flight away from London, a large group of people were clustered around a 43inch TV screen. Mostly, sitting cross-legged on the floor, watching the BBC World Service news programme. As the UK Prime Minister finished speaking and was stepping away from cameras, the room erupted. Shouting, screaming, high fives and pats on backs. Some of the men waved guns around in the air, but did not fire them in case it drew attention.

These people, in the Istanbul building, knew every detail behind the P.M's words. His speech had confirmed, undeniably confirmed, that their incursions into US territory were having the desired effect. They began placing bets on how long it would be before the American President decided to face the people of the USA.

The calamitous effects being reported had already reached Anneliese's working group. They all had the feeling the Citadel was being stormed whilst they pontificated in a room in Jackson, Virginia. They, now into the second half of their 48 hour intelligence match, needed to find an easy way to defend and then gain ground to attack.

Anneliese stood in front of the team. "Let's not let this rattle us." Her expression was determined and confident. "We are well on the way to discovering success! Right now you all feel like Canaries in the coal mine. And if we are Canaries, so be it, but just like those canaries, we will give our people the answers they need to survive!"

Anneliese was distracted by a very loud knock on the door. One of Denton's analysts whispered to Anneliese, who immediately turned and called Hana over. Loud enough for everyone to hear, she said "Hana, we have a computer and an engineer for you to go play with." Hana, with a very wide smile, waved and left the room.

As Anneliese turned to return to her seat, there was another knock. She turned again whilst everyone craned their necks. She moved away from the person at the door. "Chuck and Denton, your people have several messages for you. Well, they are addressed to Jerome and myself, but they are in your department, and I think it's right that you look at them first."

Chapter 17

Hana Delivers with Donald

The staff in the 3rd floor laboratory had been extremely accommodating. They had cleared a whole section of the room and a large work-top was available to Hana.

The laboratory supervisor had a few words with Hana. He had five staff plus himself. Did she want them to stay? Hana, grateful for the offer, thanked him, but then said it was imperative that all wore protective breathing equipment until they knew what they were dealing with. The engineer, a young enthusiastic guy looked bemused, saying "I don't need it." Hana, assertively, replied, "Yes you do. Until I say we are ok, you will take instruction!"

Hana called the staff and the engineer together. Her plan was pretty simple. The engineer would take the computer apart as fast as possible. The lab staff would, keeping up with him, attach each part to a board with the numbered order in which it had been dismantled.

Before they dressed in the safety equipment, gloves included, Hana turned to the engineer. His name was Donald, she informed everyone. Now they were ready to get going. As Donald began to work; the lab staff formed a disassembly line, the teardown board was ready and they had stickers ready to number the components.

As he worked, Donald spoke to Hana. "Do you know what you are looking for or which component you are most interested in?"

Hana, with a thoughtful expression, held onto Donald's arm. "Stop for a moment please. I don't know if this product uses convective or fan-forced air flow. But whichever it is, I need to view those components. I also need to have a good look at the heatsink which supports the extraction of heat."

Donald, now enjoying and excited by the fact that he was working with someone that understood hardware, gazed into Hana's deep brown eyes and mumbled, "I am just about to take those bits apart." Hana turned to the lab staff, saying, "Until Donald says complete, would you please board the next parts separately from the rest!"

In a few minutes it was done. Hana, with a strobe light and magnifying glass, began to interrogate the separated emission components. As she searched the heatsink she said, "That's it, found it!" but this exclamation was not euphoric. Waving her arms, she ushered everyone toward the door. With the group by the door, Hana said, "Please leave and don't come back until you are told its safe!"

As Hana and Donald exited, Hana asked, "Would you like a coffee? I owe you that; you should be proud of your skills, so please let me buy you a coffee."

They went off to the coffee shop in the lobby. Hana was exhilarated, but Donald didn't have a clue why. As they enjoyed the coffee, she explained that the computers had been sabotaged by a terrorist group. She had found a tiny capsule installed in the heatsink. Heat would eventually melt the capsule and the contents would be part of the exhaust that the operator inhaled. She suspected it was a nerve gas.

"Donald, I probably shouldn't have given you so much information. But in reality, I recognise you may have put your health and, indeed, life on the line today." Donald smiled saying, "I'm sorry I was late today, but I suppose I managed, in the end, to help."

These two were getting on well. Just making conversation, Hana asked, "So why were you late? This place is famous and even do tours!" Donald, with an embarrassed look said his van did not have a navigation device like all the new vehicles. So he phoned the office. He explained he had a compass stuck on his windscreen. They gave him coordinates. West 77degrees, North 38degrees." I tried to work that out on my windscreen compass!" Hana exploded "Stop, you may have just given me another answer." She leaned forward, kissed him gently on the lips. As she left, she passed him her card, and shouted "please ring me. I mean it, please ring me, and I'm sorry, but this is life or death!"

Jerome and Anneliese were sitting together discussing the disturbances in the UK. The conference room door burst open with such force, a picture clattered as it hit the floor. Jerome and Anneliese sat, open-mouthed, staring at Hana in the doorway. She stood, breathless, motionless, but with the widest grin.

Hana, pointing at the flip chart, burst past Anneliese and Jerome, whilst trying to catch her breath. Reaching the chart, she flipped to a clean page. She scribbled a bullet point and against it, in large capitals, she wrote THE COMPUTERS ARE BOOBY TRAPPED. THINK NERVE GAS! Scribbling another bullet point, she began to giggle loudly as she wrote DAN BIE = 41 degrees N, 29 degrees E – I THINK!

Their time was almost up. Hana, now laughing out loud, shuffled over to Anneliese and Jerome, who were now standing, staring at the flip chart.

The rest of the team started to drift back in. Chuck, Denton and then Frank. Once settled, Anneliese ambled to the front, saying, "You all have things to tell us, but based on what Hana has written, I think she should speak first."

Hana explained that she had worked on the computer in the laboratory which was at the far end of the building, upstairs. The lab staff helped as the engineer dismantled it. "I was looking for the heatsink which supports the heat extraction using fan-forced air flow. I found a tiny capsule attached to the corner of the heatsink. It would slowly melt and I believe the capsule contains some form of nerve gas. This would be emitted as part of the heat exhaust."

"As we know, 100% were supplied by the same Corporation; we need to put out an alert to prevent any further use of these computers. All units should be immediately recalled and disassembled. Essentially this will halt the spread of Havana Syndrome!"

The cheering was heard on all floors of the building. "The second bullet point is just a hunch! The engineer mentioned a compass and it seemed to fit the DAN BIE pattern. So if someone could check those coordinates it may take us another step forward." Chuck volunteered, and left the room.

Denton, as the room quietened asked to speak. "Just a couple of things. First, you won't be surprised to hear that we have confirmation that three of the computer components are manufactured in Turkey. Indeed, they are all from a sub-supplier in Istanbul. And to add another piece to the jigsaw, the heatsink is one of those components."

Anneliese let out a piercing yelp, took a deep breath then loudly said "Now we are taking off! We will soon be at mach1 and the cheers will be as loud as a sonic boom!"

Denton stepped back into the arena. "Not sure if it has importance, or is just a coincidence, but the Company supplying the computers is named The Bietronics Corporation." Following a brief silence, Jerome's singular expletive was "Wow, if that's a coincidence, I'm a Dutch uncle!" expressions around the room told Jerome he was not understood. "Oh, I'm sorry," he said. "It's an English expression that I've never understood either!"

Anneliese took charge once again. "There are a few things we should do to tidy up." Looking over at Denton and Chuck, she said, "I believe in American circles you call it, doing the housekeeping." Frank interjected, "Before that Anneliese, the engineer that did such a good job for Hana wants to leave. However, the Marines on reception say they require authority from a senior person." Anneliese, with an assertive voice announced that this could kill three birds with one stone. "Frank, would you do this for us. Go down to reception, and ask them to call the CIA director, Mr Webster. They should ask him to join us immediately. We have some really good news! Then we can get his authorisation for the engineer and several other issues."

Chapter 18

Geographical Coordinated Pinpoint

In the short period waiting for Mr Webster, Hana addressed the team. "The engineer that worked for me today really knows his business. In view of all he knows, he won't be able to leave without a lot of fuss and assurances. I would like to ask the Director to appoint him to join us, because all this hardware will need dismantling. He could carry on working for Bietronics, but be on assignment to the US government until we are through this."

Anneliese said, "Hana great idea. We will need him." Just as she finished speaking, the door burst open and the picture fell off the wall again. Jerome retrieved it whilst Anneliese welcomed Mr Webster.

With her most assured expression and alluring eye contact, she addressed the CIA Director. "First thing to say, Sir, is that shortly the Havana Syndrome will be no more. We need your assistance to close that off, then we can all breathe a sigh of relief."

Mr William Webster was in seventh heaven. Anneliese went on to explain, briefly, Hana's work with the computer and what she'd found. Also, all other information concerning the components manufactured in Istanbul. The coded message, DAN BIE and Hana's hunch that it represented geographic coordinates. As she was about to continue, there was a knock on the door.

It was one of Chuck's subordinates with a note for Chuck. The Director, getting excited by all he was hearing, was continuing to ask questions. With each answer, he realised this team were unbeatable and the best they would ever experience in the USA.

Chuck, also hardly able to believe the number of baskets they were scoring, had his hand up to speak. Green cards had become obsolete with this extraordinarily cohesive team.

Mr Webster indicated to Chuck to speak. "Sir, Hana, working with the Bietronics engineer, came up with a decipher of the possible coded message.... DAN BIE! Don't have a single clue how she did it, but it was a set of geographic coordinates. My guys have checked, and checked again. It is definitely Istanbul."

The Director, as his jaw dropped, leaned back in his chair. "So now I have lots of good news to give the President." Frank, slowly and concisely spoke. "We have a possible dangerous nerve gas sitting up in your laboratory. We need to get it taken away to make the building safe. Also, we have a Bietronics engineer who has demonstrated today he is probably the best in the business; he wants to be released, but before that, Hana wants to make a request on his behalf."

Hana stood and in the most courteous way she could conjure up, appealed to the Director. "The engineer that I worked with today is the best hardware engineer you will ever find. We are going to have thousands of these computers to deal with. He knows them inside out. We, our team, have discussed this and wish to request he be offered a management job marshalling all these computers into an area where we can make them safe. Why waste millions of dollars when this guy can oversee their rehabilitation."

Looking around the room, William Webster agreed and said he would get everything moving.

Anneliese now with a stoic expression and a voice to match, turned to the Director" The last thing we need your help with is where we go from here. Absolutely everything indicates we need a force out in Istanbul. Intelligence is solid, and now we have interpreted mystical messages from staff suffering Havana Syndrome. We require your help with approval for our team to go to Istanbul."

Mr Webster stroked his chin for a while as he peered into Anneliese's demanding blue/green eyes. "I want to give you immediate, concise and clear direction. Anneliese, you know I can't do that! The next part of this operation takes us into dangerous political territory. There has to be discussion and agreement with the President. My proposal is this, I will meet with the President and his Chief of Staff as early as possible tomorrow."

"Anneliese, you and your team have delivered today. But to go into the arena with the President and his gladiators, I need persuasive weaponry. I need you to prepare a summary of the events that led us to the conclusion we should assign your team, our CIA agents and possibly military into Istanbul. We will be taking our offensive into another countries' domain. I would also welcome a summary of the events and findings regarding the Bietronics computers and a clear and concise picture of actions necessary to eliminate Havana Syndrome."

"I know I'm asking an awful lot, but I also know you are capable of an awful lot." Anneliese, smiling at the Director, said "I guessed that would be your position. Yes, we will have the necessary reports ready for you by 7am."

The Director's car was waiting. As he approached the door, he turned, and in a loud voice exclaimed, "You guys have done a superb job. It's not finished yet but we are getting close. You have my heartfelt thanks"" He waved as he left and Anneliese closed the door behind him.

Standing in front of the team she stood quietly for a second or two. She then surprised them all. Without a word, she began a ballerina's pirouette. Slowly at first, but gaining speed so fast her flowing dress fluttered around like a large parasol in a summer breeze. Her speed diminished, and as she came to a halt, her smile consumed everyone.

"I'm not going to apologise for that because I absolutely needed to show all of you how I feel about your achievements. The Director touched on it, but I've been with you. The journey has been fantastic, and that was how I felt, and had to express myself. But now we have some more to do. I know you are all tired, but we will overcome."

"So this is my suggestion. I will work with Frank to write the first report. The Havana Syndrome report should come from Hana and Jerome." "The third report, involving a sortie into Istanbul will, necessarily, involve our whole team."

Looking around everyone, Anneliese, with a somewhat sour expression, said, "This will probably require us to work through the rest of the night. I will deliver the reports to the Director at 7am, then we should be able to catch up on sleep during the rest of the day."

"One or two things to mention. It's a general rule that each report will only take up one side of an A4 page. This first report should touch on the details we have regarding intelligence reports from the CIA undercover agents in

Istanbul. Also the efforts that have been made to protect Medical factories, together with the assignment of all service personnel to attempt to apprehend terrorists in the event of an attack on the top 3 most vulnerable facilities."

"The second report by Hana and Jerome should commence with the work that Jerome did capturing input from both US and UK Personnel experiencing HS. Then it should move to the work that Hana did on the teardown analysis. Importantly, you guys must mention the need to urgently get the capsule contents analysed and, possibly, identified. The other very urgent action is to get all these Bietronics computers out of the work place and into a safe place. Then Donald should take on the job of making every unit safe, and through a rehabilitation programme. My view is, that the rehabilitation programme should be the responsibility of Bietronics.

"Frank and I will make a start on the third report but once you are finished, just come and join us to develop it!"

Chapter 19

The US President Smells Success

As good as their word, at 6.50am they all hugged one another feeling they had completed a good, fair, assessment of all the events. Anneliese, a very bleary-eyed Anneliese, took 6 copies of the report down to reception where a driver was waiting to collect them. The rest of the team were continuing to drink coffee, as they had, all through the night!

They all settled down for slumber in their makeshift dormitory. At around 2pm the phones began to ring. Then loud knocking on the door. Hana was the first to answer the door, whilst Chuck was answering a phone. One of Denton's staff stood at the door. "Excuse me Mam" he said, "but we have had a message for you guys. The Director requests you to assemble in the 2nd floor conference room at 3.30pm for his debrief."

Mr Webster, about 5 minutes late, and looking a little flustered, apologised saying he had an important phone call just as he was leaving his office. About to begin, he slowly looked around everyone as his smile widened. "Well, ladies and gentlemen, you should be extremely proud of yourselves. The President and I went through your report together; word for word. Indeed, Mr President read it out loud a second time, commenting to the Chief of Staff and I as he picked out salient points. He was astonished at your teamwork and, in particular, the work of Hana and Jerome. All of you were magnificent, and the only reason you two were singled out was that it seemed you had some magical, mystical help from some "power for good"."

"Anyway, the end result was that the President asked me to pass you his gratitude. He has already taken action on the urgent safety issues you specified. And we were all in total agreement with your recommendations."

"The team that should get themselves to Istanbul is Anneliese, Frank, Hana, Jerome and Chuck. Your assignment is to conclusively finalise the intelligence that will allow us to formulate an action plan that nails these bastards."

The lines on his face contracted into an aggressive expression as he uttered these words. He thought for a few seconds then continued. "The President is prepared to provide all resources you need. The first wave will be military support to be based on a clandestine ship, moored near the port of Istanbul. Several CIA agents will be deployed in properties close to the US Consulate. A frigate with SEALs and US Marines will be stationed at the exit from the Bosphorus Strait, into the Sea of Marmara, using the islands for cover. If the terrorists attempt to escape by sea, the frigate will seal their fate!"

"Furthermore, the President has an agreement with the Turkish Government. Their President is giving us his total support. Therefore, we will also have several US helicopters based in Istanbul airport."

"Your teams' first task will be to spend time with our CIA agents based in Istanbul. As you know, they already have a substantial number of leads. And they will spend the next couple of days working on a plan to help you."

"They have been tracking a guy that they are sure is involved. He goes most days to a Dentistry Clinic. Their surveillance has convinced them that this property may be the terrorists cover. They have done exemplary work on this, establishing that the clinic are advertising for a receptionist with language abilities. They have applied on behalf of one of your team…. Hana! Our operatives have already arranged her Turkish passport, references, family history. In summary her complete cover!"

"As soon as you are there, they will review every detail with you, and especially Hana." The whole team, with nods and smiles at one another were obviously enamoured by the level of support work that would be available to them. Hana appeared ecstatic; almost ready to leap out of her chair.

Mr Webster, peering around at their proud faces, exclaimed, "You are looking excited, and better than that, I can see pride in your eyes. And yes, you deserve to be proud, absolutely proud! And unless you have any questions, I think we have reached the point to wrap up this meeting. You all deserve a celebration drink, and I'm sorry I can't join you. But when this is all over, I promise we will have a party to remember."

The Director, shuffled his papers together and placed them in his leather folder. Straightening his back, and looking around, he had a last thing to say. "It's Wednesday, and you will be flown out of Jackson airport on Friday. Enjoy the rest, which I know you need. And I will ensure we are all in constant contact!"

Waving as he left, Anneliese moved back to the front of the group. Always understated, she giggled then said, "Well that went well."

As they all left the conference room, with happiness and relief on their faces, Anneliese put her arm around Hana. "You are the star of our group at the moment, and I'm so glad you are. To join a new team, is never easy but you have fitted in better than anyone expected. I, years ago, had a colleague that was just like you. In fact, you seem so similar, and she was my best friend for what seemed a lifetime. I hope we can evolve in the same way. Hana, clearly rapturous and invigorated by Anneliese's comments, said, "Well, shall we all get to the bar and have that celebration drink? I don't know about the rest of you, but it will wrap up an absolutely brilliant few days!"

The next few hours were literally intoxicating. The CIA Director had left instructions that tonight was a free bar for their team. None of them went too far. Just enjoyed their evening together.

Late on, most of them had drifted away to their beds. Frank, who never needed or wanted too much alcohol had left in the middle of the evening. He always seemed to continue to work, whatever the temptation!

Anneliese had remained to ensure that none of her team fell off cloud 9. She was last in the bar, chatting with Jerome, concerned about him. He had consumed more than his fair share of alcohol and had become melancholy.

Chapter 20

Jerome's Anya Visitation

Anneliese, having known him for years, sensed that his morbid mindset was worsening and needed rescuing. "Jerome, what is eating at you? Your achievements have been sensational, but I know you are in a bad place!" Her psychoanalysis was now reaching top speed, as she searched his semi-intoxicated eyes. Her gentle glance into his eyes, initially made him drop his head. Both of them were quiet for about 30 seconds!

Jerome's face slowly lifted and peered back into Anneliese's caring expression. "I want to tell you everything but I'm worried you may think I'm not making sense. Maybe even think I am going nuts! And maybe I am. I've been days and nights trying to analyse all this but have not found an answer!"

As he finished those few words, tears engulfed his eyes and as Anneliese saw them starting to trickle down his cheeks, she knew that listening was the answer. "Jerome, please explain. I know I can help and I can't bear to see you suffering like this."

Jerome took a deep breath then reached for his handkerchief in his top pocket. "Please don't think I've lost my marbles when I tell you this, but you are probably the only person I could talk to about it." Anneliese could see how much he was hurting and reached across to hold his hand. They now both took a breath, and began to smile. Anneliese whispered, "I will never ever believe anything bad about you, or leave you. You were Anya's protégé and you know how much I loved her!"

Jerome's face livened. "That's it, Its Anya! She has contacted me every night for several days. My sleep is suffering and I'm finding it hard to keep it all together! I'm now doubting my own thoughts, my own feelings; my own mind! Although it's you Anneliese, just trying to have this first conversation is making me tremble."

Anneliese, engrossed by his crisis, gripped Jerome's hand, squeezing it so tight he began to relax. Leaning forward to Anneliese, Jerome's speech was tinged with disbelief!

"Anya comes to me as I drift into sleep. But I'm not asleep, it's not a dream. I wake up; I'm wide awake and she is sitting there on the edge of my bed. She talks about the events leading to her death. The horse rearing, her foot caught in the stirrup and being dragged across rocks and boulders and seeing her blood pouring onto them."

"I knew nothing of all that. I wasn't there. Nobody has even spoken about those horrific events. But if they are true;" he stopped as his stare into Anneliese's eyes was questioning.

Recalling those dreadful events, emotion now gripped Anneliese. "Yes, they are true, "she said, as tears welled up in her eyes.

Jerome, rubbing his eyes, took a deep breath. As he exhaled, he slowly continued. "Anya said she was in a mental health crisis, being attacked on all fronts by demons. She will carry remorse with her throughout eternity. Her attack on you, Anneliese, was caused by those evil demons and she said to tell you she knows her remorse will never be enough. But she loved you, still loves you, and her soul will, throughout eternity, be flooded with that love."

"Her soul will now continue to fight evil. She will be alongside us in everything we do. She has already worked with us to resolve some of the difficult issues we have faced. And now she is being allowed to transition her heavenly soul into a physical human presence. She said she cannot explain how excited she is at the prospect. The transition has already begun and, as it proceeds, she will gradually fade. Anya will become immersed in the body and soul of Hana!"

Anneliese clasped an emotional Jerome. As she gently kissed his cheek, she whispered, "I believe, absolutely, every word you have spoken. I am convinced it is real, not your imagination. Please Jerome, if Anya visits you again, tell her she remains in my heart and I forgive her everything. Do you know, Jerome, I spoke with Hana just a few minutes ago, and sensed some special bond between us. That feeling even prompted me to talk to her about Anya, and at the end she gave me a knowing smile that reached my very heart and soul."

"You know I have always been religious and believed that one day a glorious eternity would appear to me. Well that's happening to us right now. To have Anya's spirit in our world is a beautiful gift from the heavens!"

Jerome began to believe in the power that was engulfing them. His heart was pounding as he searched Anneliese's face. As their eyes met and made deep contact, Jerome asked "How do we both go on from here?"

Anneliese's smile was intoxicating. Holding Jerome's hands she said, "Jerome, this, for now, will be our secret. It's a secret that I have always prayed for and believed in. We, us two, have been visited by the best friend we ever had, and that has confirmed that there is life after death. A thing I have always believed and prayed for."

"As far as where we go from here, we keep this extra special revelation between us. We move forward knowing that we both have very powerful support in all that we do; Anya, in the form of Hana, will be amongst us. We could not ask for more!"

"Friday, Jerome, we will charge into Istanbul with the knowledge that our crusade cannot fail. That doesn't mean it will be a walk in the park. But it does mean that forces for good will be with us. Indeed, they will be there with us, amongst us!"

"Jerome, I don't know how I can ever thank you for this. You are a very special person that has been selected to be the messenger to get good on the road to triumph over evil. So now we should both head off to our slumber. We will both sleep soundly tonight, and in my prayers, I will thank God for giving you the task of involving me."

Chapter 21

Mystical Message - Tommy!

Thursday was a relatively quiet relaxed day. In the afternoon, the whole team assembled in the conference room. Anneliese led the meeting. "The only purpose of this meeting is to give you the arrangements for tomorrow. We will fly commercial from Norfolk to Istanbul, with a short stop in Madrid, Spain. There are only five of us and we are being treated to a first class flight. We are to behave as tourists. We will be undercover from the moment we leave Jackson. When we arrive in Istanbul, vehicles dressed as taxis', driven by CIA operatives, will take us to the US Consulate where we will spend the first couple of days. These days will be taken up reviewing CIA intelligence and developing the next steps! Any questions?" Chuck put his hand up to ask what the temperature would be. Anneliese chuckled as she replied, "About 30 degrees C, so all of you would be well advised to bring shorts!" No more questions were forthcoming, then Anneliese said, "I have one question, and it's to Hana."

"Would you mind explaining to the team how you deciphered that HS message that gave the code DAN BIE. None of us have worked it out and we are fascinated to know how you fathomed it out!"

Hana, once again in her respectful way, stood. Anneliese smiled, saying "You really don't need to stand." "No, but

I really do need to walk around whilst I explain. It was a strange set of circumstances that came together, almost like a patchwork quilt being sewn together."

"I already had immediately recognised the meaning of the numbers. Istanbul telephone numbers. Numbers that I had dialled almost every day for a year. So, I suppose, not much to be surprised about in that. The next part of this story leaves me standing in wonderland. The previous night, in my dreams, I saw a really beautiful woman. All she kept saying was, remember Tommy, remember Tommy, remember Tommy."

"When I awoke, those words wouldn't leave me. So who was Tommy? In my childhood I lived in beautiful gorgeous Prague. Tommy was a holiday visitor from England. We became inseparable. I taught him some Czech language and he taught me some English. He taught me games and I returned the compliment. A game he taught me, and all my friends, became the favourite. We would sit in the square, with several of us kids playing, and passers-by stopping to watch."

"For hours and hours, our voices reverberated around the square. I think most of the locals could repeat the words, along with us! The rhyme that initiated the game is simple, now that my English is good. It wasn't so good for us kids in those early days. But it goes like this! NORTH, SOUTH, EAST, WEST, WHO'S THE KING OF THE CROWS NEST! It goes on from there to form the game, but those words were the trigger."

"When I saw DAN BIE it came to me: D letter4, A letter 1, N means North, B letter 2, I letter 9, E means East. It's the geographic coordinates for Istanbul; once again Istanbul! That beautiful lady, that mystical person, had instilled into my brain the way to find the answer. And whilst working with Don, he mentioned a compass. That shook the answer out of my brain!"

The room was quiet and all eyes were wide with wonder. Anneliese with eyes on Jerome and a knowing smile, thanked Hana. "And what a marvellous story! Well, whoever that lady was, she has pushed you to the front as our trailblazer."

"Let's all hope and pray the mystical lady stays with us throughout our assignment in Istanbul."

"There is a second slice of help that we will get in Istanbul. The Turkish Minister of the Interior has assigned the Gendarmerie of the Turkish Republic to work with us and maintain constant contact. I am informed that a few of the Gendarmes' will escort us from the airport to the US Consulate."

"I think that just about wraps up this briefing meeting. And I sincerely hope we all experience as much future success as we have had so far!"

After a day of well-deserved rest, and then frantic last minute packing, they were all exclusively comfortable in the first class seats in the upstairs section of a Boeing 747A. Constant security surveillance was available to them in the shape of Frank. He had selected the upstairs because, as he put it, "only a few other passengers and easier to defend!"

Chapter 22

Istanbul Crusade

They landed in Istanbul around midday. The Gendarmes were there to meet them in arrivals; escorted them on a fast track through passport control and even helped collect their luggage. Then it was out of a side door, down a corridor and out to two waiting MPV vehicles. No sign of customs!

They sped off down the highway and into the city. They arrived at the US Consulate General which was in the Istinye Poligon. The address was unpronounceable like most in Turkey, but it was in the city, and they would always have help.

Entering electronic gates a couple of sentries indicated to go straight into the building. A massive white painted building that resembled a hospital. They were met, once inside, by the Consular General and three of his staff. After courteous welcomes, one of the staff members talked with Chuck. He was provided a map of the building noting the dining room and the bar. Then they were escorted to their rooms. As they walked, Chuck said he would collect them for dinner and give them details of plans for the next day. It had been a long tiring journey, so they were all pleased to enter their own rooms.

After showers and finding their way around their very comfortable rooms, they just had time for relaxation on the bed. Chuck was around to them all approximately ten minutes to seven. All their rooms were on the same floor, the third floor, in a neat line next to each other.

The dining room was a very well appointed and inviting room with well-dressed tables, menus and waitresses. They were shown to a large table that seated them all, with three seats to spare.

Everyone was suffering jet-lag until wine was brought to the table by a beautiful Turkish lady named Fatma. Her English was superb and she clearly intended to make this a night that would be a Turkish delight.

Whilst waiting for the first course, and most enjoying a second glass of wine, Chuck, glass in hand, stood and proposed a toast to success in their venture. But then he followed with some information on arrangements.

First turning to Hana, he explained that it would be necessary to place her in an apartment close to her work, to avoid suspicion. Slowly, thinking as he reviewed his notes, he turned to Anneliese. "The rest of that plan is that you should accompany Hana, both for safety and also in an advisory capacity." Anneliese could not contain herself. With a grateful smile, she first looked at Hana and then back to Chuck. "That is an idea that I cannot reject; please continue."

Chuck realised he was doing better than he had expected, so his confidence was at the top of the gauge. Now moving left to face Jerome he was about to speak, but decided instead to take a large gulp of wine as a courage builder. Now, prepared to continue, he peered at the expectant Jerome.

Frank, the quiet, but always together, man in the group, saw this as his chance to elevate the confidence of both these individuals. "Chuck, you are addressing an East Ender. He's almost a pure Cockney. Nothing you are going to say will fill him with fear. He's as hard as a piece of granite, so don't be afraid to say it as it is!"

Chuck smiled, his pure white teeth glistening as he did so. "Ok, so first I will take myself partially off the hook. These plans, after a lot of work with our CIA in Istanbul, have been prepared by our own Walrus, Denton. He has recommended that Jerome book himself into the clinic for a possible new set of teeth veneers. Anneliese would accompany him as his cousin, it would give us more support for Hana! And Anneliese could, while she's waiting around, do her best to reconnoitre the place." Jerome interjected;" They can look at my teeth and if they can improve them, I'm up for that!"

Chapter 23

Recall – Donald Impresses Denton

Back in Jackson, only a few miles away from HQ, in a disused hangar, a disassembly line was working full bore. So far, around 1000 computers had been shipped back from various locations. It was estimated that another 1500 units would complete the recall.

Don had been in charge of the whole process for about a week. All retrieved capsules of nerve gas were safely packaged and delivered to a US military site in the Mohave Desert, and destroyed. Don had organised and trained five military volunteers for the disassembly, and a further three personnel for packaging. So far, this team had managed to complete 120 units per day, and with growing experience, would soon be at 160 units per day. Don's plan then was to train the disassemblers to reassemble the units, and get them shipped back to the originating areas.

Today, Don was expecting a visit from Denton to review progress, in order to report back to the CIA Director. Don had thought through what he would tell Denton, and had decided to put his own neck on the line. He would stick with the promise he had made to himself. The impact of Havana Syndrome would substantially decrease over the next 10 days, and be no more after the 10 days were up.

Don had trained one of the Marine Corp Engineers to organise and process the re-assembly such that the computers could be shipped back to originating locations as soon as cleaning and quality checks were completed. His guess work on this was that it would take around a month. However, the pressure from above would not be excessive, and the guy he had trained was exceptionally good.

Denton arrived on time at 11am. Don took him around, explained the process and gave him all the time-scales for completion. Denton, as he sweltered in his safety overalls and visor, said, "Don, that's a fantastic result! The boss will be ecstatic!"

They came away and sat outside drinking water on this hot day. Denton had been suffering in breathing apparatus and his safety suit, and was relieved to be in the fresh air. They began to chat as if friends!

Enjoying the cool breeze, Denton, smoothing his wayward moustache, leant across the small white garden table as they sat outside the hangar. "So Don, now you are in this grubby business with the rest of us, are you coping with it; are you enjoying it?" Don, with a shocked expression, peered into Denton's eyes. "This is the best and most rewarding job I have ever had. I would never, ever, have expected to be doing such an important job. Helping my own country, and better than that, other countries that rely on us!"

Denton imitated a salute, saying, "Don you are my kind of guy, we are going to get on famously. But tell me, what did you do before you joined Bietronics?"

Don took a sip of his water and a deep breath. "Denton, I am going to be completely honest with you. I grew up in an area of Detroit, Michigan. Not a trailer park, but a housing estate that wasn't much better. It can't get much worse than

Michigan Avenue where I lived. Never achieved much at school or college. The whole area, almost every house, was regularly burgled. So I thought that was what you needed to do to survive. I became a bad boy. A very bad boy, but never got caught so there are no sheriff's records!"

"Then a light bulb turned on. With all those burglaries, people were always crying out for locksmiths, and they were few and far between. I took a locksmith course, and it hit the spot. I was good at it. No, not just good, I was great. I can get through any lock and fix any lock."

I used an old computer to help me in the locksmith profession. And I became accomplished with computers. I absolutely loved this new creation; this new technology. Although, of late, my job has been the hardware, and in view of my present work, I am grateful for that, but I also excel with software."

"Working through computer programmes has many features that are also necessary to open locks. I taught myself to hack into systems using a similarly ordered step-by-step approach applied to locks. Whether they be door locks, car locks or safe tumbler locks. And now I am a very competent hacker!"

Denton's sophisticated intellect began to race ahead. Picking up his bottle of water, he stood, bent forward and poured water over this thinning hair. He shook his head then stood up straight. His lips formed a grin as he wiped water away from his eyes. "Your skills are very attractive to me, Don. When you are finished with the hardware programme, I'm pretty sure I can find you a position on my team!"

"We can talk more nearer the time, and if you like what I am offering, you will become part of the CIA Intelligence Team. I have to get back to the office now, but think it over.

You have already been given clearance so we will just need a relaxed interview chat! Of course, there will be the usual bureaucracy, but it just involves a few signatures."

Later that evening, Frank called Denton. "Any news on the intelligence front, Denton?" "Yes Frank, I was just about to call or fax you. There's some information that needs to be dispersed among the team with you in Istanbul. Our scientists in the Phoenix laboratories have analysed several of the capsules we sent them. They are definitely a weak, slow acting nerve gas. It won't kill, but it is debilitating for a lengthy period. They have seen it before, in attacks in London, Berlin and New York. Their capsules are much weaker but exactly the same chemical compound and mix. They are certain, due to the composition replicating those previous attacks, they originate from Russia."

"Significant weight has been added to that theory with recent intelligence reports from the Istanbul agents. As we've advised before, they track the Iranian every day. He fraternises with the same characters most days. From photographs and voice recordings they have been determined to be Russians. Indeed, at least three of them are employed in the dentistry clinic as dentists or dental assistants. However, mostly they are viewed climbing the stairs to the second floor and we don't know what's up there. It seems that dentistry is only on the ground floor! One more thing; the target facility is called the Cosmo Clinic, and it's an absolutely gigantic property. The building is almost 100 yards long and 40 yards wide.

"When you meet with Istanbul CIA tomorrow, they will provide much more information!

Chapter 24

The Istanbul CIA Team

The meeting with the local CIA guys was scheduled for early morning. Coffee, breakfast fruits and pastries would be provided in the meeting room. At 7am they filed into a vintage American style room, with a highly polished boardroom table, flock striped white and blue wallpaper, and an American flag in the corner of the room. Several pictures of US presidents clad the rear wall; George Washington, Eisenhower and Kennedy included.

With a trolley against the side wall, Chuck said they were expected to just help themselves. As they were doing that, the door opened and in ambled four, very well dressed, agents.

Different to Europeans who usually try to cluster together, these guys confidently, sat in the interspersed seats around the table. The CECD visitors, with food and drink in front of them appeared uncomfortable about tucking in. Amos, the first to speak, put them at their ease. "Please enjoy the breakfast victuals, while I introduce us." He pointed at the faces as he spoke." We are Ben, Adam and Enrique." Jerome tried to return the favour with introductions, but Amos cut him short! "We'll get to your names in a moment; in the meantime just enjoy your breakfast while I talk. My name is Amos, and in our business, us four are known as the CIA Crazies!"

Amos, clearly the senior, then said with a smile, "and we probably deserve that nickname!" He paused for a moment, then sipped his coffee, which was about the same colour as his handsome face. His smiling eyes looked around the room, then he continued. "I hope you guys don't mind but while you enjoy your breakfast I will attempt to introduce your team." Smiling in his direction, he said "I know you are Chuck. We have talked many times." Moving on he stared for a few seconds at Hana. "You are Hana! You are already getting yourself a reputation, and it couldn't be better." Amos's eyes continued on around the room. Next he focused on Jerome. "I've heard all about you also! You are Jerome, the UK's Assistant Director of GCHQ. You are a very clever kiddy and now you are on our team. I am so grateful." His eyes moved on to Frank. "Our guys have been in so many abominable situations with you, Frank, that one day, I'm sure, you will be awarded the US medal of valour. I don't need to say anymore! Anneliese, your reputation is not enough. You deserve a book to be written about your exploits. Your work in Berlin is already being written into the history books. I will be very proud to tell my grandchildren I worked with you."

Amos took a few moments breather while he sipped his coffee. Then introducing Enrique to speak, Amos explained that he had been at the forefront of the surveillance, tracking mostly the Iranian and then, more recently, the Russians that attempted to disguise their meetings with the Iranian.

Enrique was a slight character with South American features and complexion. He made everyone chuckle when he said he was usually singled out for surveillance jobs, firstly because he was small and thin, and therefore, hard to see. Secondly, in the Turkish environment his features just faded into the background!

At this point Amos re-entered the chat, saying, "don't believe all of that! He is a past master at disguise, different outfits and sometimes even working from his own fast food trailer. He is the best in the business!"

Enrique responded. "I am a quiet Mexican that is easily embarrassed." All the local CIA agents burst into laughter. Anneliese and Jerome peered at one another. Both glanced around the CECD team with knowing expressions that concluded, these CIA guys are a massively cohesive and experienced team!

Now it was Enrique describing the people he had been tailing. Times, faces and places. Next he passed around photographs of the individuals and lastly a video, surprisingly, showing inside the Cosmo Clinic.

It was now 11am, and time for a welcome break. Everybody began milling around, collecting coffees, pastries and laughing and joking about all they had seen and heard so far.

A knock on the door, followed by a very slow entrance, created an infectious silence. A face appeared around the slowly opening door. An absolutely, astoundingly, beautiful woman's face. "Come in" Amos shouted. "You are just in time!" She appeared; this female with striking features, unlined skin, plump lips and winsome eyes entranced the whole room.

Her pace into the room was slow, careful and collected. Amos escorted her to a place next to Jerome. Leaning on the arm of her chair, she twisted her tiny waist to turn to Jerome, and offered a genteel handshake.

Amos returned to his place at the head of the table. With pride written all over his sparkling eyes, he said "this person is our secret weapon. She works in the clinic as a dental nurse.

After she finished her degree, she excelled in the training for her chosen profession, dentistry. This beautiful lady, was all set to breeze through life. I approached her, having researched her CV and athletic story. I knew, with what we were contending with, I had to approach her. I didn't need to explain too much. Indeed, I was not allowed to explain too much. She has been through all the training and excelled through every checkpoint. Previously, she had excelled as a gymnastics contender for the Olympics."

By now, this poor lady had her face buried in her hands. Amos, stopped, and took a very deep breath. Looking straight into Hana's eyes, Amos exclaimed, "Hana, please meet your sidekick in this operation. Please meet our Turkish operative, Ece!"

Ece's face raised with eyes glistening. Her eyes gradually moved to focus on Amos. "Thank you, Amos, for those kind words. Amos has been my mentor, and as he has explained to me time and time again; in this job I have the chance to help keep the world safe and sane. And this is now all I live for."

"I already feel it in my heart;" she looked around the room. Her eyes settled on Hana. "We will make a great team, Hana. We will help sort this whole wicked mess out, and not just alone. Everybody here will pull their weight, and we have two special people to rely on. Anneliese and Frank!" "I have read everything there is to read about you two and it is stuff history books are made of!"

Frank, the inimitable Frank, the confident impenetrable Frank, needed to speak. "Ece, thank you for your kind words, but don't believe everything you read!"

Ece giggled which seemed to beguile everyone. Ece taking some water, spoke again. "I'm sorry, but I am due to begin my shift in 45 minutes. And I need to keep them believing I am a worthy employee. So I must leave now, but I will talk with you regularly and start the real work with Hana on Monday."

"Just one more thing Hana! Having carefully reconnoitred the clinic, I am certain the key is the second floor. Every bit of the ground floor is allocated to dentistry. There is restricted access to the second floor. But it is the place where the Iranian takes the Russians. I understand Jerome will be a visiting patient, which may prove the distraction necessary for you or I to get a look up there!" Ece, with an endearing smile and slight sway in her hips, stepped off to the Cosmo Clinic. Amos asked Ben to explain the research he was doing to assist access to the second floor.

So far, Ben had taken a back seat. Although immaculately turned out in a grey flannel suit, Ben started fidgeting with his two button jacket.

With his eyes attempting to focus on them all, but also glancing down at the middle button, which was being difficult, his face became strained. In a southern drawl, he said, "you heard Ece say that we think the second floor secretes a lot of answers. I have been working with the National Turkish Government. For reasons of secrecy they have used local government, to access all the original building plans for the Cosmo Clinic. They also have, or are in the process of getting, details of all the properties' security systems and types of lock that have been fitted. Once we have all that information, life will get a lot easier!"

At that point, the button edged through the button hole and a relieved expression appeared. "Just to finish my input! I have been wearing all this nonsense; I am a casual man, so please excuse my tussle with the button." Ben, now in a calmer frame of mind said "we now want to take you guys on a tour. It will be through the city and, slowly, past the

Cosmo Clinic. The intention being to acclimatise you to your surroundings and whereabouts. So would you mind getting yourselves ready for this exotic CIA Istanbul tour!"

Jerome, with excitement in his voice said, "I offer you guys our grateful thanks. It has been a fabulous start to our journey together."

The drive, in a Mercedes LWB bus, was about 30 miles. Every inch was interesting. They drove alongside the Bosphorus Strait for most of the journey. Parks, children's playgrounds, and noticeably, ship after cargo ship heading into the Istanbul harbour. Palm trees, and then traffic jams. Several traffic jams. One after the other, but understandable as the city of Istanbul has 15.5million people----almost twice London. Passing the turning into a narrow single lane road, Amos shouted, "That is the entrance to the Blue Mosque and the Topkapi museum. If any of you guys saw the Film Topkapi, they steal a fabulous diamond. We are going to do something similar to those terrorists. We will steal their ability to operate!"

A slow tour past the Cosmo Clinic gave the CECD an appreciation of the property. A massive glass fronted building, with several MPV's parked, many people coming and going, and several drivers sitting on the wall outside, smoking and chatting.

Chapter 25

The President wants Action

They arrived back at the Consulate. As they trailed in, one of the secretaries greeted them with a concerned expression. Amos stood to one side listening to her, then quietly explained to Jerome that the Ambassador needed to talk to him. Amos excused himself.

Everybody headed off to the dining room bar for a drink! Amos returned after about 10 minutes. He called them all together. His expression reflected a level of stress. A severe level of stress!

His first words were, "the President has been on the phone to our Director. Apparently, yesterday there was an assault on a major medical facility in Georgia. This factory was our largest supplier. It has been totally ruptured and will be out of action for weeks. The news media, both the US and UK, are all over it like a swarm of wasps."

"And different to previous attacks, this time the terrorists have taken four hostages. The President wants our action accelerated. He is pleased with what we have achieved so far, but he needs more, much more!"

"The President thought that as we have identified the Cosmo Clinic, he should initiate a military offensive. Mr Webster argued that it may win the battle but not the war!"

"After some further discussion, the President eventually allowed us five more days to save his, and our, skins!"

Amos leaned back against the bar, stroking his greying black curly locks. Took a large gulp of his Bourbon, then another! As it seeped into his system, he calmed enough to smile." Now I will help you understand why our hierarchy are so rattled. I'll start with the UK. Once the news leaked out, the kids in Northern Ireland decided it was action, not words, that were needed. They began rioting everywhere. Police cars were petrol bombed. Police were attacked. So they brought in the army. The ferocity escalated. Soldiers, and even armoured vehicles, were petrol bombed!"

"The media did their best to report the facts. But of course, all that did was spread the disease. Late into the night, London, Manchester and Liverpool suffered serious protests and civil unrest. It was contained before it developed into riots, but it was borderline all the way."

"In the USA there is even worse news." Before he continued Amos glanced around the faces in front of him. took another swig of his Bourbon and casually wiped the corners of his mouth with a napkin. He pondered before he began to speak.

"All across the States, civil unrest is beginning to bubble up. The media never help, but I suppose they have a job to do just reporting the news. In Georgia, where the attack occurred and hostages were taken, the vigilante groups are out looking for trouble. They are armed and dangerous and the police and sheriffs have been advised to stay well away."

"The Media, last night, began to report numbers of people dying. Men, women and children, resulting from medical care not being available. Obviously that has only worsened the tension within the population!"

"The Southern States have begun to move into their territorial mindset. Since the American Civil War there has been a Southern backbone that has never weakened. They are beginning to become determined to defend the South. If Government cannot do it, they will. The TV and all other media, are viewing the South's protest. Everywhere in all the Southern States, the Confederate flag is appearing. The "Stars and Bars", also known as the "Blood Stained Banner", was starting to appear all over the Southern States. Protestors are carrying placards with the words, "Gettysburg" and flags of the seven states, that exhibit ties to the Confederacy, are flying on buildings!"

"The news reports also did nothing more than make the whole scenario more threatening. Gun stores and shops have been reported to be running out of stock. And in the last few hours, shots were fired outside the White House!"

"The President needs us to quickly give him some positive news to appease the media and quieten the people. It is, in his words, unthinkable that more terrorist assaults may lead to full blown riots and even civil war!"

Anneliese went to sit in a peaceful lounge. Sipping a glass of water, she sat thinking through all the options. A priority list gradually developed in her mind. The first item was to call everyone together. She would arrange the meeting for 8pm. To get things moving, she decided to find Amos. She stood and slowly turned, to place the wicker chair back in the corner of the room. Running her hands over her pert, firm bottom, she could feel her cool, pink, linen dress had become crumpled by the wicker. As she increased her hand pressure down from her waist, stroking and brushing the fabric, Frank entered the room.

For just a few seconds, testosterone surged through his veins and his heart missed a beat. Anneliese finished smoothing her dress, stretched, and then, with hands on her hips, arched her back. She quickly turned to find Frank standing completely motionless, frozen to the spot.

Self- control ran through Frank like words in a stick of rock. However, on this occasion, this momentary lecherous incursion, caused by such feminine beauty, was unavoidable and, therefore, excusable. Indeed, it was dispelled, the moment Anneliese spoke!

"Hello Frank! Are you ok? You look bewildered!" Frank stuttered "Yes, I'm fine, at least I think I am. I just had a spasm of shivers. Perhaps I'm coming down with something."

Anneliese with a concerned expression said, "I do hope not Frank. We are heading into a difficult period and I will need your expertise every step of the way!"

With a purposeful stride Anneliese, followed by Frank, set off down the corridor to find Amos. He was in the Dining room, talking to the Manager. Anneliese's assertive expression had Amos and Frank hanging on her every word!

"I want you guys to help me get everyone together in the conference room at 8pm. Amos, I would appreciate you arranging for a flip chart to be available. And would you please call up Denton such that he could join us in a tele-conference call."

⊶⊶⊰❬❭⊱⊷⊷

Chapter 26

Havana Syndrome Defeated?

Everything was organised and everyone settled around the table at 8pm. The call came in from Denton on time. Anneliese announced that the whole team were with her and the purpose of the meeting was to find a way to end this misery. Anneliese announced to the whole gathering, "the President has given us a five day deadline. When our last deadline was set, we got together, exactly like today, and achieved success. We can achieve this; we are totally capable of defeating these terrorists!" As Anneliese searched the faces for agreement, Denton came through, loud and clear.

"Hello, all you guys, I am lonely here and missing you, but I completely understand you need a backstop; and I drew that straw. The good news is that Havana Syndrome is no more! We have defeated them on that front. There is no chance of a sabotaged computer getting back into our work areas. If they are still making them, they might as well do us a favour and send them to Russia!"

Denton continued as smiles enveloped everyone around the conference table. "Our new operative, Don, did a superb job with the computers. Also the processes, logistics and constant well-written reports to me. He has been appointed as a CIA operative because having researched his skills, he not only knows computers inside out, but also is a software specialist. He is an exceptionally skilled hacker! Which is a skill we don't often get offered. And to crown it all, he is an experienced locksmith; the cream of the crop! We are all lucky he has not become a safe- breaker!"

With that, an excited Ben stood. Looking at Anneliese, he said, "Anneliese, I don't have the green card, but it's important, after what Denton has told us, that I be allowed to speak."

Anneliese reacted with a sensitive, understanding expression. "Of course, Ben, we all trust your judgement regarding the necessity to speak. So the floor is yours!"

Ben explained he had spent a lot of time reviewing the local authority paperwork detailing the security systems and locks throughout the Cosmo building. "I am by no means trained in that discipline, so I employed skilled advisors. They all conclude the steel doors are impenetrable; the door locks are top level security locks and there is a substantial amount of electronic security requiring code input."

"So putting it simply, I think we need this character, Don, here with us as soon as possible. And then if we can get through security, up to the second floor, we will probably find that computers hold all the information."

"Don may be able to do his bit with those too." Ben took a breath, then shouted so Denton could here every word. "Denton, it may have been luck, but you may have stumbled across a horse that can win us the Kentucky Derby. Right now we all need some luck!"

Anneliese, now exhilarated by what she had heard, pretended to take back the invisible green card. Once again, with a raised voice, Anneliese said, "Denton can you get Don here by tomorrow evening?" It was a single word answer. "Yes!" "So do we all agree that, when Don is here, the next stage is to access that second floor?" It was yes's and nods all around. So this was the next phase of their plan. "After Don arrives tomorrow, we will get together again. Hana starts work tomorrow and Ece already has a pretty good take on the place. Both Hana and Ece will be needed in our meeting!"

Hana and Anneliese spent the next couple of hours getting their stuff together ready for their move into an apartment. Chuck would drive them later that night.

They eventually left for an area in Istanbul; Panorama Tarik Muzesi. It was a superb apartment in a middle class area, about ten minutes from Cosmo Clinic. Chuck gave them each a paper with addresses, phone numbers etc and said that a taxi would collect Hana at 8.30am. it would be driven by a CIA agent. Chuck would come back in the morning to take Anneliese back to the American Consulate.

Hana's driver arrived early. He brought with him two sets of clothing, appropriate for a receptionist; he explained they had been chosen based on sizes reported on her medical. Mostly trousers and pristine white blouses. For today, she had dressed in her own clothing. Anneliese had helped her choose the most acceptable, reserved, but feminine outfits. Hana looked stunning in a navy blue knee length skirt with side vents and a fetching white and blue edged, cool looking t-shirt. She set off looking calm and without a worry in the world! What was invisible was the very small Derringer pistol strapped high on her thigh. It caused emotion in Anneliese when she saw her adjusting the strap. Anya, as always, was with them in spirit! Even this small Derringer was like Anya's own pistol!

Chuck arrived for Anneliese about 10am and they re-convened in the conference room half an hour later. Anneliese, Chuck, Frank and Jerome were feeling like parents that had watched one of their children move out to make their own way in the world. But once having had a chat and a coffee, their unsettled minds were quickly healed.

As Frank was about to speak, Chuck interrupted saying that Denton had sent a fax with details of Donald's arrival times. "That's important for what I was about to say Chuck, so please continue."

For the first time in days, they all were dressed in casual clothes, looking relaxed and comfortable. Chuck, in particular, looked scintillating. An Eddie Bauer light blue cotton shirt, his cuffs rolled back twice, to half way up his muscular forearms. A pristine pair of Ralph Lauren beige chinos and what appeared to be handmade light tan ventilated moccasin shoes.

Chuck sipped his coffee as he obviously felt much calmer and collected than he did in his three piece suit. "Well, Denton says we can expect Donald about 2pm. Don't forget he's never travelled so far before and will be seriously jet-lagged. So please give him all the help you can." Denton, having seen something special in Donald, had taken on the job of mentor!

Chuck asked, looking around the table, "does anyone know if he prefers to be called Donald or Don? "Denton always seems to use Donald. But Hana has used Don." Frank jumped in feet first. "That's easy, we will ask him when he arrives. Us Europeans are not too fussy unless it's some derogatory name. But I know you guys like to be called what you have grown up with. You have "so and so the second", "so and so Junior". We don't have the intellect to work all that out. So we'll just ask him what he prefers."

Everyone gave Frank an agreeable smile. Fortuitously, the trolley lady entered with coffee and pastries. The room livened as they began chatting.

Chapter 27

Anneliese Leads Cosmo Attack

Anneliese, after ten minutes, got them back to business. "We've got just over three days to the deadline. The crucial thing we now have to tackle is when we should attempt access to the Cosmo second floor. We must remember that we are now heading into dangerous territory. As well as the safety of our people, we must remember that they have hostages. We need to access their information about all their terrorist cells. Then, when we have that we must be careful not to leave any trails that make them suspect we are onto them. If we get this part wrong, they may kill the hostages!"

"Of course, this all depends on what we find on that second floor." It's time we had a coffee break; about 15 minutes. As Anneliese moved towards the coffee trolley, Jerome stood next to her and whispered "I would like a word when you have a moment." Anneliese, with exquisite agility, swivelled on the balls of her feet to face him. Looking into his eyes, her tenderness grew as she absorbed his endearing smile. "Let's go into the library; it's quiet in there!"

Sitting in the peaceful corner, Anneliese said "I sense you have had another visit." Jerome was about to speak, but Anneliese continued. "Until the last time we spoke, I was just about managing to cling onto my faith. Now I feel reborn. My thoughts of Matthew and my little Frank Junior are with me every waking moment and those thoughts are provoking me on to victory. It is the essence of all our futures!"

Although uttered in a quiet voice, every word in Jerome's voice bubbled with joy and pride. "You guessed it! Anya appeared again last night! She was excited and so happy. She has been living in Paradise but her transmigration to Hana is almost complete. She had some sadness, leaving Albie, but her joy is now overwhelming." Albie" she said "is also being allowed to be with us. He will be resurrected alongside me; he will transmigrate into Donald! His transference has begun. Mine is coming to an end. That's why I appear now to be living in a misty world. As the mist dissipates, so will I, but then I will be with you in that wonderful physical presence, Hana. And the most glorious thing is that Albie will be with us. We will all fight evil together!"

Jerome, with a lump in his throat, took a few moments to gather himself. As he took a deep breath, Anneliese's subtle perfume engulfed his senses, lifting his spirits.

"As Anya faded, she repeated, she and Albie would be with us soon!" Jerome, as his smile widened, said "Anneliese, it's fantastic. Is this really happening?"

Anneliese, turning toward the door, said, "Jerome, yes, we both know it is! I must return to the team. They will be waiting for us!"

In the middle of the afternoon, Chuck and Donald arrived. Chuck went around the room, introducing Donald to everyone. Anneliese waited until the end of the introductions then stepped forward to ask Donald if he would like a drink. He paused before answering, staring into Anneliese's eyes as if he knew her! As he snapped out of it, he said, "I would love a cold beer." Chuck immediately volunteered to get one from the bar.

Donald was looking tired and jaded. When Chuck returned with the beer, his colour returned to his cheeks. Anneliese then asked Jerome to move next to Donald, explaining that they were going to carry on with their meeting, and Jerome should do his best to explain what was going on and get Donald up to speed.

The next issue before them was when to attempt to break into the Cosmo Clinic and get access to the second floor. In the background, Jerome could be heard explaining to Donald that it was important for him to listen to this section as he would be a key member of the team.

Anneliese managed to get Denton on a conference call. He was delighted that Donald had made it, then continued to listen in!

Frank put a stop to proceedings. Anneliese said, "What's up, Frank?" Say your piece." Frank eyeballed everyone. Slowly and deliberately, and in an assertive voice he spoke; "We don't have time to look at all this through a microscope. The bottom line is we must do this in the next two days." Smiling across at Donald, Frank said, "I am compelled to say that we now have our Houdini here. Although he's jet lagged, he's a young fit fella that will recover quickly." Denton was heard to giggle.

That background distraction put everyone at ease. Frank moved into the centre of the room. Anneliese's expression said it all. She knew something was building and Frank was the one to deliver it!

Frank's voice moved up a decibel. "As I see it, Ben is sitting on all that intelligence that addresses all the security, locks, mechanisms, electronic access pads and systems. Ben needs to review all of that guff with Donald so that he can prepare a plan to get us into that second floor. We have more help coming, in the form of Hana and Ece who have been working in the place."

Frank walked across to Donald. With an assured expression, he said, "I am sorry to put such pressure on you, but, truly you have become our main hope!" Ben arose from his seat. "Frank is correct. So shall we go into the lounge and start on it. Do you think you can stay awake and be capable enough to deal with the complexities of what I will show you."

Donald stood, and with words of encouragement from Jerome, said "Yes we can definitely do it." As he finished speaking, the door opened. It was slow, with everybody waiting to see who it was that was about to enter.

The first face that appeared was Hana. Her face, then slowly her body, edged into the room, followed by Ece. Enormous smiles as both faces scanned the room. Anneliese, beckoning to both girls to join them intensified that welcome. Hana's beaming smile locked onto Donald. The spark between them would have turned the lights on for the Trafalgar Square Christmas Tree!

Ben and Donald slowly exited the room, but Donald stopped at the door looking back at Hana. She smiled at him! Not a casual smile. A smile that engulfed every part of him with dizzying speed. Then gestured to him as she closed the door.

Chuck, at dinner time, organised for sandwiches to be sent in to Ben and Donald. Also, he placed a note on a plate, saying they would all meet again at 8pm.

Ece and Hana joined the team after dinner. Anneliese looking around everyone then spent a moment talking to Denton. "I think we should listen to Ece and Hana. They have been closest to the target today and may have new information." As she asked who would like to talk first, the door opened and in strode Ben and Donald.

Ece stood by the flip chart. With a calm voice she began. "I've been at Cosmo for a while now. I know the ground floor inside out, but I've come up against a barrier every time I have attempted to get close to the second floor. Today I was given a schlage card that gives me access all around the ground floor. I tested it but it doesn't give me access to the door at the foot of the stairs to the upper floor. And it requires an access code."

Hana now stepped forward. "As you know, I've only had today. I have managed to find a place where we can hide people. Past the dentistry surgeries there is a room where all the dentistry garments are kept. All on hangers. We could hide everyone in there. Tomorrow, I will receive my schlage card that provides ground floor internal door access, including the closet!"

"And a few feet past the closet room is an external fire door which leads out the back to an area of waste ground. Around that door are electric switches and three junction boxes. Probably for fire alarms, burglar alarms and, maybe separate alarms for the second floor."

Chapter 28

A New Star Appears – Ece

Now Ece was ready with some more input. "I have made it a routine practice to sit on the wall outside in my break. Although I don't smoke, I have pretended to be a smoker because that is where all the smokers go. Mostly taxi-drivers, some patients, and the Russians when they are around. I sat a few feet away from the Russians today and managed to record them. These micro-recorders are superb, but I also had to use some distraction on the Russians. They occasionally tried chatting to me, so I made a point of flashing my legs whenever they looked my way".

"Hana is pretty good with the Russian language, so shall we listen to the recording and see what she makes of it!" Ece smiled and glanced around as she turned the voice recorder on.

They all sat listening intently to the three minute recording. As it finished, they turned their eyes toward Hana. It was a good clear recording, despite the droning traffic noise through most of it. Smiling, she repeated Ece's last words, in Russian, purely to evidence her ability with the Russian language.

Jerome glanced at Anneliese who, although staring at Hana in a mesmerised way, had a slightly emotional expression. Jerome leaned towards Anneliese and whispered,

"What's wrong?" Her face brightened as she turned to face him and with a half laugh, returned a whisper. "Hearing her voice speaking Russian, I was definitely back in the room with Anya!" Jerome, with a poignant expression, slid his hand across the table and, for just a few seconds gripped her left hand.

All the while, Donald had not been able to take his eyes off Hana. She was now in the middle of saying that she would summarise her interpretation of the Key things she heard. Ben and Chuck simultaneously reached for their pens and note pads.

"The Iranian was named as Abdul Karim. He will leave Istanbul tomorrow morning on a flight to Philadelphia. He is meeting some friends to understand how immunity is spreading. And another friend who worked on putting the units together; to determine if he is getting all the components he needs and whether the assemblies are being shipped. His last comment referred to his mother who had arrived from Volgograd and would be staying for a while! She will have time to meet his sisters."

Chuck and Ben, both stood; Ben remarked, "Hana that was fantastic. I suppose all of you around the table realise there was a lot of double talk in all that; they were trying not to give anything away. But, in reality, there is enough substance in what Ece recorded to give us some real clues." Ben continued, "The urgent thing now is to get this information to Denton so he can ensure our Iranian friend is tailed from the moment he steps off the plane." Ben and Chuck then checked each other's transcripts and agreed they had captured the essence of Hana's translation.

Chuck walked round to Ece to collect the tape recording. He would get that over to the CIA Intelligence Analysts along with the transcripts. "In the meantime" said Chuck, as he beamed a smile around the room, "I will call Denton and read the transcript over to him. In his lonely Walrus life, he will appreciate a call and deserves the Kudos he will get from our Director."

Chuck ambled to the door, saying "Ben will stay with you and give you some thoughts on the Russians double talk." Ben said, "In a very short time we will receive our Intelligence Analysts take on all that was said. I am sure you all have your own interpretations; but shall I give you mine before we move on to plan tomorrow. As Frank said earlier, and I totally agree, I think our incursion into Cosmo Clinic must happen in the next 48 hours."

Ben, about to begin, poured himself a glass of water. A couple of gulps then got down to it. "The Iranian flying into Philadelphia is understood. The question is why Philadelphia. The friends, a terrorist cell, must be stationed close by. He and they are bemused with the fact that HS is not worsening. So far, they don't seem to know we have found the cause. Next thing that's obvious. There is a Bietronics employee, working on assembling the heat sinks with capsules into the computers. Alternatively, he is just inserting the capsules in the heat sinks. I doubt if that's the case! Nobody would be keen to handle those babies without adequate protection."

"The really interesting part is mother arriving from Volgograd. Russian ships cross the Black Sea from Volgograd constantly. They are referring to the mother ship. And if they are, it's already here, moored in the Istanbul Port…. The Port of Haydarpasa! So far, it has probably been used to ship the capsules and heat sinks."

"The last sentence that Hana interpreted will set the President, the whole Government and my CIA bosses alight. Tonight and tomorrow the sparks will fly, and we should be ready for them to want to impose extreme measures, that we may or may not find palatable. My analysis of that last sentence involves the hostages. They may already be on that ship or being transported to it as we speak."

"The one clear-cut thing is that the President will not countenance them taking the hostages across the Black Sea to be held as hostages on Russian soil!"

Anneliese took charge again. "Thank you Ben for that, undoubtedly, superb analysis. I hope you all agree with this direction; until we hear from the hierarchy I believe we must continue to travel along the road we are on. So let's start to talk about how we go about the Cosmo Clinic second floor investigation. You will notice I am not calling it an attack or an incursion. That is deliberate. This exercise demands that we access that second floor, gain every possible bit of intelligence and then exit the place without leaving any clues, any footprints, any evidence, that we have been there!"

"If direction from the top requires us to change, amend, or even think the whole thing through again, we will do it. But let's not allow that thought to prevent us from getting a formidable plan together for our investigation of the Second floor."

"So let's go back to our old favourite, the flip chart. I will scribe if someone would like to volunteer to commence with any thoughts or ideas."

Frank was the first to speak. "Let's start by writing down who is involved in this operation, and the part each of them will play."

Chapter 29

Rescue the Hostages

Things were really starting to hot up in the team meeting in the Istanbul American Consulate Building! Whilst in Washington, the President had been up for hours, trying to figure out how much worse things would get!

An urgent call from William Webster, the CIA Director, was on the line. The President put the call on loudspeaker and lifted the handset. Leaning back in his high back leather chair, he wondered if this could actually be some good news.

"Morning William, how are you?" "Mr President, my Senior Intelligence officer has received a communication from Istanbul that sounds very promising." Mr Webster carried on explaining every detail of the Russian translation which had been confirmed by Denton's language interpreters. He followed with the interpretation of the guarded double talk provided by his Intelligence Analysts.

As he listened intently, the President began to smile to himself. "Lastly, Sir, the Iranian is flying to Philadelphia early tomorrow morning and will arrive around mid-day, next day. We've not had time to get exact timing but my people are presently contacting the airline! And we now have a name for him.... Abdul Karim!"

Now the President had every bit of the information, he said "William, I'm going to put you on hold for a couple of minutes." Pressing the hold button on his squawk box, the President placed the phone down.

He stood and began to pace around the Oval Office. As he massaged his chin, his brain was racing through every note in this stanza. He stopped opposite his chair and reached across the desk for the phone. As he did, he leaned forward to re-connect with Mr Webster.

"William, you and your people have done a great job; so now we can make use of that intelligence. Please contact the Secretary of Defence, the Secretary of Homeland Security and the Chairman of Joint Chiefs of Staff. On second thoughts, when I put the phone down, ask my secretary, Jean, to do it. You are much too busy!"

"Oh, and tell her to tell the Chairman to bring all the Chiefs of Staff. I want them all in my office at 2pm. We are on a War footing!"

"You, William, should get here for 1.45pm and bring your man Denton! If you get cracking now, you should be able to make it. Take a helicopter and land in the White House grounds." "I will, Mr President. We will be there."

At 1.45pm the CIA Director and Denton were sitting in the Oval Office with the President. "I wanted a few minutes with you guys to discuss an issue that I need some help with. I believe we are all confident that the hostages are held on a ship in Istanbul harbour. But which ship? Denton, from this very moment, can you mobilise your Intelligence Analysts to work like beavers to find the ship. Involve whoever you like. I have talked with the Turkish President and he is promising every possible assistance. Customs reports, Dock reports, times ships docked, bills of lading, what customs inspected, the types of cargo etc. the key is to find a ship from Volgograd carrying computer components."

Denton stood, saying "I will get our people moving right away." The President, with a satisfied grin said, "but Denton, when you are sure it's moving at a pace, come back in with us." Denton beamed at the honour! As he opened the door, all invitees were heading towards him. He held the door open, as everyone passed and thanked him.

They all gradually settled. The Defence Secretary, Harry Penrose couldn't wait. "Mr President, what's got you...." The President held up his right hand as if he was a traffic cop. The room silenced. "The first person to speak will be William" said the President as he nodded to him.

The CIA Director stood and, having given this briefing before, quickly recounted the intelligence. The room remained quiet as everyone digested it, and their minds sped forward into, "what will happen now?"

The President slowly paced around the Oval Office, his head down in deep thought. His face lifted and he scanned all the faces around him, about 16 in total. He began to speak, very quietly and slowly at first, "If we were in the trenches in World War 1, and I was your Captain, I would shout, its time, time to go over the top! I would lead! you would follow, and maybe, we would all be going to our death. Well, it's like this ladies and gentlemen! We are not going to our death. But people in our country and in the United Kingdom are! And four of our fellow citizens may be hostages on a ship in Istanbul, not knowing if or when they may die."

"We have to go over the top of our trenches for their sakes. I am the person to lead you and, as such, I will tell you right now what we are going to do. And you will lay your lives on the line for our people as you follow me across that battlefield."

"When the Iranian arrives in Pennsylvania tomorrow, I want CIA operatives following his every move. I will give him until 3pm. If he meets anybody they must be tailed. Nobody must be lost from view. If we get to 3pm without any issues, I want him arrested and interrogated. I want to know where the hostages are being held. I want to know where the terrorist cells are within the US. I want to know who initiated these attacks, although I'm already almost certain it is Russia working with Iran."

Just as the President finished speaking, there was a knock on the door and Denton entered. The Marine Sentry held the door open. "Come in Denton, please. Anything new to report?" Jennifer Askew, the Director of Homeland Security asked, "Mr President, would you do the introductions so we know who we are listening to." "Jennifer, I am so sorry, Denton is not a regular in our meetings, but he is a regular on my phone!" The President, with a wide smile, continued. "Denton is our most respected and creative Intelligence officer and Senior Analyst. He played a massive part, along with one of our colleagues from CECD, Jerome Janowski, in defeating Havana Syndrome. If these guys had not worked their magic, this country may have been without a President. They were due to install me a new computer, and I would probably have ended up long-term sick!"

"Sorry for that diversion, but now people know you and will remember you. So do you have any new news?"

"Mr President, yes, I do; and you may want to factor it into your thinking. Our CIA/CECD operatives in Istanbul are planning a clandestine operation at the Istanbul Cosmo Clinic, which we believe is the Command Centre used by the Russians and the Iranian."

"Denton, I am going to stop you there, for just a few minutes! There is another action that I want the Joint Chiefs of Staff to progress immediately." Continuing, the President, as he sat on the edge of his desk, uttered, "I think your report, Denton, may deserve quite a bit of time."

Easing off the desk and walking across to stand before the military and naval chiefs, the President said, "Please, all you gentlemen, work together on this. I want a frigate and a corvette stationed at the entrance to the Black Sea. With as many SEALs and Marines on board to cope with the hostage freighter if it tries to make a break for it. I will leave all the details to you!"

Chapter 30

Cosmo Covert Operation

"So now Denton, we are back to you!" Denton stood and glanced around the faces. "As I was saying, our team in Istanbul have begun developing a covert operation. The objective is to access the Cosmo Clinic, which we believe is the terrorists Command Centre."

"I don't have complete details of the plan yet, but the intention is to uncover any information that will identify the terrorists vessel moored in Istanbul Port. Further, to obtain identification details for any or all of the terrorists. Lastly to ascertain any details that will lead us to the terrorist cells in the U.S."

"We already have two plants in the Cosmo Clinic. Two elite undercover agents that secured the intelligence regarding the Iranian and the voice recording of the Russians. Another agent will join them tomorrow, posing as a patient. The second floor of the building is the target, which appears to be well protected in terms of security locks. One member of our team attempting access is a top-class locksmith and computer hacker. It is intended to initiate the operation in the next 48 hours. The exact timing will be established after we give them feedback from this meeting."

The President strode across to the French Doors and stared out at the Whitehouse lawns for a few seconds. As he slowly turned, glancing around the room, with raised voice he exclaimed, "Denton that sounds absolutely splendid! I know your guys are superb at their jobs and this CECD team have helped take them to an even higher level."

"Denton, would you quickly go out to Jean and ask her to try to get Anneliese on the phone."

"While he is doing so, what do you all think? Please let me hear your comments." All the Presidents men, in unison, began to slap the arms of their chairs. Vocal support emanated from them all.

The President's phone rang. He snatched it up! "Hello Anneliese, it's so good to speak to you again." The Oval Room's audience were hanging on every word. "I just wanted to thank you and your CECD team for the amazing results you have delivered." The President went quiet for several seconds as he listened. "Oh Anneliese, thank you for correcting me. I know that through this episode you have all pulled together as one team, both CECD and CIA. You are a great leader of any team, and we can't thank you enough."

"Just one more thing Anneliese. Denton has given us a fairly detailed overview of your intended operation, but is there anything new you may wish to tell us?" The President listened intently for about thirty seconds then with a sincere tone said, "thank you Anneliese. One day soon, I will arrange for us to meet and talk face to face. Goodbye."

The President faced his men. "That lady, in her capacity as an on-call Senior CECD Agent, is absolutely outstanding! Her reply to my question was she thought it prudent to wait until they have seen the feedback from this meeting. Then she would attempt to dovetail together a seamless plan that has the hostages' safety as a priority."

Chapter 31

Frigate in the Black Sea

It was a late, hot, humid evening in Istanbul. The team had been crawling through every possible question since early afternoon.

Anneliese entered the room and, clearly in good spirits, elegantly floated to her favourite place. The flip chart! Before any other business, Anneliese wrote in large bold, black letters. The President was exceedingly complimentary. Our team are the toast of the USA!

With a sweet smile that captivated everyone, she wrote the next line, WE WILL FEEL LIKE THE CANARY THAT HAS ESCAPED FROM THE CAGE. WE WILL SUCCEED!

The chuckles grew in intensity as Anneliese sat down; her head still in the clouds. "Chuck, do we have the transcript from today's White House meeting yet?" "Yes, we do," replied Chuck. "Well it's over to you to read it out loud; then we will write any issues on the flip chart."

Chuck slowly and carefully read through the single page report which summarised the meeting; the President's signature was appended!

Anneliese stepped back beside the flip chart. Frank, clearly and concisely opened on issues. "If they arrest the Iranian at 3pm, that is too late for us. If they manage to squeeze anything out of him Hana, Jerome and Ece would have been stuck in that closet for almost 5 hours. That's too long to leave them there where they could be found by security, cleaners etc."

Ece joined the discussion. "Frank, I don't think you are correct. I am not involved in the first infiltration wave." Frank rubbed his forehead saying, "Ece I'm sorry, you are correct." Looking at Anneliese, Frank said, "Can we go over the assignment detail again?"

"Ok", said Anneliese, "Jerome and Hana will be secreted in the closet room. You, Frank, with Chuck, and backup from our four local CIA agents, and mastermind Donald, will work from the outside in. Ece will leave Cosmo at around 6pm as if it's the end of a normal working day. She will work with me in our Command Centre. Everyone will have radios and mobile phones. Everyone will have cameras and mini-video recorders. This is important. Are you all completely clear?" Frank said, "Yes and I'm sorry; must have been a senior moment!"

Anneliese smiled at Frank, then asked if anyone needed any supplies of any kind. "Based on what we've discussed we have tomorrow to get completely organised. Tomorrow, Jerome will go to the clinic to have his first appointment. Get to know how the system works. Ingratiate himself with as many people as possible. Then Wednesday, he will return, having committed to a full set of teeth veneers. From there on, you and Hana will organise the first step into this operation."

Anneliese, now with a stern face and voice said "I will ask the question again. Does anyone need supplies of anything?" With a really mischievous look in her eyes, she turned to Frank. "Based on what you said earlier, do you need any incontinence pads because you may have to wait around for quite a while?"

The first person to erupt with laughter was Frank, but everyone followed. He strode across to Anneliese, grasped her around the waist and pulled her close. Looking around the room at everyone, he gradually stuttered into speech. "Yes, she's right, we have been through a lot together, over many years, but I'm not near that point yet!"

As the humour died away, Jerome asked, "Should we have weapons?" Hana was the first to reply. "I have my revolver and unless someone tries to become amorous, they will never find it." Frank and Chuck said "We will have firearms." Jerome, looking meek and mild, said "Perhaps I need something!"

Frank walked to Jerome. "You always want to look good, I did this once for Anneliese's husband, Matthew. You should have the same thing. A Beautiful watch! A Breitling, that you can use in emergencies. It is filled with a mild nerve gas, not murderous, but will knock someone out for about an hour! Matthew used it in Arizona and it did the trick. Anneliese, can you arrange for the invention specialist to get one here for tomorrow?"

"Yes, Frank. The CIA have their own creative engineer in this building. Chuck tomorrow morning, would you take Frank to meet him so the specifications can be determined."

Early next morning, Chuck and Frank met Jerome for a coffee. They were meeting with the creative engineering people at 8am, on the third floor in a large room next to the laboratory. Then mid-morning, Jerome would depart for his first appointment at the Cosmo Clinic.

Independently, Ece and Hana had set off for the clinic, ostensibly for a normal day's work. They would make time to check everything was ready for the following day's operation.

Chuck, Frank and Jerome arrived at the creative engineering department. They tapped on the fluted glass panelled door and it was opened by a bald headed man in large horn rimmed spectacles. He shook hands with them, introducing himself as Austin Hemsby.

Frank explained what they needed, Austin smiled saying, "I know exactly what you require. I think Frank, it was one of our units you used on that assignment in Wickenburg, Arizona. And I have exactly the same piece of equipment sitting on our stock shelves, let me just go and find one."

He returned with a very handsome Breitling Chronomat. "It's the Seamaster derivative; a splendid timepiece." He then began to explain how to operate the attack mechanism, but Frank interrupted. "Austin, I'm sorry but Jerome is short of time. I know how to operate it and will take him through it later in the day."

Austin, holding up both hands, said, "Certainly." "And if you need anything else just call up and see me."

In the lift, on the way down to the ground floor, Frank explained how to set the attack mode. "Seems pretty simple." said Jerome. "Yes, but also pretty dangerous, "replied Frank. "We will go over it again tonight. I will hold onto it until then!"

Jerome's car had arrived to take him to Cosmo Clinic. He would book in with his UK address, false name and passport. He was just having a good holiday in Turkey and at the same time, hopefully getting a fabulous set of gnashers!

Chapter 32

Iranian Apprehended

Jerome headed off and Frank walked back inside to the coffee shop. He'd just collected his usual medium Americano, when Anneliese and Chuck came trotting over. "Frank, can we go somewhere quiet to talk?" Anneliese swivelled around, Frank walked between her and Chuck. Anneliese, quietly spoke as they walked. "The Iranian has just been captured and arrested. When they got to him, he was attempting to contact someone on his mobile phone."

The three of them entered the first empty office they came to on the ground floor. Chuck closed the door behind them as Frank asked Anneliese, "So what happened then?" Anneliese, with hand outstretched, passed the question to Chuck. "Well to finish what Anneliese was saying, we don't yet know if he spoke with anyone, although we do have the phone and may be able to get info, from it."

"The sequence of events went like this." Chuck, his expression totally neutral continued, "As he was leaving the airport, towing his case and holding a briefcase he bumped into someone and his case tipped over. He bent down to it, but as he did, he must have noticed his two tails stop abruptly. He moved off again trying to throw the tails off. But now he was discreetly watching their every move."

"As he was passing the entrance to the Metro, he made a run for it. Left his suitcase at the top of the stairs, but was still carrying his briefcase."

"The station was busy and our men lost sight of him on the platform. Then they saw him in the third carriage as the doors closed and the metro pulled out. Our operatives radioed back to base. Central Command sent some operatives to the next station's exit and at the same time, contacted the Metro Company who stopped the train in a tunnel and remotely locked the doors."

"By the time the Metro people managed to stop the train, it had gone through the first station, but was brought to a halt in a tunnel just before the second station. Our people walked down the tunnel and a Metro security guy used a keypad to open the doors of the third carriage. After a bit of resistance, they dragged him off the train and down the tunnel to the platform. He hadn't resisted for long because several passengers joined in. It's amazing how angry people become when their train journey is disrupted!"

"Anyway, we have both his case and briefcase and our guys are going through them right now. He will be interrogated through the night and, possibly, all day tomorrow!"

Chuck said, "I'll let you know if anything more comes through." Anneliese, with a slightly concerned expression, said, "The thing that's worrying me is that possible phone call. If the Iranian alerted anyone, we may experience more trouble tomorrow than we bargained for." "Just have to keep our fingers crossed." Replied Frank.

Two hours later, Chuck found Anneliese again. "The interrogation is not throwing much up so far. The Iranian thought he had a way out. He suggested we offer to exchange him for the hostages. Russian contact was made but they have not responded. They are not even admitting any responsibility."

The CECD team and Chuck assembled again in the conference room at 5am Thursday morning. The next two hours were spent reviewing the plans for the day, going over every detail, time and again.

Frank had drilled into Jerome the procedure to operate the Breitling. Donald sat next to Hana and at one point Anneliese dropped her felt tip pen and it rolled under the edge of the table. As she stooped to pick it up, she glanced under the table and noticed Hana and Donald were holding hands. She appeared from under the table top with a very satisfied smile!

Anneliese decided to ask the question once again. "Has anyone got any questions, concerns or anything they need for today's operation? Donald was the only person to speak. "From talking with everyone last night and this morning, it seems they have all been allocated some form of weaponry. All I have is my tool belt! I would like something to help with our protection, if it comes to it."

Anneliese glanced toward Frank, who turned to Donald. "Have you had any training with a firearm Donald?" He released Hana's hand and began to stand. Hana's gaze followed his every movement as he quietly, but confidently moved to stand in front of the group. "I know I'm new to your business, but I grew up in a rough area. I had to learn to take care of myself. In Detroit City, almost everybody carries a gun."

"I joined a gun club at my college, which taught me all about safety with firearms and gave me some target practice. I moved on to join the Marine Cadets and won almost all their shooting competitions. I lost touch with all that when I went off the rails and became a bad boy for a while. I managed to get my life back on track, and now I'm here with you. So yes, to answer the question, I can shoot!"

Frank decided on one more check. "What firearm would you prefer?" Donald didn't take a moment to think. "To conceal easily, a Colt Detective Special, snub-nosed revolver. But, in case we get into serious trouble, I would also like a Skorpion 61 Machine pistol. I lived with one of those beauties for 2 years. It sat in my glove box and saved my life several times over. Usually just showing it was more than enough!"

"Donald, you will receive both in the next hour! I am honoured to have you with us!" Hana sat glowing with admiration for her new found romantic suitor.

Anneliese announced that she wanted to go over a few more things with everyone before Ece and Hana left for Cosmo Clinic. "Following on from Donald's request, another thing came to mind," said Anneliese. "Ece, I know you will be coming out of the Clinic and joining me to ensure everything ticks along as planned. However, just in case anything goes wrong do you have, or need any protection, any kind of weapon? You will all remember the details I gave you regarding the backup plan. As well as Frank and Donald on the outside, on the perimeter will be stationed our local CIA chums, Amos, Ben, Enrique and Adam. They will all have radios and phones. Any issues, you can contact them or Ece and me."

"But as you, Ece, will be in Cosmo until your shift ends, do you need any defensive weapons?" Ece's smile got everyone's attention, which translated into a long infectious giggle. She stepped out in front of them all. "I can handle guns but not too well. You will recall I was a gymnast, mainly on the mat." She began to move across the floor, flicking her legs above her head, twisting, sliding and pirouetting. She stopped and loudly banged her heels on the floor, then high kicked again. The toes of her shoes caused flickering light spots all around the room!

She stopped, bent over pointing at her toes, and with a glorious smile as she pointed at her shoes, said, "These have been my defence for a few years now.... My sharp shoes! Austin designed and built these for me. I have used them several times. They are a perfect match for my agility." Everyone studied the shoes, the toes extended into 3inch razor sharp blades. Ece began chuckling again. "I got the idea from the Russian, Rosa Klebb, in 'From Russia with Love', and as we are battling Russians they seem appropriate."

Ece's interlude was greatly appreciated, and she welcomed the applause.

Hana and Ece, wishing good luck to the team, left for work. At the door, Hana turned and eyeballed Jerome. In an assertive voice she said, "Don't forget your appointment; be there before three, so you can look around!"

Chapter 33

Russian Lost, Ship Leaves

A few minutes later, Amos appeared. Addressing the team, he said, "It's never good news, as always both good and bad! Denton called saying that with the help of the US phone company, they now know the Iranian did connect with someone for almost 50 seconds. Not when he was stuck in the tunnel. That was a failed call. The successful call must have been when he was getting on the metro or actually on it. He has probably issued out an alert, so we have contacted the frigate, and put them on action stations. We are now watching for any Russian vessel preparing to sail."

"The bad news is that we have lost the Russians that we had been tailing. Maybe they are on the Russian Merchant Ship. Or maybe they are in hiding, waiting for a time to make a run for it."

"There is a piece of good news! Our people have gone through all the paperwork that the Iranian had. They have found lots of coded and encrypted work that they are analysing as we speak. It may lead us to the name of the ship or the terrorist cells or both."

"So far they've not managed to squeeze anything out of the Iranian. He seems to think he is in the driving seat and keeps offering deals. His latest offer is that we deliver him to Iran in return for the whereabouts of the terrorist cells. But he is insistent that Iran is not implicated in any way! This whole affair was him being employed by Russia for financial reward! Our people are considering that option!"

It got to 4 o'clock. Anneliese got a call from Denton. In a sombre tone, he said his Intelligence Analysts had been working through the Iranian's paperwork. One specialist code breaker had uncovered what he thought may be the Russian merchant freighter. Amos's agents had been informed and were following up with the Istanbul Port Authorities. However, the news had just come through that the ship had been given clearance only ten minutes earlier and was on its way out into the Bosphorus Strait.

The ship was named the "Ledi Anastasia," destination, Volgograd. Amos was in the process of alerting the US frigate and corvette sailing close to the Kizil Islands at the entrance to the Black Sea. Ben was on another phone talking to the USAF Commander in the Istanbul airport.

Three Chinook helicopters were being scrambled to assist the frigate and corvette.

Attempting to appear totally innocent, the "Anastasia" was cruising at normal commercial freighter speed, toward the Black Sea. Then the frigate and corvette appeared in front of it!

At around the same time, Jerome was probably wishing he was bobbing around in the Bosphorus. Instead he was trapped in the dentist's chair, mouth wide open and the lady dentist prodding and poking around in his mouth. He had always done his best to look after his teeth and the dentist said she was quite impressed. Her English was fairly good, and next she explained she wanted to take a few x-rays. Ece smiled at Jerome as she placed the metal plates in his wide-open mouth. Whilst she did that, the dentist left the room for a couple of minutes. Ece whispered, "After this you are finished, then we just have to go to get your estimate. Then I will get you hidden!"

It was now almost 5pm. The lady dentist, indeed, a stunningly beautiful lady dentist, that no man would mind suffering pain for, returned to the treatment room. She carefully took 4 different x-rays explaining that she was a perfectionist and she wanted Jerome to be an advert for her work! It was now 5.10pm. This lady dentist now spoke with Ece, then turned to Jerome. "I just want to show you the different veneer colourings; I would recommend you try to select the colour that matches your teeth. Your teeth are already a wonderful white, but as we go through the process you will have some chances to change your mind." Ece brought in the colour pictures and palette. It was now 5.22pm. Jerome picked what he believed was a colour match. The dentist disagreed and asked for Ece's opinion. She attempted to give professional help and they finally came to an agreement. It was now 5.35pm. Jerome was given a card with his next appointment, shook hands and thanked the dentist, who obviously was not his cup of tea. He wandered behind Ece to the finance office to wait for the estimate and deposit requirement.

Sitting waiting on seats in the corridor, Ece said, "I thought Anneliese was coming with you!" Jerome replied that, with the amount of activity now the Iranian had been captured, she thought it best to stay in the Command Centre.

In reception, Hana and a few other employees were beginning to close up. There were about six patients remaining in reception, and another four in the clinic rooms. Jerome and Ece were patiently waiting outside the Finance Office.

Chapter 34

Hostages Taken in Cosmo

At precisely 5.58pm, the main entrance door crashed open! Hana had just been going to lock the door. A senior colleague was accompanying her, as she was still training.

Four men burst through the open door, almost knocking the girls off balance. With aggression, shouting and swearing, they shoved the girls back into the reception area. All were wielding firearms, pointing them around at everybody and anybody. Three of the men were threatening with machine pistols and the fourth, chinning a machine gun, pushed the door slightly open and began spraying fire outside at anything that moved.

These men were all casually dressed, although dishevelled. They were so tired they could barely stand. An older one, dropped to his knees, panting and out of breath!

One of these characters, a blonde guy in his mid 20's, was still fit enough to scream fiercely at Hana, her colleague and the three patients remaining in the waiting area. He herded them towards the access door to the stairs. His screaming continued, but now to his crew. He was telling them to go into the dental clinicians areas and round everyone up. Hana was the only one that understood him. He was Russian!

The spurts of gunfire at the door and the screaming hullabaloo brought the old man that ran the corner coffee shop stumbling into the reception area. One of this crew ran to him, and as he stood trying to figure out what was going on, this Russian brought his machine pistol crashing down on the old man's skull. As he sunk to his knees, the gun was swung to scythe into the back of his neck.

Just a few moments later, the Russian in a leather jacket was ferociously pushing, kicking and shoving the people he had rounded up in the dental clinician's area. Totally disorderly, and with hands above their head, their small crowd entered the reception area and were harassed to join the others by the stair's entrance doors.

This group included Ece and Jerome. The whole group, petrified, stared at the old man from the coffee shop lying unconscious, face down and bleeding profusely.

The terrorist who had commanded the post by the main door, closed the door, kicked the bottom to check, pulled out several keys and operated three locks. He already possessed keys to the main door!

With a marching swagger he strode to the captives group and stood in front of them. Speaking in English, and with a threatening expression, he began to intimidate them. With an arrogant tone, he advised them not to try anything silly. "Do exactly as you are told and all will be fine. Do anything else and you will die." Pointing at the old man on the floor he said, "You do not want to force us to drop you on the floor next to him."

"We are now going to take you all upstairs. Do not talk, keep calm and we will make you comfortable on the second floor." One of the Russians entered a password on the keypad, and used a key on the double locking system. Ece had watched and memorised the whole thing!

The twelve captives were taken up the stairs, three people at a time. The leading Russian entered codes to the second floor door and again operated the key locks. The twelve were herded into the second floor area. A large open plan area, with about a third of it sectioned off and two distinct offices adjacent to that area against the rear wall. The windows all along the front of the second floor were covered with blinds.

The Russians made the whole group sit on the floor against the rear wall. One of them went to the front wall, marginally opened a blind then a window, giving a six inch gap, large enough to rest a gun in.

Hana, sitting next to Jerome, whispered "Don't do anything yet. Let's size it all up first!"

Back in the Command Centre, Anneliese was completely swamped with messages coming in regarding the Battle of the Bosphorus, and now the Russians' incursion and hostage taking in Cosmo Clinic.

Denton had established a permanent line to Anneliese. But he also was drowning in calls from the CIA Director, the President and all of the Chiefs of Staff.

The latest information on the attempted escape by the Russian Ship, the "Ledi Anastasia", was that she had been trapped by the U.S. frigate and the corvette. Both vessels had fired warning shots. The frigate had used radio communication to tell her Captain to return to the Istanbul Port. But no answer was the stern reply! So then they tried semaphore. Three times!

Ten minutes after the third attempt, the Anastasia slowly began to turn back to the Istanbul Port.

Phones were now buzzing and ringing everywhere. Denton was now on a direct line to his CIA Director and the President. Anneliese had a massive volume of calls coming from CECD headquarters and Commander Farrell.

But the calls were becoming confusing. Some were asking about the Anastasia. But some were beginning to ask about the Cosmo Clinic. Anneliese decided she must give priority to the Cosmo Clinic. Frank, Donald and Chuck were parked on the waste ground at the back of the building. Amos and his team were waiting on the waste ground perimeter.

The Turkish Police, the gendarmes, were at the front of the building. They and several CIA agents had chased the Russians from Istanbul Port, and now they were all surrounding the building. The Cosmo Clinic was under siege!

Frank decided it was time he moved from watching to doing. He took to the radio and instructed everyone to stay in their positions and not to do anything to cause violence. He, Chuck and Donald were heading back to the Consulate to consult with Anneliese and their bosses. They would keep in touch and return shortly.

Chapter 35

Cosmo Siege, Strong US Unrest

Sitting in a meeting room in the Consulate, with radios crackling all around them and mobile phones laying on the table, the small group sat together. Concerned expressions on them all; Frank was first to speak. "What do you think Anneliese? What's our next move?" "First, I think we should consider the environment they are all trapped in. The patients are confused and terrified. The same goes for the Dentists and staff in there. They have no idea what may happen. Their minds are on a knife edge, mostly thinking the worst. Some of them will be trembling with fear."

"Our guys also will not be able to avoid fear. But, for them it will be controllable. They have been trained to use it to rationalise the situation. Hopefully they are guiding one another to sit tight and wait to see if anything develops externally. They know we will be in the process of establishing a plan."

"The terrorists know, that from the point of view of dominance, they are able to dictate with fear. But they also know it only applies internally within Cosmo. They are just as fearful and uncertain as the patients when it comes to the external environment."

"A major thing in our favour is we can dictate and apply a siege mentality. I would not think they have much food, if any. They cannot leave or go anywhere. Sleep will be difficult. The hostages will disrupt their thinking constantly. With every day that goes by, our negotiating stance will become stronger."

Just then, Denton came on the line. "As usual, it's good and bad news. The Russian freighter was escorted back to Istanbul and docked about 15 minutes ago. The Captain and the whole crew have been arrested and are presently being taken to Metris Prison. Our four American citizens have been taken into care and are being escorted to the American Embassy. They are all in good spirits and seem to have been well treated. We will debrief them and get enough evidence to put all the Russians on trial."

Denton went quiet for a few seconds as he got his breath. "The President has been informed and is delighted. I guess you are all together to discuss how to manage the events at the Cosmo Clinic. The Russian terrorists that are in there had been followed by several of our agents switching around, changing cars and changing places. The Russians had been hoping to join the "Anastasia" at the Port, but as they arrived, all they could see of the ship was its rear end as the Captain got nervy and threw in the towel."

"The four Russians made a run for it, just as a shift at the Port ended. They mingled in with the hundreds of workers going out of the dock gates, and our agents lost sight of them. Anneliese, if you don't mind, I will stay on the line to help with your discussion on next steps."

Glancing around the room, Anneliese massaged her brow as she began to speak. "Glad to have you with us Denton, and grateful thanks for the update. Based on where we are now, what is clear is that this situation affords us an opportunity to negotiate release of the Cosmo hostages avoiding any resistance or bloodshed."

The room was absolutely silent as everyone carefully listened. In her usual manner, Anneliese stood and began to amble around the room. "As the American hostages have been released, unharmed, we have some leverage. We could make the terrorists the following offer! If they will release all the Cosmo hostages, unharmed, we could give them safe passage to the "Ledi Anastasia" such that they can sail away, back to Russia. That would obviously, also require release of the ship's crew."

"Another option, with this deal as the basis, is that we would also be given information on the terrorist cells in America."

Anneliese stopped alongside the flip chart and wrote both these options on a clean page. Holding the felt tip pen towards her lips, she said "I don't like either of these options. It means they get away scot free!"

Denton shouted down the line "and I don't think the President will buy either of those! I will explain why in a minute."

Anneliese began to slowly pace the room again. "The key issue is that all other alternatives put lives at risk. We have three competent agents in Cosmo, unknown to the terrorists. We have operatives on the outside that, no doubt, have the skills to access that formidable second floor. We have the possibility to contact the terrorists and offer a financial deal that would make the four of them very rich! We can just wait it out, using siege tactics. Lack of food can work wonders! Denton, I am going to scribble these on the list. Why don't you talk to the President and his Chiefs? We will need their direction in any event."

Denton said, "I will get onto it straight away. Then I will call back in about 15 minutes because I need to update you all on some stuff going on in the U.S."

Frank, peering at Anneliese said, "I know what I would like to do. I would like to apply the same strategy and tactics as we did with the Iranian Embassy siege back in 1980. Get some of your Delta Force guys, or our S.A.S. and drop in on them. Anneliese smiling, said "Frank, I knew you were going to say that. It's your motto "the best form of defence is attack" and it may yet come to that." She stopped and wrote another line on the flip chart. Chuck, grinning said, "Frank you are definitely a military man that will never make a politician!"

Anneliese went back into pacing mode. "Listen guys, I am just thinking out loud. I doubt if we will get the go ahead on any option for quite a long while. The American hostages have been released and are safe and well. I know it sounds cynical, but the President has something to appease the American population. His troubles at home may, therefore, settle down. The flip side of that is, if any further attacks occur in America! I doubt that will happen, because by now the U.S based terrorists will have got the message that we are making headway and are on their trail."

Denton came back on the line. "Hello everyone. I have talked with Mr Webster. He and I then had a conference call with the President and the Homeland Security Chief. It's now afternoon in Washington and soon it will be too late for you. But he will get everyone together tomorrow to get things moving. Right now, he says he's happy to let the terrorists sweat for a bit!" With a knowing smile developing, Anneliese looked around at the faces. Denton said, "Is it ok for me to continue?" "Yes, go ahead," replied Anneliese.

"The supply of medical equipment continues to worsen in both the U.S. and UK. The substantial number of factories and facilities taken out of action will continue to impact medical services for some while yet. The waiting lists on both Continents, for some serious operations is into years.

Death rates are continuing to climb. Morgues and funeral parlours can no longer cope, and the media, TV, newspapers and magazines, have more stories to tell than in a child's library. The pressure on Secret Service Agencies and military is now enormous for the following reasons."

"In the UK the Police and Military are constantly required to marshal protests, demonstrations and quell rots. Their minds and resources are being taken away from the real job…. Fighting crime and protecting the country. The prisons are at busting point and criminals are being given early parole. That is inviting more crime onto the streets."

"In the U.S. the picture is worse. Almost everything I have said about the U.K. also applies to the U.S…. but with one big difference. Most of what I am going to tell you now is being constantly discussed by the President and his team, behind closed doors!"

"There is a definite damaging rift appearing, both in the political world and with the man on the street. I've seen this type of thing before, the priority order of issues to be dealt with will change, depending on the politicians' perception of importance. What I'm really trying to say is that this difficult international incident in the Cosmo may slide down the priority list. We will be left to make our own decisions, and possibly to be blamed if things go wrong."

The civil unrest in the U.S and the growing divide between Northern and Southern states is creating massive political concern. The threat of Civil War; the Southern States ideology, based on belief in "the right to bear arms," is a serious threat to U.S democracy. And, once again, behind closed doors, indeed, our own CIA doors, there is a strong suspicion that the growth of this unrest is being orchestrated and funded by a subversive organisation. Or perhaps a country attempting to destroy us.

Anneliese, in a tone that reflected sincere concern, said, "Denton, on behalf of us all I give you our heartfelt thanks. I sense you are worried for your country, and I can see from Chuck's expression he is feeling the same. Whilst we concentrate on our next steps, you can be assured, us Europeans, and especially the UK will always be your ally!"

Chapter 36

Killed, for Want of a Pizza

In the Cosmo Clinic it was late. The terrorists needed to get some shut-eye. The patients were exhausted; all so tired, most had fallen asleep on the hard wood panelled floor. Jerome, Ece and Hana lay close together pretending to sleep, but watching the terrorists every move.

Just after midnight, the terrorist wearing a black leather jacket, put his Udav machine pistol on the floor. He wrestled his jacket off and threw it on a metal tubular chair, unlocked the door, exited and locked it from the outside.

He returned ten minutes later, with armfuls of dentist white coveralls and some cushions taken from chairs on the ground floor. He threw them down in front of the hostages, miming they were for their sleep. He did the same trip again, bringing back more, but this time for the terrorists.

Donald, sitting next to Frank in the Consulate Command Centre was tired and getting edgy. So far, all he had done was listen. But now he had to speak. "Anneliese, may I say what I think we could do?" Anneliese smiled and nodded.

Donald with a very serious expression said, "Let's try talking to them tomorrow. All day tomorrow! Get megaphones and loud speakers outside Cosmo. Then our people and the other hostages won't think we have forgotten them. Ask them what they want. Talk about things they want; food in particular. If we get nowhere, tomorrow night I should get us quietly through that rear door. We can hide somewhere, maybe the closet or the toilets!"

"We know they have locked themselves upstairs. But one or two of them may come down, looking for food or coffee or some other thing. When they do, we can take them out, then carefully, get through the doors to the second floor."

By now, Frank had a thoughtful, interested look. "Ok" said Frank, "That's an idea that may be worth developing. Chuck, would you be able to arrange hordes of gendarmes, police vehicles, loud speakers etc for the morning. Have them all outside at 9am. We may need linguists to talk to the terrorists throughout the day. Anneliese, perhaps you would prepare the sorts of things we should cover with them. One thing we should do is try to get them to agree to us setting up a phone line to them."

"Also Chuck, would you get me a sniper rifle from the armoury. I would prefer an SVD with a PSO 1 x 4 scope. It will be a last resort as we don't want them to kick off and start shooting hostages. But if any action takes hold, we may need to pick one of two of them off!"

"So, do we all agree, we go down this road tomorrow; then depending on how it goes, we will talk again tomorrow night." As they all nodded agreement, Donald exclaimed, "I have to get her out of there soon.,... I mean we have to rescue them all soon!"

Anneliese, with an enigmatic smile uttered, "We know what you mean Donald. We all feel the same!"

Sure enough, the commotion and noise began just after 9am. Barriers had been erected across the front and side of the Cosmo Clinic. Seven police cars behind the barriers, two armoured personnel carriers with Marines for good measure! TV cameras' were in situ in the road opposite.

Anneliese had seconded two linguists from the CIA Intelligence team and, initially, all the attempts to get the terrorists talking were in Russian. It all started with megaphones but by 10am the loudspeakers had been connected up to power supplies and microphones were being used.

For the first two hours, there was no response from the terrorists. All they did was to, occasionally, push a terrified patient to stand at the window. First a German lady, then a beautiful Turkish girl.

Just before mid-day, Anneliese took the linguist to one side and said "Major on food. They must be hungry. Do they want Pizzas' or sandwiches sent in." Anneliese reminded the translator to regularly say please and to remind them that several of the hostages are getting on in years and they wouldn't want them getting ill.

Hunger eventually drove the Russians to respond. A window was opened and their leader stepped forward, but with a hostage held in front of him. This was the guy that could speak broken English. "Yes we want Pizzas' and drink. Coca-Cola! It come to the front door!"

Anneliese prompted the translator. "Ask if he would give us his phone number to make arrangements easier." He did just that, loud and clear over the microphone. No response!

The pizzas' and drink arrived, it was agreed they would put them on the front step. The Russian appeared with the terrified young girl in front of him. There were two large cardboard containers. She picked up the first and as if locked together, they edged back through the door. All the time, Frank had him in the sights of his SVD sniper rifle. They began the same dance out to the second box. As they moved to the step, almost as if they were in harness, she tripped and fell forward. Trying to hold onto her, he dropped his machine pistol.

This brave young girl had had enough! She sprinted off towards the line of Gendarmes, and with her first few steps, inadvertently kicked his gun a few feet away. Getting off his knees, he scrambled to pick up his machine pistol. All the watching Police, with TV cameras recording every moment, dropped down behind their vehicles.

As this brave girl was trying to break through the barriers the leather jacket leader was lifting his gun off the concrete. Still on one knee, he started to take aim at her. But before he could pull the trigger, a single silenced phut noise saved her!

Frank's last minute, very accurate sniper shot had found its target. The leader of these Russian terrorists had fallen to a Russian SVD sniper's rifle. Frank's shot had been perfect. Now THERE WERE ONLY THREE!

The beautiful young girl, traumatised and trembling, was quickly lifted through the barriers by a plain clothes agent and taken to safety, behind one of the armoured cars. A chair was brought for her, but she seemed unable to release her grip around the CIA operative's waist. Her head pressed against his chest, as tears flooded his shirt. He let her sob until it eased along with the trembling. Gently lowering her into the chair, he wiped her eyes with a pure white cotton handkerchief.

He then passed it to her, and as he did, she looked up into his face and her eyes began to smile. It transformed into a relieved giggle just as another man arrived. He stood over her, stroking her dark hair. "You are an extraordinary, brave young lady. "How old are you, Miss?" Frank was trying to get her talking, to take her mind away from the horror she had been through. "I am nearly 18, Sir." Frank, with a surprised expression replied, "Your English is Perfect, Miss. Well done!" She was beginning to relax and talk. "It is my subject at college, Sir! Who are you, please?" "Oh, I'm just one of the police here to get you all home safely! And what is your name, Miss?" "It's Aylin," she replied. "Well, Aylin, I will never forget you. I will always remember you as the brave young lady from Istanbul. I have to get back to work now, but I may see you again later." Frank, with sincere sparkling eyes, looked into hers as he held her hand for a few seconds. He then drifted off into the crowd.

The second floor in Cosmo was in silence, other than two middle-aged ladies who were sobbing! The terrorists began arguing, then shouting, then screaming at one another. One of the terrorist's, a bald stocky character was clearly angry; pacing the room, going to the edge of the window to peer around, then rattling off in Russian at the other two.

One of the tearful ladies, seated on the floor with her back against the wall, began being sick. Jerome took his dental overall and placed it on her to protect her clothing. The bald Russian bruiser ran up behind Jerome, screaming something in Russian and pointing to where Jerome had been sitting. Jerome, kneeling beside the woman as he straightened the coverall, stubbornly ignored him.

He stood behind Jerome, shouting orders and pointing to the place next to them. Just then, a negotiator began calling out again on the power megaphone. This was not what the Russian wanted to hear. His anger boiled over! His expression twisted into a demented look.

He turned away, taking a step back. Now with room, he ran forward and exploded a powerful, ferocious kick into the middle of Jerome's back. Hana saw it coming and dived, attempting to grab his foot, but the thrust was too powerful for her. Hana scrambled to her knees to hold Jerome, attempting to comfort him!

The Russian backed away, as he shouted and pointed his finger at Hana. The second lady, holding her friend, shouted back at him. "You vicious, cruel bastard, hell is where you're going and it won't be long!" This lady had an American accent. So now they had another American hostage to rescue!

Ece carefully moved next to her. The Russians, now in a group had moved to the other side of the room and were talking. Ece whispered to the woman, "We have friends coming; some Americans. Please just do whatever we say! We will look after you!"

Ece held her hand and smiled. "For now just grin and bear it. It won't be long. And don't be scared." Ece looked away, took a breath then whispered again, "my name is Ece and this is Hana." The American woman returned a smile and whispered, "I am Susan, thank you!"

Jerome slowly recovered, and along with everyone, spent hours into the evening listening to the constant megaphone and loud speaker appeals.

⁂

Donald's Cheese Wire

Just after sunset, Anneliese, Frank, Donald and Chuck sat together again. They soon had Denton on the line and asked if any instructions or advice had been received from the hierarchy. "Absolutely nothing, "replied Denton. Anneliese went on to explain Donald's thinking, discussed in their previous meeting. The phone line went quiet for around 20 seconds. They were all looking around at one another as he returned to speak. "Sorry you guys, this is Denton back with you! I had to take time out to think, and pull up my lucky orange socks. They work, you know! That's why I wear them! But back to business." He was about to carry on speaking but the laughter on the other end of the line engulfed him. As it dwindled away Denton continued, "I want to assure you guys that I am not negative on Donald's plan. But, I can think of a myriad of issues. That said, I am not on the spot. You guys are. I have nothing better to offer!" He stopped in his tracks. "I am beginning to sound like a politician!" Down the phone line, they heard him take a deep breath.

"What I was going to say is that going ahead seems the only alternative. Some weight has been added to your plan because I have received intelligence that says that two of the hostages in Cosmo are Americans, and a further two are British civilians. So if your incursion works, you will be the toast of both the U.S. and the U.K. Whatever the outcome, I will back you!"

That was enough for them! The team set off for the Cosmo Clinic. Their cars parked, in the dark, at the far end of the waste land at the back of the clinic. As they parked, Frank asked Donald, "Have you got your weapons?" Donald patted his leather travel bag, full of tools and firearms. Donald partially unzipped the bag, saying, "I've brought this as well." He pulled out from the bag, a roll of cheese wire! "What's that for?" asked Frank. "If a Russian comes down, I may need to take him out quietly. Gunshots will not help our guys upstairs." Frank, with a wry smile, said, "Good thinking."

Chuck said, "Good luck" and gave a thumbs up as they stepped out of the Jeep. Amos, Ben, Enrique and Adam, in another vehicle, would sit and wait, in the dark, under trees on the perimeter of the piece of waste land.

Donald and Frank, both dressed all in black, approached the rear door. Donald disabled the burglar alarm and had them through that door in 20 minutes. Inside all was dark. With Frank's flashlight, they moved forward toward the stairs.

Just before the stairs was a dental clinician's room, with a large adjustable dental chair. As they moved on, the next thing was the stairs. Frank shone his flashlight under the stairs, then they both backtracked into the clinician's room. Frank whispered to Donald, "I can hide under those stairs. If I squeeze right under the first two steps, I cannot be seen." Donald, also with a whispering voice, said he would hide under the dental chair in the clinician's room. They both moved to their places.

All was quiet throughout the night. Donald was itching to get through the entry door to the stairs, it was the most difficult one with a numerical key pad and a double lock. Donald decided he would stay put until about 5am; then if there had been no sign of terrorists coming down, he would take a crack at it!

In the meantime, Frank was his usual patient controlled self. Even though he was curled up in a small confined space, under the stairs, he hardly moved a muscle for hours.

Just before 5am, Donald's patience ran out. Quietly, he crawled out from under the dentist chair; reached into his bag and stuffed a length of cheese wire into his hoody pocket. With his bag in his left hand, as he slowly edged past Frank, he whispered, "I am going to have a go at the door. Frank moved out and rubbed his knees and legs to get the circulation moving.

Donald first tried his bunch of skeleton keys. No success there, so now he was working on the lock with a special steel pick that he had developed in his job as a locksmith. This tool had proved, time and again, to be invaluable. As he wiggled it around in the lock, the door at the top of the stairs began to open. Donald's heart pounded, as he withdrew from the lock, kicked his bag across the floor and moved behind the solid steel door.

He took a deep breath, as he listened to the footsteps moving quickly down the stairs. It took a few seconds for the terrorist to punch his number into the keypad. Donald held his breath as he heard the key entering the lock. The door slowly opened. Donald pulled his cheese wire out and wrapped it around both hands.

It was the bald, stocky terrorist. He slowly moved out, as he reached to push the door behind him. He was about to take a full step forward and turn to complete the closure of the door. With his back to Donald, this was the chance!

Donald's execution of this manoeuvre was perfect. Indeed, his execution of the terrorist, was perfection! In a split second, the wire was flipped over his head and Donald's two hands, relentlessly, pulled it tight around his neck. With a knee in his back, he had no chance, and made no sound.

Frank appeared, reached down to the bald brute to check his neck for a pulse. It was absent!

Chapter 38

Shoes, Gun and Watch

As Frank smiled through the dawning dimness, the noise of two gunshots from above them, set their pulses racing again. Frank was first off the spot, charging through the open door and up the stairs. Donald's mind snapped out of shock and he grabbed his machine pistol out of his bag. Two or three seconds behind Frank, his thoughts were only for Hana!

The entrance door to the second floor had not been locked. They burst in, but could not see Hana or Ece anywhere, until they focused on the partitioned area at the end of the second floor. One of the middle-aged ladies was pointing to that area as they sprinted, 30 yards across the floor.

What Frank had seen was Jerome standing at the door of the partitioned area. They ran to him, and peered into the large room. Both the terrorists were prostrate on the floor. Hana and Ece were both sitting against the wall, appearing as if they had spent the night smoking cannabis or taking cocaine. But at least, they were both alive.

With the door slightly open, Frank peered at the terrorists. One had been shot. The bullet entered under his chin, into his skull. Frank went to him, covering with his revolver. Looking back at Donald, Frank said "This one is dead as a doornail." The other had been stabbed in the stomach, but like the girls, he appeared to be drugged. He had a machine pistol lying close to him. Frank got on his mobile to call for assistance.

Later, Frank, on the radio to Anneliese, explained all he knew. She was going on her way to the hospital to check on the girls.

They had successfully completed their assignments. The Gendarmes and some of the CIA agents helped them all out to transport, taking them to hospital. Chuck, Amos, Ben and the rest of the CIA operatives came in and spoke with Frank. They would not stay around. Instead, they would return to the conference room and give Denton the good news.

Frank and Donald escorted a worried Jerome down to the reception area. They sat him in one of the easy chairs and Frank got him a coffee from the machine in the Coffee Shop. Frank then, down on his haunches in front of Jerome, asked "What happened with Hana and Ece."

Jerome shaking, probably due to post traumatic stress, said, "Frank, those two bastards, early morning, must have decided Hana and Ece were easy meat." Having to recount the events, Jerome continued, trembling. Frank grabbed his hands. "Jerome, stay strong; I know it's difficult but tell us what happened."

"I'm sorry" said Jerome. "But I've never seem a girl treated like that before," "Those shits dragged them into that partitioned office area. Ece fought all the way, but they grabbed her hair and towed her into that room. They made both of them stand facing a wall, their hands on the wall, then began to abuse them. Both terrorists, smiling, forced their hands between the girls' legs."

"But those fuckers didn't know what they were dealing with." Jerome's face brightened and a smile broke through.

"Ece, our little agile gymnast, knew when to catch them off balance. She banged her heels on the ground, then, like lightning, spun around. The long blades protruding from the end of her shoes hit his stomach. He collapsed in a heap. Holding his guts, covered in blood!"

"That distracted his mate. Hana pulled her derringer from under her thigh belt and blasted him into oblivion. Earlier I had been told not to move or they would kill both of them. But when I watched all this. I ran over to the door. As I did, I saw the one lying bleeding, reaching across the floor for his machine pistol. I pulled my watch off, pulled out the timer button, threw it at him and closed the door. I am so sorry! They have suffered nerve gas, all of them! Ece and Hana as well. But otherwise he would have shot them."

Over the next hour, everything settled down. The crowds, TV and Emergency service vehicles dispersed. The army vehicles and troopers stayed a bit longer, but left when the CIA operatives gave the word. The Gerdarme Commander spoke with Enrique from the CIA, saying they were off to find the owner of the Cosmo Clinic property, to interview him.

Chuck came to Frank and explained that his CIA Operatives would take charge of Cosmo, and through the night, go through the second floor to find anything valuable in terms of intelligence.

When Frank thought everything had been wrapped up, he seconded one of the Turkish CIA operatives to take Ece, Hana and two other women to the hospital. Frank, Jerome, Donald and Chuck followed him in a CIA car.

The hospital was only 15 minutes away. Sitting by a small ward, an English speaking nurse came out to them, saying that some of the older hostages would be staying the night, but that Hana and Ece had received special recovery drugs and were fine and ready to leave. There had been no physical injuries other than a few bruises.

Donald asked, "Can we go in and see them?" "No," replied the nurse. "We have been very busy tonight and they will be out in a few minutes."

Ece came out first, with her arms around the shoulders of the American lady, Susan. They stopped as they reached Jerome. Susan threw her arms around Jerome's neck, kissed his cheeks and said she would be forever grateful. Next was Hana! Donald grasped her and lifted her off her feet, kissing her neck, then cheeks then lips. He was almost lost for words. All he could say was,"You are ok! You are safe!"

But the ecstatic affection didn't stop there. Susan joined Donald and Hana. "Thank you, both of you, so much. I will talk about how wonderful you are, for the rest of my life." As tears began to stream down her face, she turned to Frank. "What would we do without brave, beautiful people like you? God bless you all."

Susan was going to get a taxi, but they gave her a lift to her hotel. She had been through a lot, but now she had a story to tell for the rest of her life. Her friend was staying in hospital overnight for observation, but she would collect her in the morning. Waving, they set off for the Consulate.

Next morning, they all, eventually, congregated in the coffee shop. Although bleary eyed, everyone's spirits were high. The chatter was non-stop.

Chapter 39

Back to US Quick!

Anneliese arrived. She stood at the door for a few seconds, then hurried across to Hana. She bent forward and grasped her, kissing her cheek. Hana kissed her back. Jerome smiled, quietly recognising the mystical love that engulfed them. Anneliese turned to Ece and cuddled her, then Jerome. She stood, as her back straightened; "You guys are the most fantastic people. That was a difficult assignment and you overcame all the odds. All odds that were stacked against you!" she now turned to face Frank, Jerome and Donald.

"Under the circumstances, your performance, your execution, was superb. When I think about the stress and pressure you were under, knowing those people upstairs may have been killed if you put a foot wrong, was amazing; indescribable! But, please always remember that those people you rescued, yesterday, will always have you in their memories and their prayers."

After they had enjoyed their breakfast, Anneliese asked Chuck when he thought he would receive information on the searches and investigation concerning the Cosmo second floor. "And another thing! The terrorist that Ece sliced open; how is he doing and where is he being held?"

Chuck, stroking his chin, exclaimed "Well Anneliese, I can answer the last question. That terrorist is being held here. In the basement we have both cells and a medical centre. He had an operation last night and is presently said to be stable. As soon as I get a report on the findings at Cosmo, and our analysts have completed their reviews, we should all meet again to determine the next steps!"

Anneliese, having made some time for a bite to eat, sat talking to Hana and Ece. With some simple salads in front of them they were explaining to Anneliese, in women's detail, the extent of the violations they had suffered and the disgusting things the Russians had muttered in English, to them.

Anneliese's phone rang, just in time to ease the tension. It was Denton. "I just wanted to say that the President is speechless at your team's achievements. His words to me were that the resilience your team has shown is beyond belief! As we talked, he was about to continue, but stopped and took a couple of seconds to gather himself. I could tell by the quiver in his voice that he was upset and the constant pressure was invading his ability to retain control."

"As he exhaled, he blurted out, Denton, I need you to get them back here quick. The Rebs (meaning the Southern States) are rampaging and attacking anyone or any business that originates from the Northern States. We still need to find the terrorist cells that are operating here. Our medical factories and facilities continue to be threatened, and you CIA guys don't seem to have a clue to their whereabouts or what they may do next."

Denton broke for a moment. Then said, "The President seems to be falling into a black hole and losing faith in all us CIA guys around him." The line went very quiet!

Anneliese's mind went into overdrive. Twenty seconds then she called out, "Denton, don't let this get to you! Tell the President, and I think you should get Mr Webster to have the conversation, that we are bringing our team back. We will immediately be pulling back to the U.S."

"But to give him confidence, explain that I think we need the terrorist from the Cosmo episode extradited to the U.S. as soon as possible. We need to do some tough interrogation on him. He should arrange that with the Turkish President! Also Denton, I need you to get into Bietronics and find and arrest the guy that has been assembling the heat sinks into the computers. Then, he should be interrogated to determine how he got involved."

"The CIA over here in Istanbul now need to interrogate all of Anastasia's crew. I'm pretty sure they will know nothing and not be involved. They were probably just a merchant ship doing a job. But it's worth checking."

Denton thanked Anneliese. "I will get us all back to Jackson in the next couple of days. Denton, don't get despondent. Just remember how far we have come. And we will soon, sort this whole thing out!"

With Frank's help, Anneliese called everyone together late afternoon. She quickly explained that the assignment, had come to an end and they were all being recalled to America." Frank will make arrangements for our flight which will be around mid-day tomorrow. We will all transfer to the U.S., except Chuck. He will stay on to tidy up here with the local CIA, and make sure arrangements are in place to extradite the Russian terrorist as soon as he is fit to travel. Then Chuck will follow."

Turning to Ece, Anneliese said "I know you were part of the local CIA team here in Istanbul, but you are requested to return with us to America. It sounds as if we will need your help!"

Ece's expression had been sombre until she heard those words. Her eyes sparkled as she raised her fingers to her lips and blew them all a kiss!

"In a moment we will break for dinner, but before we do, are there any questions?" Nobody spoke, but then Chuck said, "After dinner could I have ten minutes of your time, as I have some information from the investigations in the Cosmo second floor. Also the owner of the building." "Thanks, Chuck," said Jerome, "We are keen to hear about anything that's been found." All around nodded!

Frank had spoken to the chef, kitchen staff and waitresses. They would be allocated the small dining room all to themselves. As it would be the last night in Istanbul, Frank had invited Amos and his local CIA team. The chef would prepare a sumptuous three course dinner, combined with three choices.... And a selection of wines!

Following constant banter and, at times, hysterics, there were a few speeches expressing gratitude. To the local team, who stood and took a bow. To the CIA.CECD team, for their dedication and teamwork with the locals!

As the room settled down and everybody appeared to have a drink, Chuck slowly arose out of his chair. "As we are in solitary tonight, I thought I'd give you this debrief now. It won't take long as there's not much to tell. But I'm sure it will develop over the next couple of days. Anyway, the first thing to tell you is that Amos and Ben interviewed the owner of the Cosmo property. The ground floor and second floor were two distinctly separate leases. The Dental Company had taken a long term lease, and the owner had accepted a short term rolling quarterly lease for the second floor. The second floor deal had been concluded with an American. His name was obviously false, and it was paid in cash. He visited only once, but we have been given a good description. He certainly did not look anything like Robert Redford!"

"So, Amos concludes the owner is totally innocent, and only guilty of being naïve! Now to the heat sinks and capsules. They were assembled on that second floor, a dangerous job, done by some low-paid locals. They wore some protective clothing and gloves, but probably saw it as an easy job with reasonable pay. After assembly, they were air freighted to America."

"Our CIA Analysts have extracted some encrypted messages from computers and the coding specialists will probably need another few days to work on them. One chink of light is that they have extracted some e-mail addresses and, therefore, may be able to track down physical human beings."

"Now, just one last thing to say," said Chuck. "We have all dug deep and found complete success working with you, Amos, and his team; whilst we were panning in that stream with you, a 24 carat nugget was staring up at us. Just as with diamonds, the name will always be remembered. It's called an Ece!"

"I'm sorry if I'm talking too much, but this has, by far, been the most wonderful part of my career. And the icing on the cake is that within all the euphoria that success brings, we have all seen something even more special....pure romance and unequivocal love! Hana and Donald; here's to both of you and your life together!"

Chuck raised his glass of red wine, and with a gleaming wide smile, nodded to them. Everyone stood and acclaimed the lovers!

Anneliese's smile gradually lit up the room. "Do I sense that we may be moving toward an American wedding?" Donald glanced at Hana who began chuckling, as her hands moved to her eyes to shield her embarrassment. Donald stood, both hands on the table bracing himself. Looking around everyone, with his vocal chords groaning, he eventually managed to splutter,"Well yes, I've asked, and Hana has said yes! As it appens, I'm over the moon, and, as it 'appens, we have agreed to see this assignment through first."

Hearing those words, Anneliese first peered at Jerome then raised her eyes to the ceiling, whispering, "So pleased Anya." Frank shouted, "I've heard those words many times before! And Donald, you even managed a cockney accent! And I'm grateful, for the sake of our assignment, that the wedding plans are rather "Vera Lynn"... "Don't Know Where, Don't Know When."

The whole team erupted! One after the other, everyone shook hands and embraced the loving couple. After another half-an-hour of celebrations they all sauntered to their rooms for a good night's sleep, before the long flight to America.

Chapter 40

Invitation, on the Plane

As they were settling in their seats on the upper deck of the Boeing 747A, its Captain appeared with Frank. They found Anneliese sitting, chatting with Jerome. The Captain said he had a message, and slowly lowered himself next to Anneliese. "When we arrive in the U.S., the President has asked if you would go directly to the White House to meet with him. That invitation is for all you guys. If you are agreeable, I will be landing us in the Andrews Air Force Base, in Maryland. You will all be escorted, in the President's vehicles, to the White House."

Anneliese gave a calm, understanding response. As she searched Frank's and then Jerome's face, she nodded at them; then said, "Captain, please reply saying "it will be an honour and our pleasure."

The Captain eased out of his seat but then had a second thought. "I don't know if you are aware Mam, but there was another attack on a medical facility last night that sounds as though it was pretty serious, and is causing a lot of consternation." Anneliese thanked Captain Dexter, saying, "We did not know, so thanks for that important news. You have given us some time to think." As he turned away, the Captain reached for his hat's peak in a polite salute.

After the in-flight dinner, Anneliese and Frank agreed they should get everyone together. They all assembled around the rear seats near the galley. A smile that reflected the pride in her eyes, was the first thing everyone noticed. Anneliese coughed to clear her throat, then spoke with an air of authority. "There are not too many of us so I am just going to refer to you as my friends. You are all my fabulous close friends, and I have been given the privilege to pass on to you an invitation. Not an invitation to a wedding, but that may appear sometime in the future." Anneliese, with a loving smile, glanced at Hana and Donald!

"However, this invitation is one you all deserve! The unbelievable achievements that you have risked your lives for, has resulted in an invitation to the White House.... To meet the President."

"When we land, it will be in the President's allocated area in the Andrews Air Force Base. We will be taken straight to the White House to meet the President."

Anneliese continued. "From the information I have received, the first stage will be pleasurable and something you will be able to tell your families, children and grandchildren about. But there will be a second stage. Both the U.S. and U.K. continue to have serious issues regarding the impact on their people due to lack of medical equipment. The terrorists, around the U.S.A, are still causing havoc. It's my guess, the President will urge us to work on this with all agencies and military."

"When he talks to us in stage two, I am sure he will give a much better explanation of the scenario than I have. But whatever it is, just keep remembering what I have told you many times before, and you have now proved in Istanbul. We are capable. We are the best!"

A quietly spoken Jerome, clutched as many of his colleagues as were near to him. The rest, climbed across seats to wrap their arms around the group. Jerome said, "The tour that you have led us through has been so amazing; it has been overwhelming. Of course, we will all follow you, and do whatever it takes. We have all talked before and will complete this assignment together!"

It was time for the stewards and stewardesses to step forward. Wine for everyone! After an hour of socialising, the film came on and most drifted off into oblivion.

The dreamy, fuzzy awakening, began to spread through the cabin. Blinds were sporadically lifting and morning light was seeping in. Movement, all around, was growing. Some toilet trips, but mostly a tall brunette stewardess drifting around delivering breakfast menus'.

The few on board this flight to Washington D.C. were offered constant luxury. Juice and Buck's Fizz to overcome infectious yawning. An extensive choice on the menu. Hot towels and complimentary cosmetic pouches.

Breakfasts were individually ordered and served. No sign of the infamous galley trolley!

Hana and Donald were the last to wake from under their shared soft Egyptian cotton blanket. They, consequently, were the last to be served their sumptuous salmon and eggs benedict breakfasts.

Now everyone was seen to have breakfasts, Captain Dexter strolled the aisles asking, with personal charm, if everything was ok, or if anything else was required. At this point, Donald was heard to say, in a comical tone, "Who the hell is flying the plane then?"

Captain Dexter chuckled as he turned at the beginning of the aisle. "We will be landing in about an hour, so for the next half-an-hour, George has taken my place. I'm going into the galley, whilst I have time, to have my Big Mac and cheese!"

As he grinned and tripped away, the team gave a round of applause! The descent through the pure white puffy clouds experienced some minor turbulence. With Captain Dexter at the controls, the engine thrust slowly diminished, and now, as they banked south-west, all Washington buildings and highways below were clearly visible. Ece, Hana and Donald clustered at the windows, fascinated by the views from on-high.

The dinging for seat-belt signs, and an encouraging stewardess soon had everybody strapped in their seats. The plane slowed as the Captain lowered the flaps, and they hovered like a hawk viewing its prey below. Then came the clonk of the undercarriage locking. Landing was so soft it was hardly noticeable, followed by the increasingly thunderous noise of reverse engine thrust.

The Boeing came to a complete stand-still, and within a minute, the Captain and three stewardesses were amongst them. Helping them access luggage, and generally chatting to everyone.

They were all getting ready to head down the stairs when Captain Dexter approached. "It seems its, no expense spared, for you guys" as he, once again saluted them. "Two limousines have arrived to ferry you to the White House. One is the President's own vehicle. "Cadillac One", better known as "the Beast". The second vehicle is another luxury Cadillac limousine. Both have Marines as your drivers and escorts. Apparently, it was originally planned by transport to meet you with Stagecoach, the President's luxury bus."

"But the President directed that he wanted the absolute best for you." Cackling and chuckling seized them all, until

Frank's thoughts were diverted to Jerome, who was standing at the back of the queue. Frank with a look of amazement, stared through the group to Jerome.

Frank, addressing everyone, pointed to Jerome saying, "I'd like to introduce the best dressed Assistant Director of GCHQ there has ever been." Jerome, with blushing embarrassment returned a timid smile. The team moved aside to view Jerome. He was now wearing a superb three piece worsted hounds tooth suit. Complete with black, highly polished, buckle shoes, gold pin collar shirt and glorious lavender coloured, striped tie and pocket handkerchief. He would have graced an audience with Queen Elizabeth II.

Frank, casually dressed, just like everybody else, said, "Jerome, how did you magic that outfit?" Jerome replied, "It's all about training. I carry this stuff with me all the time, just in case. And I've learned, over time, to use the plane's tiny toilets as if they are changing rooms in Harrods." "For me," he continued, "meeting the President is a once-a-lifetime event, so I want to look my best!"

Ece now moved forward and grasped Jerome's arm. Jerome glanced at her, then took a long lingering look. "Frank, I'm not the only one overcome by an invitation to meet the President. Please, everyone, meet my gorgeous partner for the evening." Gasps, especially from Anneliese and Hana, underlined how precious she looked.

Ece, now in make-up was astonishingly beautiful. Wearing a black, knee length evening dress, and two inch high heels, her peep toe shoes were screaming, "we will find her the man of her dreams." But for now she was very satisfied hanging on Jerome's arm. A deep breath then a mischievous smile as she began to speak. "In my case" said Ece, "I managed to change, with the stewardess's help, in the galley. Jerome would not let me share his toilet!"

Captain Dexter escorted them to the Boeing door as a stewardess opened it. The plush carpeted aircraft steps were in front of them with Marines, top and bottom, saluting as they passed. One at a time, down to the limousines.

Mr Webster, the CIA Director, was at the bottom to greet them. He ushered the ladies plus Jerome into "the beast". They had to wait a few seconds as the two Marines at the top of the steps, escorted Ece down, helping to steady her, as she carefully descended in her high heels.

Frank, Donald and the other two Marines approached the second limo. The front passenger door opened, and out stepped Denton to greet them. "I'm invited to this reception too," he said, as he embraced Frank and then Donald. "And as it's our team. I wouldn't miss it for the world."

The cavalcade sped off with police cars in front and behind. In around 20 minutes they entered Pennsylvania Avenue. Very soon they were approaching the floodlit architectural treasure, known as the White House.

Everyone, even those that had visited before, were in awe of this occasion. The Marines escorted them into the Reception Hall.

Mr Webster and Denton gained them all automatic clearance through security and led them off to the Blue Room. Most of the team stood, quietly nervous, until Mr Webster said "ladies and gentlemen, colleagues, please relax and take a seat!"

They only had to wait 2 or 3 minutes and the door opened. The President of the United States of America, President Hayden, stood before them.

Chapter 41

Gulf, North and South

With sparkling eyes, and a smile as wide as the Potomac River, he edged towards them. In the centre of the room, he stopped, raised both arms, and strode to Anneliese to embrace her. Then, with a relaxed gait he moved around the whole room, shaking everyone's hands.

A few rear-ward steps and he was back in the centre of the room, ready to speak. With a controlled giggle he said, "Welcome to my humble home! I feel like I know this amazing team almost as well as I know my White House team. The reason is, Denton has spent several hours briefing me on some of you. Some I already knew, Anneliese, Frank and our own Chuck, who for good reason, remains in Istanbul. But now, due to Denton's diligence I know almost everything about Hana, Ece and Jerome." He glanced around at them.

"I cannot tell you, with any words that would suffice, how proud I am to have met you, and know you. And the primary reason I have asked you here today is to tell you, personally, how grateful I am for the effort you have put in, the work that you do, and the risks that you take. I would love to tell the whole world but that's impossible in the world we live in. But there is one thing I know! Those people that don't know your work, will feel the difference you make. So I offer you my heart-felt thanks!"

Jerome, with tears of joy in his eyes, could not contain his emotions. He stepped forward, out of the circular formation, and began to applaud. Within seconds, the whole group joined in, as the President showed wide-eyed appreciation.

As the room quietened, Mr Webster stepped forward saying, "Mr President would now like us to talk about some new issues we are needed to work on. For that part of this evening, we will go to the Oval Office. So please, if you are all ready, just follow the President and me."

On entering the Oval Office, they were greeted by the chairman of the Chiefs of Staff, Paul Davis. President Hayden walked to his desk, then turned to face them. "Please, make yourself comfortable. Move your chairs to the centre, if you wish."

As the President settled behind his desk, he exhaled, as he stroked his chin, with a somewhat serious expression. "You people have been away for a while, but I know you receive regular reports concerning the state of the nation. Well, putting it in my own words, it's pretty dire at the moment. You guys have done an excellent job, but mostly on areas that our citizens don't see, or hear about. Yes, and that's also true for the U.K. Our civil servants and Embassy staff are no longer under threat. You located the terrorists Command Centre and closed that down. Now it's been ostracized from the terrorist cells in the U.S. life will become much more difficult for them. But they are still here and seem intent on carrying on with their attacks on our medical equipment manufacturers."

"The bottom line is, putting it simply, now you are back I want you to do what you do so well. The country needs you to find them and put an end to their atrocities."

"There is another angle I need to alert you to, although Denton will expand on what I'm about to say. Here in

America, a dangerous gulf has been developing. In all my years on this earth, I have never seen anything like it before. It's reminiscent of the Civil War Years. The South versus the North."

"The underlying lack of medical attention is the catalyst. But CIA intelligence reports, from all over our country, indicate that this fire is being stoked by serious levels of funding from a fundamentalist regime. Subversive groups and radicals are being paid to destroy the United States of America. Their primary objective appears to be to eliminate the word "United". If they succeed, democracy throughout the world will be threatened."

Denton has detailed information to share with you on this subject. Also results of interrogations and terrorist communications found in Istanbul since you left. At this juncture I will finish, because you have had long stressful days, and so have I."

Anneliese stood, and graciously thanked President Hayden. "You can be assured Mr President, we will do everything possible to get a result. We will, every one of us will, put our hearts and souls into this."

President Hayden replied, "Anneliese, I would not expect anything less from you and your team. But there is one more thing I want to say. I would like Denton and Anneliese to lead on this assignment. So please accept my direction with a good heart."

The President searched everyone's faces. Then in an appreciative tone, turned to Denton and Anneliese saying, "I have complete confidence in you all. But now, we should have something to remember this day by." Turning to Paul Davis, he chuckled as he asked, "Paul, do you have a camera, or can you get a photographer in here, on the quick?" The CIA

Director entered the arena, peering at the Chief of Staff, who was shaking his head. "I will get us one," said Mr Webster. As he left the room, the President walked around them all, with brief chatting and embraces.

The third person he engaged with was Hana. "My dear," he said, "I've heard of the terrible time you had in Istanbul. You are a very strong person, so now I'm going to say let's forget that, except to say how sorry I am for what you had to go through. But on a brighter note, I am told, you and Donald!" He stopped, and with his hand out, called Donald over. He continued, as he held Donald close, "I am told you have found love and are planning to marry sometime soon!" With embarrassment written all over their faces, they both nodded saying, "Yes, Sir."

The President released Donald from the shoulder hold, and stood back two or three feet. Everyone was in awe; expectant as he spoke. "When this is all done, dead and buried, I will pay for the wedding." There were gasps from everybody. "And if Donald and Hana like the idea, the wedding could be held at Camp David and you will all be invited. Talk about it amongst yourselves." Then cuddling Hana, he said, "Thank you. Just let me know."

A knock came on the door, and in strode Mr Webster with a photographer. Photo after photo and they would all receive copies.

The last photo opportunity was with Ece. President Hayden held both her hands and almost waltzed her into the middle of the group. In Ece's two inch heels they were about as tall as one another. After several takes, the President asked the photographer to stand back. Facing everyone with his arm around her shoulders, he announced, "I've had many fantastic reports about the ability of this young lady." Ece slightly swivelled to look straight into his eyes. He eased her the rest of the way to face him. "Ece, Intelligence tell me you always jump in feet first. Well, all I can say is, that so far, that has achieved superb results." He gained a breath and looked back into her eyes. His head dropped, staring at her shoes. With a wide grin he said, "But I'm really hoping that those exclusive high heels you are wearing don't contain the Rosa Klebb Knives. If they did I would be very apprehensive about being this close!"

Continuing to hold Ece's hand, he slowly moved to the corner of his room. He shouted to Mr Webster, "Would you ask for the drinks trolley?" It arrived in a few minutes. In the meantime the President loudly exclaimed, "I've had a very rough few weeks, but now I'm among friends. Do you mind if we have an hour or so of fun and dancing?"

With that, he pressed a button on his stereo. Mostly, the music was soft and gentle; Frank Sinatra but with some Mary Wells thrown in for good measure. Soon Jerome and Anneliese, Donald and Hana and, of course, the President and Ece were tripping the light fantastic.

The photographer clicked away the whole time. So now, everyone would have pictures for their family photo albums!

It had been a fabulous evening, and at approximately 10pm, they were all ready to return to their Jackson street. Their beds were beckoning after a long, tiring, but exciting day. A day they would treasure in their memories for the rest of their lives.

Marines drove them, in two Ford Crown Victorias', to the Staybridge Suites. Denton accompanied them, and as the bell boys were collecting their luggage, Denton shuffled Anneliese away from the group." I need you to join me in the morning for a meeting with Mr Webster. I will pick you all up at 8am and you and I will meet Webster at 9am." Denton turned, but then hovered and whispered, "Don't tell the others about the meeting with Webster!"

Chapter 42

Is There a Traitor?

In the morning Denton arrived in an Explorer. Another Ford Explorer driven by one of the HQ security people was just a couple of minutes behind. Denton explained, these two cars would be for the team's use. They were driven to the Jackson HQ. Ece was excited as it was her first visit, and she chattered throughout the ten mile drive.

All of them went straight for the coffee shop. Anneliese said, "When you have had your coffees, would you assemble in our second floor room and start to put any ideas concerning how we find their cells, up on the flip chart. I will be with you shortly, but first I have a meeting with Denton to develop some strategies."

She joined Denton at the foot of the marble staircase, and they headed up.

Mr Webster's office was on the top floor, and they ambled up together. Denton was very quiet all the way. Anneliese began to sense something was wrong.

The Director's secretary showed them straight in. Mr Webster also appeared to be in a sombre mood, only offering a quiet welcome. Anneliese stared directly at William Webster and then Denton, trying to stimulate some form of response.

Mr Webster, with a frown wrinkling his forehead slowly began. "Anneliese, whatever we tell you now must not go beyond these four walls." This opener raised the tiny hairs on the back of Anneliese's gorgeous silky smooth neck.

The Director, glancing at Denton, tried to raise a smile, as he looked into Anneliese's eyes. "I will start by saying that the information I am about to give you has been discussed with the President. The issue goes like this. Denton has gradually become concerned with what he perceived as unusual incidents and coincidences. He's taken me through his work and now, with sadness, I have to admit I agree with him. The bottom line is, we believe someone in our team may be leaking information to the enemy." His face soured as he massaged his temple." Denton, let me pass this to you to give more detail to Anneliese."

Denton tried to smile but could only manage one that was wry. "Anneliese there are many pieces to this jigsaw and no factual evidence. I will try to run through it."

"There are two totally circumstantial elements linked to Hana." Anneliese screwed her eyes up as she blurted out, "No, there's no possibility!" Denton stopped her saying more. "At this stage we are just providing a commentary that is a potential negative against the person. We must remember, for the moment, we are not definite we have a leaker!"

"As I was saying, Hana's mother was Iranian. There was the Iranian in Cosmo, and we recently determined that the assembler of heat sinks was Iranian. Hana can speak Russian and as we know there are several Russians within the terrorists. Lastly, the terrorist she shot in Cosmo was killed outright. All our training dictates avoiding a kill, if possible, to allow us a chance to interrogate. Her single shot was deadly, and from a few feet away!"

"The other prime suspect we have is".... Anneliese stood and kicked her chair away. "I can't see it being any of our people," she said, as she peered into the Director's eyes. "As I was saying, and this hurts me much more than you, Anneliese; the other suspect is Chuck. The only intelligence we have goes back some years, indeed, when he was first appointed. Our Analysts did the usual deep dive into his background. He was born in the U.K. Has an older brother. He has always said he lost track of him years ago. He moved to the U.S. with Father and Brother. Father died of cancer two years after arriving. He has always said he doesn't remember his mother. However, our Intelligence Analysts are almost certain she was one of the hostages killed in the Iranian Embassy siege in London in 1980. She had been a cleaner in the building, and only one other hostage remembers seeing her. Her name has never been found but several documents were saved that showed her as a cleaner on the employee list, with her name shown as Iran."

"Chuck's Father was black heritage, from the Caribbean, the Bahamas. As the Bahamas are part of the Organisation of American States, it wasn't too difficult to emigrate with his kids to the U.S.A."

Denton took a sip of his coffee, and wiped the corners of his mouth with a paper serviette. Mr Webster now interjected. "Denton had suspicions for some time, but the lid came off with some new intelligence from Amos. He had interrogated the Russian that we captured!"

"He did it alone, because the Russian asked for that. The Russian wanted to negotiate. He told Amos, we have a double agent and, if we agreed to release him, he would give us the name. We have not answered him because the President wants to hold him, in case we can obtain more information identifying the terrorist cells, and maybe, the organisation funding the subversive activities. And the President expects us, in the meantime, to wash our own dirty linen, and find the double-agent ourselves, if there is one!"

Anneliese's expression was now less emotional and more business-like. "So gentlemen" she said, "Where do you think we should go from here?" The Director stepped straight back in. "Anneliese, Denton has done hours more work on this and he has summarised all of it on a single page document." As Denton passed it across to Anneliese, Mr Webster tried to assure Anneliese. "I don't want you to think we are flying into this on a wing and a prayer. So let me first give you a few minutes to read Denton's paper, whilst I organise some more coffee."

The page detailed many controversial events. The terrorists worked around the protected facilities. The Bietronics assembler had gone walk-about, just before he was to be questioned. The latest attack on the Baton Rouge facility happened just after CIA and military security was withdrawn. The Russians had been trying to escape to their ship without any reason to be spooked!

With coffee now replenished, and in front of them, Anneliese searched Mr Webster's face and then Denton's. "Ok," said Mr Webster, "Amos will send Denton a transcript of everything they found in Cosmo. He thinks Chuck may be deliberately slow-walking that, or indeed, cleansing it before we see it. I would like you, Anneliese, to review all the detail and ascertain if it can be useful. Secondly, I would like you both to take Donald to Chuck's apartment and go through it with a fine tooth comb. I am bringing Chuck back in two days' time so that Amos can continue his work. Clearly, you have to set this up with Donald so that he does not realise its Chuck's apartment. After he gets you in, he should be told to guard the entrance, from the car. Third on the list is Hana's room.

You need to get her out for an evening while you get in her suite!"

"Are you both in agreement?" Anneliese and Denton nodded. Mr Webster was now in full flow. "You two can't let this distract you from the key objective. Obviously you will have to keep this issue in the forefront of your minds as you work with your team on each of the next steps. Essentially, what I'm saying is you must keep the pressure on finding those terrorist cells here in the U.S."

Chapter 43

Check it Out!

The meeting was at an end. Anneliese stood, and glancing at the Director, then Denton, she uttered "Well, that was a really tough one. But I can see you are correct; we can't ignore this! So, thank you gentlemen, for all your hard work and the exemplary way you explained it. Denton, are you coming down to the team with me." "Of course," replied Denton.

They ambled into the second floor conference room together. Everyone, seemingly led by Jerome had been beavering away. The flip chart page was full. Anneliese, with a relieved loving smile, said, "Is there any coffee left. I've already had my allowance for today, but now I'm hooked and need more." Ece rushed to the coffee pot, gurgling away in the corner.

Denton and Anneliese sat next to one another, peering at the writing on the flip chart. Anneliese picked up on the third bullet point. "Yes we should do a more intensive interview with the assembly operator. See if he knows more about the previous operator. Also, we need exact details of his operation. What he does, movement by movement." Denton picked up on another point. "Who does own Bietronics? What nationality? His address and we should interview him."

Several other items were discussed but it was decided to hold them in abeyance. Denton went off to get his analysts and Frank to work on the owner of Bietronics and once they had enough data, he would receive a visit. Tomorrow, Hana and Ece would fly to visit the Bietronics factory, to interview the new heat sink assembler. However, today's plan involved Anneliese, Denton and Donald taking a visit to Chuck's apartment, late evening.

Later, Anneliese chased down Jerome. "I have an urgent assignment which I know I can trust you with." A look of regret in her eyes gained Jerome's close attention. "Please don't ask me or anyone here any questions. Denton will give you paperwork detailing what is known about Chuck's background."

"This is all strictly confidential; top secret. Get in touch with your best counter intelligence analyst in GCHQ. Explain to him the secrecy and security importance. You should do your best to stay in touch with him as he works on this assignment. He or she should investigate Chuck's background right through from birth to when he emigrated to the U.S.A. Jerome, put your heart and soul into this. Everything and anything may be important, especially potential links to other countries or other nationals. It needs to encompass his whole family."

Jerome didn't wince! "We will access all Somerset House files, Public Records Office, Companies House, and follow all trails." Jerome was about to run off to begin when Anneliese grabbed his arm. "I need a complete report no later than 48 hours from now."

With great urgency, Anneliese got on the phone to Denton. "Jerome is on his way up to you. Please let him have your file on Chuck." "But Anneliese;" she cut him short! "Yes, I know I've broken the rule, but we need details on his UK background, and Jerome is Assistant Director of GCHQ. We can't do this job without him and if I can't trust him, I can't trust anyone!" Denton replied, "I completely understand, and agree with you but, you know, I will have to report this to Mr Webster." "Ok, fine Denton. I'll get on with the assignment until they come to lock me in the tower!"

Denton gave a muffled chuckle, then the phone went dead. 15 minutes later, he knocked on the "war room" door. This was the nickname given to Anneliese's assigned office! "When should we talk with Donald?"

Anneliese adjusted the bra strap on her left shoulder as she thought. Glancing at her watch, she said "we should go when it's dark. Let's have dinner first then leave about 8pm. Leave me to explain what we are doing. The story will be, we've had intelligence linking this apartment to one of the subversive groups that are supposedly watching CIA HQ."

As soon as dinner was over, Anneliese leaned over Donald's shoulder as he chatted with Hana. "Donald, I need your assistance for a couple of hours." It was said loud enough for Hana to hear. She just smiled and nodded, saying "see you later then." Donald stood and followed Anneliese to her "war room". Once inside, Anneliese, as she tidied her desk, grinned, saying, "Denton and I need you to break us into an apartment. We have some unconfirmed intelligence about one of the subversive groups that are giving the President a headache. Just need you to get us in. I don't think it will come to anything."

Donald, with a glint in his eyes, excitedly replied "I'm glad to be of help and that my expertise is appreciated. The last few days have been a bit quiet for me." Anneliese remarked "Don't worry Donald, we are heading for a very busy period." She put her arm around his shoulders and they wandered to the door.

About 30 minutes later in an upmarket area south of Jackson, Donald was wiggling his home-made lock-crackers tool. 24 seconds and he had the door opened. Another 8 seconds and he had disconnected the burglar alarm. As Denton and Anneliese began to enter Denton turned to Donald saying, "Sit in the car and keep watch. If you need to give us a warning just sound the car horn."

Denton and Anneliese were experts on where to look and what to look for. Denton had the computer on in seconds, and was peeling through emails. It took them just over 10 minutes. At around 9.30pm the three of them wandered into the bar, needing a drink. Hana was there waiting for Donald. As they grasped one another, Frank couldn't resist saying, "please get a room!"

Frank got Anneliese and Denton drinks, then all three sat in the corner of the bar. Frank slowly sipped a Michelob as he viewed Denton gulping a large Bourbon. When he concluded Denton and Anneliese were comfortable and ready to hear more work talk, he quietly announced "Your guys, Denton, are great! They certainly know their stuff!" Denton, after more gulps of bourbon, was relaxed and overjoyed to hear Frank's commendations. Frank continued, "More and more information exploded in front of me, as they worked their magic. The owner of Bietronics is a character who came to America as an immigrant. His name, when he arrived, was Ahmed Biesef. He legally changed his name, in the early eighties, to Arnold Pavlova. He originally trained with and worked for IBM, and very quickly became their super-star programmer and software specialist. From there it was onwards and upwards."

"When I left them, playing tunes on their keyboards, they had found that he came into America with a younger brother and a father. And apparently it was looking as if their mother, who had died in the U.K. was Iranian. When I left them, they were still digging and delving."

Denton took another gulp of Bourbon, then turned to look into Anneliese's eyes. Her expression was just as knowing as Denton's.

The evening wasn't finished yet. Hana and Ece came to join them. "We are going to the Bietronics factory tomorrow. Anything you want us to cover with the assembly guy?" As Hana finished speaking, Anneliese stood to join them. "Just use your feminine charms to get him talking. About everything and anything. What conversations did he have with the previous incumbent, did he talk about family, hobbies? How did he get the job? But also what were his operations when the heat sinks arrived. Step by step. Then we can piece together who did what. Was it the terrorists inflicting the nerve gas capsules, or did the Bietronics Company know what was going on and were party to it?"

Chapter 44

Hana Clear, BLUE Important

In the morning, Denton and Anneliese met early in Denton's office for a short meeting. They agreed they would work together, to summarise all reports into a single dossier. Denton was going to make a start on the findings on Chuck's apartment.

Anneliese would re-convene with Denton after she had completed her incursion into Hana's room.

An hour later she was back in their hotel. Anneliese pretended she had forgotten something, and leant across the reception counter to get her room key. Instead, she took Hana's key!

Standing in the peace and quiet of Hana's room, her eyes began to fill with tears. She wanted to cry out loud, but suppressed the emotion. With a hand clasped over her mouth, she wandered around. On the chest of drawers, photos of Hana's parents and her sister. She stared at them, her mind confused with thoughts of both Hana and Anya.

She pulled herself together and began a serious professional search. Everything she moved, she placed back in its original place. There must not be a single hint left behind, of her search. The last, and most important feature of the investigation was Hana's paperwork in the credenza.

Anneliese's expression was sullen as she read through loose papers and a notebook.

Later, feeling grimy and with a nasty taste in her mouth, she sat facing Denton. "There was absolutely nothing there, Denton! The room was as clean and tidy as her life!" Before she could say more, Denton said, "I know you are hurting Anneliese and so am I. That feeling of guilt will stay with us forever, but we had to do it to be able to assure every one of her innocence."

Anneliese rolled her eyes and attempted an accepting smile. "I micro-filmed addresses in her papers; all were Prague. Her parents and sister are all now in the Czech Republic, close to Prague. They live on a small farm and there was a photograph of the place. Even a picture of a cheeky, bouncing chocolate-coloured Labrador dog!"

Denton signalled to Anneliese, saying, "Move round to this side of the table and we can push on with putting the dossier together. It's looking to me as if it's going to throw up the answers we need. Frank has nearly finished his review of the Bietronics ownership. Ece and Hana will return with their report tonight. Jerome also says he should have completed tonight."

"So, for now we can crack on with our review of the report that Amos sent, regarding what was found at Cosmo. With the papers placed between them, Denton read out loud anything he deemed interesting. At those points they would call a halt and discuss the topic.

After a while, Anneliese stopped and stood. "I need a coffee," she replied, as she strolled to the coffee machine in the corner of the office. With a pensive expression, she asked Denton, "Where are the emails?" "Oh, I forgot to mention, they are with the Intelligence Analysts. They were all encrypted and so I got them working on them! I'll give them another half-an-hour then ask how they are doing."

Just as Denton was picking up the phone, there was a knock on the door. Denton opened it and exclaimed, "Hello Tiny Tim, I was just about to ring, but you beat me to it. You may be small, but you are quick, which is much more important." Denton smiled, saying, "Thank you Tim! Some good teatime reading!" as he closed the door.

Their eyes began to skirt quickly over the report. "Well that is really interesting," said Denton, as his finger jumped to points on the page. Several of the emails had the words "Kodsiniy". My guys say it's Russian for;" Anneliese, with emphasis in her voice, interjected. "Code Blue!" Looking across at the papers, Anneliese said "It's in almost all the emails! Must have been used to initiate some form of action."

The smell of steaks cooking was wetting all appetites. The few around in the bar were about to go to the dining room. First Frank arrived, followed three minutes later by Hana and Ece. Frank, carrying a bristling folder, took it straight to Denton saying, "Some real eye-openers in there."

Denton, walking out, was met by Jerome who also handed over his report. Denton went off to his office to ensure the reports were safe and secure.

The steak dinners were a speciality of the CIA HQ kitchen. The T Bone steaks were a revelation. Large and juicy with amazing pepper sauce, coupled with fruity Californian Cabernet Sauvignon; kept everybody in culinary ecstasy for over an hour. With everyone together, the stories were constant. Nothing security contentious. But relaxing anecdotes that enhanced this team's bonding.

As dinner came to an end, and one by one, they drifted off into the bar, Denton approached Ece. "I know you and

Hana have had a long day, but I need your report tonight. I'm sorry but our deadline is tomorrow, requiring Anneliese and me to work on all the different reports through the night!"

Hana joined Ece, and held her hand, as she put her arm around Ece's shoulder. Donald then approached. Hana turned to him saying "Ece and I have an hour or so to get our report to Denton. So go and enjoy a game of pool with Frank and Jerome while we finish up." Denton, with the relieved look of a grandfather whose grandchildren had listened, turned to Anneliese. "Shall we carry on, to get this paperwork finished?" Anneliese, with a sensitive smile replied, "There's nothing better I can think of doing. So let's go!"

Denton and Anneliese settled into reading all the reports, gathering increasing excitement as a picture began to emerge. Anneliese stopped Denton as he was in full flow. "We can't give Mr Webster and the President all this paperwork. Denton, I think we should extract the salient points that give the President all the information necessary for him to make decisions."

Denton, although looking tired, nodded and smiled at Anneliese. "So" he said, "This could be one of those all night sessions." Anneliese, still looking fresh and full of fight, replied, "No Denton. I know I can do this in two hours." Just as she spoke, there was a knock on the door. It was Ece. Denton answered. Ece, with a reserved smile said, "Sir, this is Hana's and my report on our day in Bietronics." Denton responded with a grateful expression. "Thank you Ece, but please call me Denton. We are colleagues, but also, friends."

Chapter 45

BLUE It Is!

The dossier was completed by Anneliese in just under three hours. It had taken her a bit longer as she had spent some time thinking about issues that arose in her mind as she was writing the summary document.

As she finished, Denton said, with relief in his voice, "Fantastic, amazing Anneliese! Shall we go to the bar for a drink before we hit our sacks?"

"Not just yet, Denton. There are two things I need you to attend to. Please make a note of them. "Denton picked up his pen as he opened his notebook." We never heard anything about the documents that were taken from the Iranian, Abdul Karim, when he was arrested. I think you should contact your people involved in his arrest to see what they know. But, for the time being. Keep everything away from Chuck."

"The other thing is just a hunch that came to me out of the blue, as I was working through the reports." With a wide grin, Anneliese exhaled and continued. "The word blue in my last sentence is very appropriate. It struck me that the Bietronics owner's surname is Bluesef. And several of the emails from Cosmo referred to Code Blue. There's one more thing. Frank mentions in his report that your Intelligence Analysts, Denton, had accessed all Bluesef's personal assets.

The element that keeps niggling at me is that they found Mr Bluesef owns four motor cruisers!"

"Now what I am going to ask sounds a monstrous task. But it may prove to give us a gigantic result. We should check all marinas around the coast line of America and identify any Motor Cruisers with "Blue" in their name." Denton took a sip of his coffee.

Anneliese, with certainty in her tone, continued, "Your guys must be able to access all marinas rental documents. If that doesn't work, they can go through Bluesef's bank accounts to try to find any payments to marinas. And if neither of those work, as a last resort, we could get all Coastguards to physically check out marinas in their vicinity."

Denton peered straight into Anneliese's eyes. With an expression filled with admiration, he said, "Anneliese, you are an absolute genius!"

"And if we find three cruisers with blue in their name, all registered to Mr Bluesef, I will get surveillance on them immediately. I'm going to set this in motion. I will see you, Madame Genius, in the bar in 15 minutes. Please have a large bourbon waiting for me."

When Denton returned, he strode across the bar floor and grasped his large bourbon. Anneliese was enjoying the company of Jerome, Donald, Hana and Ece. As Denton swigged a big mouthful of bourbon, his cheeks bulged. His face went pink as it received a torrent of bourbon mixed with the adrenalin already soaring through his system.

Ece sensed Denton's euphoria. "Denton, have you just won the state lottery?" Her expression was mischievous but attractively nubile; she was beautiful! Denton's veins now received a tsunami of testosterone, the like of which he hadn't experienced in years.

Denton, until now, had not been stimulated by Ece's beauty. But now his gaze ventured to her mini-skirted thighs, minute waist and satin-smooth bosoms, pushing against her slightly low cut dress. His eyes toured gradually upwards, until they met hers. As her dark eyes smiled, his mind was captivated by the contours of her plump lips.

Anneliese had been watching all the while. Always fascinated by human attraction and an expert in recognising the signs of desire, she walked to Denton, grasped his arm and led him away to the bar. Denton's eyes continued to glance across to Ece as Anneliese said, "I think, Denton, you are suffering from fatigue!" "No, I'm ok" replied Denton. "I've given my people the assignment and they have made a start. I also managed to contact the arresting agents. They told me that Chuck had reviewed the Iranian's files found in his briefcase, but had found nothing." "Ok," said Denton, "leave it at that."

Denton stood thinking for a moment! "I'll be back in a minute of two!" On his return, with a pensive expression, he told Anneliese he'd talked with Tiny Tim. "They never let any possible evidence out of the building. The Iranian's files are locked away upstairs. Tim and his guys will dig them out and do a complete investigation for us. We'll have it in the morning." "Now, Denton, get off to bed and we will press ahead in the morning." She waved as he disappeared up the stairs.

Early morning, Denton sat together with Anneliese in the "war room". They were planning to read right through the dossier, and dossier summary, again.

Frank knocked on the door and was greeted by a jaded looking Denton. In his usual casual way, Frank brought a broad smile to Denton's face! "We've got them" he said. "We've found the terrorist cells; three motor cruisers!" A body behind Frank took a step to the right and was now visible. Frank clutched the back of his neck, pulling him forward. It was Tiny Tim.

Denton gestured to them to enter the "war room". "Go on Tim, tell Denton and Anneliese about the proof you have found."

"Well," said Tim. "My team powered through all the marina registrations. We found three and have all their locations. The three are Blue Bird, Blue Sky and Blue Yonder. They are all registered to Arnold Bluesef of the Bietronics Corporation. To validate this, we trawled through his personal bank accounts and corporate bank accounts. The Corporate accounts turned up trumps. He bought the motor cruisers as a company investment and all associated costs are charged to the Company. But a piece of evidence that seals the fate of Mr Bluesef was in his private bank accounts. He paid for the rental of the second floor of the Cosmo property!"

Denton looked at Anneliese, without saying a word. He picked up his phone, whilst continuing to stare into Anneliese's eyes. Just a few seconds, then she exclaimed, "Yes, phone the Director and say we need an immediate meeting with President Hayden. Denton, you know he will want good reason, so be ready with the answers."

The conversation was short and excited! Denton turned to Tiny Tim, an affectionate nickname that had developed from the gigantic wisdom and knowledge he constantly exuded. Before Denton could utter a word, Frank, again clasping Tim's shoulders, exclaimed, "This guy, Denton, is worth his weight in gold." Frank, peering at Denton, began to chuckle as he turned to face Tim. "Sorry, but in view of your weight, I should have said diamonds!"

Denton, waiting for the call back, asked Anneliese if she had any questions for Tim or Frank. "No, we couldn't have asked for more. Tim, it came just at the right time!" Frank and Tim turned as if they would head for the door. But Tim stopped. "There is one other thing, but it's shrouded in secrecy." Anneliese and Denton shared a stare. Anneliese glanced at Frank and then Tim.

With a soft and gentle voice, she uttered, "You can tell us anything Tim!" "The thing is" said Tim, "My guys are going through all the papers found when the Iranian was captured. I found his phone, and with the Bell Companies help, investigated all the phone call entries. There was one call that the Bell Company could not access because it was security protected by the U.S. Government. I stared at the number and thought I recognised it. So I checked the Government register. The Iranian, around the time he was arrested had called Chuck!"

Chapter 46

Concrete Evidence, Mr President!

Anneliese and Denton both drew breath. Anneliese thanked Tim and said, "Frank, go buy this guy a drink. He is a wizard. But, please Tim, don't mention any of this to anyone."

As they departed, the phone rang. They would meet with the President this very evening at 11pm! They should travel by helicopter from Jackson to the lawn at the White House.

At 10.55pn, Denton, Anneliese and Frank bustled under the down draught and across the lawns. Two Marines escorted them in, across the reception area and through the glistening white-walled corridor to the Oval Office.

Mr Webster had arrived in Washington an hour earlier to meet with the Director of the FBI and the chairman of the Chiefs of Staff. The meeting, in the FBI Building on Pennsylvania Avenue was short and sweet. William Webster, clearly effervescent, had asked both chiefs to be ready to support armed conflict with the terrorists. Whatever military and air support was required needed to be battle station ready.

Mr Webster was a few paces behind the advance party. He stood in the doorway as the President greeted Anneliese with a double cheek kiss and lengthy embrace. Frank and Denton had moved to the side and were politely standing to attention against the office wall.

The President invited his guests to sit, but continued to slowly pace the room. Looking at Anneliese, then the other two, the President said "William convinced me to have this late meeting, but did not give me any details as he was concerned about security. That alone, told me this was critical. So which one of you three musketeers are going to brief me?" Denton turned to Anneliese, gesturing and saying, "Please go ahead!"

In her usual manner, Anneliese sauntered to the middle of the room to face the President, about five feet away. "Mr President, we have prepared a complete dossier and summary for you. We made adjustments just before we left, to incorporate the late, but very important information that drove us to ask for this urgent meeting!"

"I don't think we should spend valuable time going through the whole dossier now. Rather, I would prefer to cover the intelligence information that you may feel requires an immediate response." The President glanced around the room, and seeing nods of agreement, said, "Anneliese, please continue."

Anneliese explained the detailed evidence regarding Arnold Bluesef's terrorist activities. She continued to identify the terrorist cells that had initiated the attacks on medical factories and facilities. She also provided an outline of the concrete evidence that linked Mr Bluesef to the motor cruisers that were used to launch the attacks.

The President's jaw tightened as his expression hardened. "Well we now know who they are and where they are." The President took three deep breaths, then continued.

"Now we have to answer another difficult question. What action should we take?"

"Mr President, there is one more, very distasteful element we should divulge to you." Anneliese, as she spoke glanced at Mr Webster. "One of our own Secret Service Agents has played a part in all this. We are not sure why, but, once more, we have irrefutable evidence of his guilt." The traitor was Chuck.

"My goodness," exclaimed the President, "You guys have been busy! My legs need to sit and I need to relax!" He stiffly moved around his desk and sat.

"Let's get back to the question of what we should do now." His eyes looked to Frank. "As a long serving military person, what Frank, would you suggest?"

Frank stood and took a step forward. "Mr President, taking the easiest step first, I would recommend Chuck is arrested as soon as he arrives in the U.S. tomorrow. Then we can begin interrogation. Continuing the order of events. The next priority is the capture of the three terrorist cells. We could just blow their motor cruisers and the terrorists to smithereens, using a gunship helicopter. That would be easy! But I think capture of as many of the terrorists as possible is preferable. Put them all in Guantanamo Bay and interrogate them. Make this public, here and in the U.K."

"When we choose to attack these terrorist cells, it must be completely simultaneous. This will avoid them sending out alerts. For the same reason, the arrest of Arnold Bluesef must be simultaneous with attacks on the three terrorist cells!"

"Once we have all these terrorists in custody, we have a chance to establish who is leading and funding the subversive groups; causing so much division and disturbance in the U.S."

Frank took a step back. The President's eyes moved to William Webster who blinked, then nodded agreement.

President Hayden stood and slowly paced towards the group. Facing them, he smiled. "I agree with everything you have done and said. I don't know how we managed to mould together such a talented group, but I thank my lucky stars that we did!"

"You should return to Jackson now, and I will convene my staff and get an action plan together. William, I would like you to stay here with me to help orchestrate the whole thing. And Frank, when our militarists have established an assault plan, I would like you to lead one of the groups. I will get back to you all with details in the morning."

Chapter 47

Operation PARALYSE Plan

They arrived back in Jackson after 1.00am. Denton and Frank went for a nightcap. Anneliese decided to go straight to bed for her beauty sleep. Denton and Frank, still running on adrenalin, were chatting as they strode into the bar. Denton couldn't believe his eyes. His heart started to pound. Ece and Jerome were still in the bar. Denton, with a wobble in his voice asked "What are you guys doing up this late?"

Ece, with a heart-warming smile, said "We just had to hear how it went." As she spoke, her right hand stretched out and loosely gripped Denton's left. "Was it difficult, stressful?" Frank interlaced with their conversation. "No, it went fantastically well. The President agreed with all our recommendations. He complimented us several times on the work we have done. He is a man of wisdom," said Frank, "And America is lucky to have him." Ece peered into Denton's eyes, repeating Frank's sentence. "A man of wisdom just like you Denton.... and you, Jerome!" As Denton trembled, Ece turned to Frank saying, "Yes, and you too have wisdom, Frank, but you are more an action man." With that, she stood saying, "It's time for bed."

Denton tossed and turned for hours. His mind overcome by the emotional attention he was receiving from Ece. But concern intervened in his ecstatic emotions, constantly reminding him of the age difference and that he may have imagined her romantic interest. He wanted this to be so so real!

Early morning, Denton reminded himself, several times, that he was an experienced professional. His first port of call was to Tiny Tim and his Intelligence team. Tim was pursuing delving into Bluesef's wealth and business interests. They were also digging into Chuck's family and background. Tim was particularly keen to learn more about Chuck's mother and was trying to establish any links to Arnold Bluesef. Chuck's bank accounts were also being visited and mapped.

Later Frank joined Denton and Tim. As they chatted, Frank's memories started to come into play. After a while, Frank interjected saying, "Guys, please help. Let me talk aloud. Some things are coming back that may be useful. I was part of the S.A.S. team involved in the Iranian Embassy siege in 1980. I remember there was an Iranian lady that had been held hostage and was shot trying to escape. The story I heard was that the Iranian's wanted her shipped back to Iran. She had begged to stay in the U.K. saying that she had escaped from Iran and had been given asylum in the U.K. She had stated she was part of the Iranian Royal Family, toppled in the 1979 Revolution. She died very soon after."

Tim eyeballed Frank and then Denton. "Frank, that is remarkable information. I will work with Jerome on that, and we may find a link to Arnold Bluesef, or even Chuck. This may lead us to a motive!"

At precisely 11.00am William Webster called Denton. "Please get everyone to assemble in the second floor conference room. I have had details and instructions from the President."

The whole team gathered just before 11.00am. The Director strode in, stood in the middle of the conference room clutching some papers to his chest. "I know you have received praise before, but I want to give you my personal thanks. Your work will save lives; thousands of lives. Indeed, it makes me emotional, to say it. But I have never, and maybe never again, will work with such a superb, cohesive team." He reached for his handkerchief, blew his nose and wiped the corner of his eyes.

Drawing breath, he dedicated a smile to Anneliese. "In all this we have had ups and downs, but mostly, thank God, ups! The down is that one of our own, Chuck, will be landing in a few minutes and will be arrested. Sometimes there are bad apples, but you found this one before it became infectious. Secondly, the vicious Russian, is being extradited today and will be imprisoned in Guantanamo Bay whilst he is interrogated. They say things that go round, come round. For him, it's confirmed. Cuba is where Havana Syndrome began and that's where he's ending up."

"Now that's out of the way, we will move to the operation your work has taken us to. The assaults on the three terrorist cells will begin at precisely 5.00pm tomorrow. The expert psychologists have recommended this time. Most of you will be involved. But in somewhat different ways. I would like Anneliese, Frank, Denton and Jerome to stay behind. I will take them through the detailed plan, and in the meantime, you lucky girls can have some lunch."

Hana, Ece and Donald slowly edged out of the conference room. Their faces showed some confusion and displeasure. They had scarcely passed through the door when Donald turned and re-entered. "I apologise Mr Webster; I have to say something." Everyone stared at Donald with surprised expressions.

With a somewhat annoyed look, Mr Webster said, "Yes, Donald, what is it?" "Sir, I know I haven't been in the service long, but Hana and Ece's recent work has been astounding. Hana lifted the lid on H.S. and both ladies showed tremendous bravery and fortitude in the Cosmo hostage situation. And I may not yet understand the etiquette in this power house, but I also have made a solid contribution."

"We all want to carry on making a substantial contribution, but I don't think we can, if we are treated as juniors and excluded." Then with a wide grin, Donald cheekily remarked, "And sir, we don't take up much room in your office!"

The Director's scowl slowly transformed into an accepting smile. Peering around at them all he said, "Donald, you are perfectly correct. You are all crucial to our success, and I apologise, profusely! Please come back in and join us." Anneliese, in particular, gazed at them with a smile as wide as the pride in her team!

William Webster drifted across the room, still clutching a folder of papers to his chest. He pulled one page out of the folder and handed it to Frank. "Please read aloud to give everyone the Government's plan and commitment."

Frank, with Anneliese peering at his paper, started. "Each of the three squads will be made up as follows:

- On Standby, an AH64 Apache Gunship Helicopter, manned by 2 pilots and 4 SEALs

- A Coastguard vessel, blocking exit, manned with Coastguard team plus 4 SEALs

- A Power inflatable manned by 4 SEALs

- Attack Team, manned by 8 Special Ops Marines, 2 CECD Agents, 2 FBI Agents, 2 CIA Agents

➢ Frank to allocate CECD personnel to each team. Denton, Mr Webster and Jerome will maintain radio contact at each location, with CECD and FBI personnel throughout. Denton will select the CIA Agents for each team.

➢ Mr Webster, Denton and Jerome, will, over the radio, announce the commencement of the operation. If any of the terrorist motor cruisers, or indeed terrorists, appear to be escaping the Apache Gunship will be brought into play. CECD personnel must raise the alert. The operation will commence at exactly 5.00pm. Make sure your watches are synchronised.

➢ Simultaneous with the operation, the CIA Agents surrounding Arnold Bluesef's property, will arrest and detain him and any other person in the property. They will be taken, under guard, to the Richmond, Virginia city jail. To be taken later to CIA HQ in Jackson for interrogation.

➢ Terrorists detained in the attack operation will be flown from local Air Force bases to Guantanamo Bay detention camp.

➢ Frank will direct all operations with his team.

➢ Anneliese will direct all operations with her team.

➢ Jerome will direct all operations with his team.

• This Operation is Code Named PARALYSE

The three locations are:

BLUE BIRD	BLUE SKY	BLUE YONDER
Delaware Bay	Santa Barbara	New Orleans
Near Dover	Rosa Island	Mississippi Sound
Delaware	California	Louisiana

You will be flown out to your respective locations tonight. You must be at the Langley Air Force Base at 7.00pm.

The Director asked "Do you all agree the plan and resources? Any questions?" The room remained quiet. "I'll leave now to prepare." Looking at Frank and Jerome, Mr Webster said, "You need to sort out your teams and then get up to the equipment section and armoury; get yourselves fully equipped, including military clothing! I will be in the Blue Bird team down in Delaware Bay. Good luck everyone. Just keep telling yourselves, these terrorists are not only threatening democracy they are threatening every family in the civilised world!"

Chapter 48

Terrorists Defeated, Ece the Star

Fully equipped with long range radios, AK47 Auto Rifles, CZ75 Machine Pistols, boots and camouflage jackets, the teams were in the air by 7.15pm. Military transport was being used by the Special Service Marines and SEALs. Apache helicopters flew each team to a U.S. Air Force base close to their target.

Frank and Ece had the longest trip to Santa Barbara in California, requiring a re-fuelling stop. Anneliese and Hana's destination was New Orleans, also requiring re-fuelling. Jerome and Donald were assigned to Delaware Bay, alongside William Webster, the CIA Director. The FBI and CIA agents were flown to their destinations together, in Chinook helicopters. Denton was to be secreted close to the New Orleans target, allowing sufficient radio range to both Santa Barbara and Delaware.

That night they all slept, but only a few hours, at their allotted Air Force Base. Support was provided, and they were all fed a rough and ready military breakfast and lunch. Most of the day was spent checking and cleaning their equipment, especially their weapons.

Mid-afternoon, the team leaders assembled their teams and took them into open spaces. They were now all going to follow a directive from Frank, to the team leaders. A short but intense exercise program, of star jumps, press-ups, rapid running on the spot, leg lifts and squats... all designed to awaken their muscles, after their cramped 18 hours. The next phase caused some laughter, especially among the girls. The leaders handed around tins of black grease to, as Frank put it, make them feel like real soldiers ready for combat duties.

As the afternoon wore on, for some of them, nerves started to jangle, feeling the pressure. Frank had warned the team leaders. In consequence, they put effort into talking to each and every one of their team. Putting them at their ease, with constant reassurance.

The 5.00pm "Operation Paralyse" time line was based on Jackson time. They had all synchronised their military Omega watches before leaving Jackson. This would avoid the small time difference between the three target locations. The only exception was Jerome, who had insisted on wearing his gas filled Breitling. He was coming to rely on it! However, its time was set, as with everybody, on Jackson time.

At 4.40pm they were transported in camouflaged personnel carriers, to points around the target vessels.... the target cruisers. Marines and SEALs were already stationed around using every piece of vegetation, rocks, boulders and trees, for concealment.

At precisely 5.00pm synchronised Jackson time, the radio crackled and the assault began.

The Marines and SEALs used the surprise tactic, with constant firing, shouting and screaming as they, en masse, boarded the moored motor cruisers. The CECD, CIA and FBI were not far behind. In the case of Delaware Bay, and New Orleans, both incursions were achieved in ten minutes. The terrorists were herded off the vessels, arms in the air, and then searched. Military prison trucks arrived minutes later. None of the terrorists put up any sort of fight. A lot of shouting and screaming at the soldiers had occurred, but these trained professionals ignored the abuse and pushed and shoved them in the trucks.

It was nowhere near as easy in California. Two minutes before the operation began, a terrorist rushed down the gangplank and released the mooring rope. As the Marines and SEALs charged towards the vessel, it powered into the tributary, heading for Rosa Island. Frank, immediately called up on the radio. "I need an Apache now!" Three minutes and it arrived, hovering 20 yards away from Frank, who ran beneath it waving his arms.

A winch line was dropped and Frank ran, jumped and clung to it. But so did Ece. She followed and jumped, clinging to Frank's knees and trousers!

They were only flying for two minutes, but Frank could feel Ece slipping down as the wind and downdraft put pressure on her fingers. He reached down and could feel her hand. He grabbed a handful of her hair as they hovered over the motor cruiser. The helicopter pilot descended until he was about 20 feet above the cruiser's rear deck.

Frank let go of Ece's hair and released his grip on the winch line. They fell together. Ece's gymnastic training was invaluable. She landed on her feet, bounced and tumbled. Helping Frank to his feet, Ece said "Are you ok, Frank?" He nodded, Ece set off, creeping along the starboard side of the boat, pointing to Frank to take the portside.

Both of them were aiming for the bridge, but before she got that far, a cabin door opened. Two ugly bastards charged at her. Just one blast on the machine pistol and they fell to their knees in front of her. Frank was now at the bridge, where two guys were piloting the cruiser.

With looks of surprise on their faces, both left the helm and flew at Frank. His Beretta revolver was in his hand by his side. Calm and steady he lifted the pistol and fired. The first man fell, with a bullet in this thigh. The second terrorist, with Frank's weapon aiming directly at the same place, threw his arms in the air shouting, "Don't shoot, don't shoot."

Frank, with Ece behind him, pushed this guy out onto the deck. The helicopter continued to hover above. Next, without warning a machine gun opened up, and a body fell from the upper deck. Another body was slumped over the upper deck side-rail. Two guys had come out of the upper deck cabin. The helicopter co-pilot had seen them and had finished the operation. The guy that had fallen from the upper deck, had recovered enough to aim his pistol at Frank. He had no chance! Ece fired from her hip; she finished the job!

Frank covered the two survivors, who were quickly taken into custody by the coastguard. The cruiser was towed back to the marina. Frank and Ece were air-lifted back to the Air Force Base. The co-pilot and Ece lifted Frank from the Apache. His left knee resembled a grotesque Halloween mask, with swollen blue lumps either side of his knee cap. The pilot called a medic who sprinted across the tarmac.

Chapter 49

Traitor and Subversives

It was almost 2am. Everyone was extremely tired, but with adrenalin now dribbling through their veins, fatigue had surrendered to a latent high. As they all congregated in the CIA HQ bar, emotions were running high. Embraces, praises, congratulations and loud conversations, growing in intensity.

The bar double doors creaked open. Everyone quietened to look! In the shadow of Ece's smile stood Frank; with Ece gripping his arm, they moved forward into the light; Frank's left side movement relied on a shiny silver crutch. It was as if they were watching Long John Silver in the movie, Treasure Island!

Applause, in the first instance soft applause, that grew into a crescendo. After a minute or so, Frank held up his right arm and the room quietened. "You are a fabulous team. It has been my privilege to work with you. But now you can help me recover from my busy day. Barman, I'm buying a round!"

With crutch tucked under his arm, Frank was helped onto a bar stool. The bar door opened once more. It was Denton. Ece turned, putting her hands on Frank's shoulders. "Are you ok?" she said. Frank nodded as he swallowed some beer.

Ece took off like a bat out of hell! She threw herself, heart and soul, at Denton, her soft white hands grasping the back of his neck. Her cheek pressed into his for a few seconds, then her lips mingled with his. The kiss was sensitive, borne out of intense concern and fear for her loved one! Her face slowly pulled away from his, as her eyes peered into his soul. Denton's gaze was misty, but Ece's was uncontrollable. Tears slowly began to drift down her cheeks. With a quiver in her voice, Ece spluttered "My Denton, I was so worried about you, are you ok?" "I'm fine, I was just as worried about you! But I was even more concerned that when I saw you next, you would brush me aside, because I had imagined the whole thing" Ece replied "Denton, absolutely no way, I want you forever!" Denton appeared stunned, as the room filled with a torrent of sighs.

Frank stood, with some support, from Anneliese. Picking up a spoon from a table, he loudly clinked his glass, saying "My colleagues, my friends, I just want to say a few words." Quiet surrounded them. "You were all heroes today and will be remembered forever. But I have to mention someone special. Our own little Ece saved my life today, twice! I can't in any way explain how courageous and accomplished she proved to be. We are very lucky to have this young lady working with us. So let's have a last drink to Ece!"

The morning began in a blistering way! Tiny Tim, had been in contact with Denton, whose first stop was Anneliese. "Tim has worked on Chuck's early background, and Arnold Bluesef's. Jerome and his analysts back in the U.K. have given him quite a bit of help. None if this is an absolute certainty, but the facts head us to conclusions that appear safe.

Before he could continue, the CIA Director, Mr Webster arrived. "I've just had President Hayden on the phone,. He wants us to assemble the team, to pass on his message to them."

"Denton, would you pass the word around to meet in the second floor conference room at 2.00pm."

The room was full of chatter. An expectant air filled the room as Mr Webster arrived. "I'm not going to take much of your time. I expect that, after the last couple of days you are winding down and enjoying yourselves. However, the President has asked me to give you a message and it is one I will really enjoy giving." "Word for word, he said he could not find a way to express how proud he is of you all. He is going on TV to report to the nation, and the world, that the terrorist activities have been completely terminated. It has been an honour and a privilege to work with you all. But the bottom line of his message is that he wants to express his, and the nations, gratitude face-to-face. You are all invited to the White House on Sunday. There will be a short Church Service to give thanks, followed by a reception. I would add that my sentiments are exactly the same, and I am looking forward to the pleasure of your company; every one of you, on Sunday!"

Next morning, Tiny Tim rang Denton to ask if he could come down to brief him on recent intelligence investigations.

"We have been deep diving into Bietronics finance. We found that they have a subsidiary, registered in Turkey. Funds have been hived off, transferred to Dubai and then to a bank account in Delaware. Denton, you can imagine how difficult it was finding these set-ups and tracking all the funds, transferred in varying currencies. The good news is that we have secured names and addresses for the people that have access to the Delaware bank account. We have a strong suspicion that these people lead the subversive groups in the U.S. If so, it means, Arnold Bluesef is funding the subversion in this country. Subversion that has caused so much unrest and violence. Probably, if we capture and intern the leaders, all the unrest and disruption will end. We already have Bluesef in custody and he is being interrogated as we speak. And now we have evidence of subversion, he may be persuaded to turn States Evidence."

"Moving on to the background of Arnold Bluesef and Chuck. Bluesef was born in Iran to an Iranian mother. Jerome's guys have put a lot of hours in with the French. His mother had been admitted to France with a child, having claimed asylum. We think she met the American in France. The French Intelligence Analysts followed the trail back into Iran. They don't have conclusive evidence, but the pieces of the jigsaw they have assembled indicate she was a princess in the Shah's dynasty. They believe she was one of several daughters of King Mohammad Reza Pahlavi, and that she was exiled and extradited following the toppling of the Iranian monarchy during the Iranian Revolution in 1978."

"Now I'll get to Chuck. He was born in London, England, and his birth registration document shows the name Charles Pavlova." Tim smiled at Denton; "sounds sort of similar to Pahlavi, eh Denton! The American was his father."

"Immigration in the U.S. turned up documents showing that he arrived here on a U.K. passport. He was accompanied by his father who travelled on an American passport. The real interesting bit is that he entered America, not just with his Dad, but also an older brother, indeed 13 years older. He had travelled on a French passport and the name registered with immigration was Abdul." Tiny Tim took a deep breath, then bursting with pride said... "Abdul Pavlova!"

At that point, Denton laughed saying, "Well, you've pulled a rabbit out of the hat, Tim! I think we both deserve a coffee, and it will give me time to collect my thoughts on all that information."

"Ok, Tim, let's carry on" said Denton. "Well, the father died in Maryland when Chuck was ten. The brother, Bluesef, brought him up until late teens, then he got a job with a security company, did well, moved on to the Sheriff's department in Dearborn, Detroit, and did very well. Then we appointed him into a junior intelligence position in the CIA. And guess what! He did very well, and was promoted to Agent."

Denton, smiling, then burping, as he leaned back in his chair. "Sorry, Tim, please excuse me! Coffee often does that to me. So Tim, what do we think became of the mother?" "Well, she just disappears off the radar in 1980. Frank gave us some anecdotal possibilities. He was serving in the S.A.S. and was part of the team involved in the Iranian Embassy siege in 1980. He recalls that an Iranian lady wearing a burqa was hit by a stray bullet and died. The Iranians wanted her transported to her homeland, but as she had been exiled, that had been refused. So she is probably interred in England somewhere."

Denton, had been smiling all the while. "Tim; that is exceptional work. Please tell all the teams involved, UK, French and, of course, your guys, that this seals off another corner in this leaking creek."

Denton continued. "Now Tim, I have assimilated all that information and we need to use it to get things moving. First, would you send a summary to the President's office? A one-page fax. Next, the guys interrogating Chuck need to be given all this; they can use it to make him aware that we know he has committed treason. And it's just the same for Arnold Bluesef. Let the guys that are working on him have the details."

"Last but not least, all the people on your list that have been orchestrating South versus North subversion. Have them all arrested and freeze the Delaware bank account. Indeed, tell the arresting officers to arrange for all the subversive's bank accounts and assets are to be seized."

Tim strode toward the door, turned, and with a wide grin said, "Denton, it will be a pleasure."

Chapter 50

Celebration, Sunday, Wedding to come!

That evening, after dinner, all the team were enjoying a relaxed life. Denton was sitting with Jerome, and Tim, tracking through the information that Tim had imparted that afternoon. Jerome had been involved with Tim, so had knowledge about the whole scenario. Quietly speaking to Jerome, Denton asked, "So what do you think Chuck's motives were for the disastrous events he became involved in? I loved the guy, he was superb at his job. Nothing phased him. He had no fear, and we all enjoyed working with him. So what set him on this destructive path?" Jerome, for a few seconds, thought about where he had come from, all the different characters he had experienced, his whole life scurried through his mind.

"Denton," he said, as his memories overwhelmed his emotions, "I believe most of what you do may come from your early life. And family ties have a massive effect. Maybe he was never able to step around the death of this mother. He was young when he lost his dad, so the greatest influence in his life may have become his brother. And of course, his early years were spent in splendour with a Royal family in Iran."

Tim interjected "One of my Analysts came up with an explanation. There was a theory going around at that time that America gave support to the revolution. I think that is absolute rubbish, but due to the negative atmosphere with Iran, at the time, a belief, within the Royal family may have developed. If Chuck and his brother had been indoctrinated with that thinking, possibly they were fixated with the need for revenge. If we let our minds gain control, they can take us into extremely dark tunnels. And that would have been exacerbated by the death of their mother. Killed on U.K. soil. Just working to put food in their mouths."

Denton, with a sad, understanding expression, uttered "Tim that's a plausible explanation. It's a great shame that Chuck and his brother have wasted their exceptional talents seeking revenge, in the vain hope it would alleviate their pain!"

"Anyway, let's get on with our work in order to finish this atrocious business." Tim got up and strode toward the door. Denton with a wide smile said, "Tim, I'm very grateful. That was a great piece of work. Please pass that on to your Intelligence Analysts."

It was a beautifully sunny, warm Sunday morning. At 8.00am a gleaming black Chrysler mini-bus arrived at the Staybridge Suites; the next stop being the Jackson CIA HQ to pick up Denton and Tiny Tim. Mr Webster had stayed in Washington overnight, as he had meetings there the previous day.

A Chinook flew them from the CIA heliport to the White House, landing on the Eclipse lawn. They were met by four Marines who explained that the church service would take place near the White House, in the open air. The Reverend of St John's Church, just across Lafayette Square, would be holding the service.

The Marines guided everyone to the place where the service would take place; on a section of the Eclipse lawn adjacent to the White House. They were offered coffees, just before the President marched out to join them. After a welcome from the President, his First Lady, and the Reverend, the service began.

Everyone joined in the short service, even though some were not of the Protestant religion. The Reverend, recognised this and thanked everybody, saying it was wonderful that people of all races and creeds could join together in worship! There was a single hymn enhanced by the singing of a small choir.

This hymn had been selected by President Hayden. After the ceremony, he told them he had selected it because it paid tribute to them. The hymn was "Pilgrims Progress". The key words that meant so much were "He who would valiant be 'gainst all disaster, let him in constancy follow the master!"

The service and, in particular the hymn, lifted their spirits. At the end of the service they assembled in the Blue Room. It was a magnificent room. Not too roomy; just right for their number, with splendid décor and a delicious buffet set on a table against the wall. A drinks trolley, manned by a male server in a splendid scarlet, braided jacket, was in a corner.

The President circulated, attempting to put everyone at their ease. Mr Webster had been in conversation with Hana and Donald. Suddenly an enormous smile captured his whole face. There seemed absolutely no way he could contain it, as it spread from ear to ear.

Trying to remain composed and aloof, but without any chance of success, William Webster attempted an uncontrollable saunter across the room to the President. He whispered, "Mr President...." "Fantastic news William, thank you!"

President Hayden seemed to have caught the affliction affecting William Webster. He took just a few awkward steps into the centre of the Blue Room, and said "Ladies and gentlemen, if I could have your attention for a few minutes." Plates of food were placed down in every available space and everybody, showing respect, fell silent.

The President's face told a story. He was excited. He, being the ultimate professional when it came to public speaking, looked around, inhaled, and then eased across to Anneliese. "Please, Anneliese, come and help me with this." He took her hand and they both edged back to the middle of the room. Anneliese had a quizzical expression, but waited for any sign that may provide the answer.

President Hayden spoke! "You had my message yesterday. I meant everything, from the bottom of my heart. All I want to add is that I am humbled by your work, your strength, your character! You alone have saved us. But with what I have just been told, I am reminded that you are human. You are not machines, like tanks or robots. You put your lives on the line for your beliefs. And I could not be more honest when I say I will take that with me to the grave. You are wondering, what the hell I am talking about. Well, it's this. Love is manna from heaven. It surpasses anything we humans try to do, or think important. Love conquers all! And what I have just been told is a wonderful ending to this excruciating difficult time for all of us."

With that, still holding Anneliese's hand, he stepped forward towards Hana and Donald. The President, with a quiver in his voice, exclaimed "Hana and Donald will be married in three weeks' time. The wedding will be at Camp

David. And I know you are as ecstatic as I am. You will all receive personal invitations. You will be invited to arrive the day before the Saturday wedding. You will have the run of the place, so please come and help me and Mrs Hayden get this organised. We, together, will make it a wedding that they, and you. will remember forever."

Anneliese, with a sparkling smile embraced Hana, kissing both her cheeks as she held her tight. President Hayden grasped Donald's hand and stretched to hug him round the shoulders. Typically, they formed a man, woman, man, woman, line for a photo shoot. The White House photographer, with his Nikon camera held at his shoulder, then gestured to the whole team to assemble round the betrothed for a group photograph!

Chapter 51

Toronto, then Urgent Return

The American judicial system trudged on throughout the following two weeks. Denton spearheaded the work required by the Government prosecutor. Witness statements, detailed CIA evidence, financial and banking information. None of the agents details would be provided, due to them being covered by national security. By the middle of week two, Anneliese, Frank and Jerome had completed their input. Anneliese and Frank flew off to Toronto, Canada, intent on seeing their loved ones. Jerome decided to remain in Jackson. To support Denton with all the report writing. Ece stayed by Denton's side! The bride and groom-to-be, flew to New York for a semi-relaxing few days. The semi-part involved selecting their outfits for the wedding. A glorious shopping expedition!

It was now Wednesday of the third week. Indeed, it was Wednesday morning when Jerome phoned Anneliese. They went through the motions of polite chat, with Frank Junior shouting in the background. Baby talk, but although only approaching four years old, cutely understandable. "Hoo is it mummy, can I speak to him?" Anneliese told Jerome she was now in heaven, spending time with Matthew and Frank Junior. However, as they spoke, Anneliese sensed from Jerome's tone, that something was wrong. "What is it

Jerome? I can tell from your voice that you are worried about something!"

20 seconds of silence followed, then a deep breath; Jerome stuttered at the outset. "You are the only person I can talk to." Another 10 quiet seconds followed. "My sound sleep last night was interrupted. But this time it was"…. another deep breath as he faltered. "Anneliese, it was Barry!". He stopped again. Anneliese's mind reversed to the painful events that had taken Barry from her. Jerome sensed the intensity of her grief. "Anneliese, would you be able to get back here tomorrow. I know we need to get to Camp David on Friday, but I need to explain all to you, and I can't do it over the phone." Anneliese, by now, had collected herself. "Yes," she replied, "That was our plan anyway. I'm bringing Matthew and Frank Jr. with me. I can't bear to leave them here again. I will meet you in Jackson HQ around midday. Is that OK?"

Jerome breathed a sigh of relief. "Oh, thank you Anneliese, I can't deal with this without you. I love you, thank you so much."

Anneliese, with a slowly developing pensive look, placed the phone down. She, with thoughts piling into her mind, settled in the quiet of the family room. After staring into space for several seconds, she arose and with a quickening pace, went into the lounge. Matthew and Frank Jr. were on the carpeted floor playing skittles. She sat on an armchair close to them. With a concerned tone, Anneliese said "Matthew, I need your attention for a couple of minutes," Matthew, with a questioning expression asked, "Darling, what is it?" "Jerome just called. There's no easy way to say this, but he has an urgent issue and needs my help. I need to get down to Jackson this evening." Matthew grimaced, but then realised this must be important. "Ok dear, get moving and I will call you a cab to get you to the airport. I'm fine with Frank Junior." Anneliese, squinting her eyes as she thought, asked, "Can you call Frank. But after I've gone; and say I will call him later."

Anneliese left the lounge and at the bottom of the long curving maple staircase, picked up the phone and rang Jerome. "I will be with you early evening. I'd rather sort this today; better than the night before arrival at Camp David." Jerome sighed with relief and said he would meet her at the airport.

Chapter 52

Supernatural Assassination?

It was just over an hour from Washington Dulles airport to the CIA HQ. Anneliese, during the drive, asked Jerome to explain, but he asked if it would wait until they were back in HQ. He couldn't drive and talk about this without losing concentration.

They arrived at the Jackson HQ at about 5.30pm and went straight to the coffee bar settee. As they tackled a welcome coffee, Jerome, with a worryingly serious expression whispered, "I don't want to talk here, Anneliese. Can we take one of the small conference rooms?"

Sitting in the quiet of the first floor conference room, opposite Anneliese, Jerome sniffed and wiped his nose with a pure white handkerchief. "It was just like the visit from Anya." Jerome sniffed again, then continued. "Something seemed to push my feet. As I stirred and turned, there he was, Barry, sitting on the bottom corner of the bed. I couldn't believe my eyes. He looked and spoke the same." Anneliese sat fighting her emotions, as did Jerome!

"Barry's diction was clear, concise and succinct. He started by saying he now lived in the Beta World, the celestial world! We live in the Alpha world. Both worlds are saturated with both good and evil! Russian scientists had, originally developed Havana Syndrome. It was a primitive weak nerve gas. Iranian scientists thought they would develop a stronger more potent nerve gas that could be implanted, whenever they wanted, into modern electronic technology! Whenever they wanted to do damage around the world!"

"They tampered with the gas, thinking they were only increasing its potency." "However, being adventurous with the chemical compound, they had included a new hydrocyanic poison. Only a minute infusion! But, for some reason this overheated and intercalated the properties, which were a stimulus we now call cyberotics. These had the effect of entwining the minds, thoughts and sounds of beings in both Alpha and Beta Worlds. The basic ingredient that works for good, is unconditional, deep, soul drenching love!"

"The over-riding catalyst for such a loving person is having been in the vicinity of H.S. gas. The completely opposite equation is true for a human being that is not necessarily evil, but can be transformed into evil."

"Barry then went on to explain why he and Anya had come to me. Apparently the purest love, between people, would blend their souls. Then a Beta soul would be able to penetrate an Alpha Body and Soul." That had been initiated for Anya and Albie. But, in my case, there was gentle brotherly love from several people, Anya, Albie and you Anneliese. Therefore, I was selected as a conduit for messages from the Beta world. The catalyst was H.S. gas that I had ingested in my office work. But only minor amounts."

Jerome stopped for a moment, staring at Anneliese's expression. "Are you ok with this?" "Oh yes, Jerome, I am now a passionate believer that just wants to hear more."

A smile of relief adorned Jerome's handsome face. "Well, Anneliese, you will love this part; but now I've said that, I suppose it may be emotionally difficult. Barry said to tell you that he had considered joining Matthew as your soul mate. But he didn't want to disturb your happiness with Matthew and little Frank Junior. You deserve every minute of the ecstasy you are experiencing. Moreover, he said, he could now be your "Watcher". Which means he is responsible for watching over you and your family, to fight evil and ward off any demons." He said, "That is my destiny, and I wouldn't want it any other way."

Jerome could see tears breaking into Anneliese's eyes. "Anneliese, the next part was the main reason he came to me. He told me, the "watchers" can see into the future. On the day of the wedding, there will be an attempt to assassinate President Hayden! He did not know who, or when it would be, but it would be someone that had been in contact with H.S. gas. And had been overwhelmed by the evil Beta energy forces!" Anneliese's expression became intimidated by concern! With a seriously worried tone she exclaimed, "Jerome that has just tipped me over the edge. I will have Matthew and Frank Junior with me, which is frightening me to death." Jerome replied, "that was exactly Barry's concern. He said we had to convince Frank, and work with him to ensure impregnable protection for the President and everyone attending."

"Barry had a further suggestion. He said there would be a crèche available for young children. Persuade Matthew to stay with him. Either tell him the truth or find a way to explain why. An alternative was for you to lie to Matthew and get him to arrive very late for the ceremony. The third alternative was for you to find a way to cancel their attendance."

Anneliese didn't seem enamoured by any of these options, "I never lie to Matthew," said Anneliese, "I should talk to Frank. Can you come with me? I'm not going to attempt all the mystical stuff. I just need to hear his thoughts and see if he can convince me we can find a fool proof answer to prevent any serious conflict during the wedding!"

Ten minutes later, they had Frank on a conference call. Anneliese, with an urgency in her voice, asked, "Frank, can you get here late tonight or early morning. I'm sorry, but I know you and Lucia were looking forward to the wedding, but a security issue has arisen. I will give you a few details, so you can think about a plan. I have received intelligence that there will be an assassination attempt on the President's life sometime during the wedding ceremony and reception." Frank coughed and interrupted. "I've not seen or heard anything, Anneliese. Where has this come from?" "Please Frank, just believe me. You trust me, and you know I wouldn't make this up. I'm confident it's a real threat."

Chapter 53

The Wedding. Now, Ece in Love

The phone line seemed to go dead, but Anneliese knew Frank was giving the issue serious thought. Frank, with quiet, slow diction said, "I will get down to you tonight. Lucia will understand we have an urgent issue. We were going to travel down with Matthew and Frank Junior, but she will handle all that, and she's just at the end of the phone. So will you be able to meet about 1.00am or tomorrow morning?" "No Frank, it's very urgent, so 1.00am is fine. Come straight to the first floor conference room in Jackson HQ and we will take you through it!"

Frank strode in at 12.55am. Both Anneliese and Jerome felt the tension ease as they embraced him. Frank stepped back, noticing the emotion in their eyes. Jerome usually comical, but now uncharacteristically quiet, staring at Frank, could not speak! As they hugged again, Anneliese uttered, "Let's sit down and have a coffee as we compose ourselves." Anneliese floated across to the bubbling coffee, as Frank leant across to Jerome, saying, "Fella, whatever it is we will solve it." Jerome sniffed as he pulled out his top pocket handkerchief and smothered his eyes and nose. His smile returned as Anneliese placed coffees in front of them.

Anneliese never ever lost her poise, and hardly ever her composure. She began to explain. She had confirmed intelligence concerning a possible assassination attempt.

She explained her concerns for Matthew and Frank Junior. She was concerned for all attendees. Close to 40! Frank listened intently and never asked a single question. He trusted Anneliese and Jerome implicitly!

Anneliese, further continued to explain her options regarding Matthew and Frank Junior. Indeed, the options that Barry had suggested!

After some discussion, Anneliese, Frank and Jerome agreed on a plan. The wedding service was due to commence at 3pm, in the open air, close to the outdoor cooking and picnic table area. After the ceremony, at about 4pm, everybody would move into the Camp David main lodge for the reception.

The President and his wife, Eleanor, would be flying in on Marine One, his own personal helicopter which would be heavily protected and staffed by Marines. They would be arriving at 2.40pm. The flight would take them North-West of Washington, through the mountainous terrain near Thurmont.

The reception dinner, speeches and songs from three celebrity entertainers, would take through to around 6pm. Anneliese would tell Matthew, that he, Lucia and Frank Junior should arrive just after 6pm. The proceedings before then would not be suitable for a young child. She would alert Matthew to the possibility of trouble, and to tell Lucia that Frank agreed the 6pm arrival. He had arranged escorted travel from the airport; a drive of about 1hour 30 minutes. Later Anneliese phoned Matthew. He took it on the chin, knowing Anneliese would not have arranged it like this unless there was no alternative. As Matthew prepared for the trip, he strapped on his shoulder holster with Beretta revolver, which he kissed as he placed it securely in the leather.

The President and his lady arrived at 2.40pm, and were escorted to the wedding venue, surrounded by six marines, and several CIA Agents, forming a wide loop around the entourage.

Frank had already spoken with the Marine Commander and agreed that additional troops should surround the venue all evening. With any signs of unrest they should prevent anybody leaving. This would all be activated in complete secrecy and the Marine Commander was the only person allowed to be privy to this operation!

It was a gloriously sunny, warm afternoon. The President and his lady clasped hands as they strolled down the aisle past the family and guests. The wedding of Hana and Donald, proceeded under a metal archway festooned with red and pink roses.

It was the perfect wedding. As they were pronounced "man and wife" Donald overcame his nerves and his trembling hands became still, he slowly lifted them to Hana's face and his lips hovered over hers for two seconds. A gentle kiss sealed their love!

The President and his lady, Eleanor, were the first to stand and applaud. Everyone followed, and a few cheers exploded from the guests. The married couple thanked the Reverend, shook hands and turned. The walk through the aisle was followed by Mr President and the first lady; the rest of the audience ambled behind.

As the loving couple exited the aisle, between the audience chairs, they passed under an archway of Marines and ceremonial swords forming the "tunnel of love." The President, Eleanor and guests chuckled loudly as they also feathered their way through the arch!

They were all led to a reception room. It was unbelievable, amazing, and had been decorated with white silk sheets across the ceiling and tasteful silver banners with the couples' names, alongside white balloons, all around the walls. Beautiful flower arrangements, and name cards on every table.

This element of the wedding day would only involve speeches followed by the main dinner course and small summer salad. It, and the rest of the evening, had been planned and organised by the President's First lady, Eleanor. After the main course, everybody would move back outside into the sunshine and be seated at the picnic tables. These were close to the bar and a stunning open kitchen and barbeque with a rear wall covered in irregular shaped grey slates. The front of the kitchen was designed as a log cabin with an open front serving area and drop leaf tables for food display.

Dinner in the Reception room was preceded by the speeches. Denton was best man and was accompanied at the top table by Ece. Neither Donald nor Hana's parents were available, but Anneliese had been asked by Hana to stand in. Anneliese was joined by Jerome, again, a request from Hana. Theirs was a joint speech. Anneliese made a poignant start, describing how Donald had quickly and efficiently unlocked Hana's heart and how, on the day this lovely couple met, the tumblers had fallen into place at first sight! Jerome, with a comical characteristic effeminate performance, launched into how honoured he was to be asked to stand in as Hana's father. He rambled into the story about the fact that he had been originally named Richard but didn't like the name! Then he told how, as a teenager he would arrive home after staying out all night in nightclubs. His mum would be in the kitchen making his Dad's breakfast, and as Jerome crawled in, she would also shout "Well yer 'ome then," He continued, "My Mum was always supportive as Hana will be…. when Donald and Hana eventually have kids." He giggled as he continued, "That expression my Mum continually used, saved me from that name Richard! "Yer 'ome, stuck in my head and became…. Jerome!"

The audience were quiet for a few seconds, then belly laughs began to echo all around.

Next, it was the turn of the Best Man, Denton. He began by telling how impressed he was with Donald's abilities and although having had difficult early years, had aspired to greater things, working for his country. The speech finished on a high note. A surprisingly high note!

Denton turned to face Ece, taking a gentle hold on her hand as he did so. "I wish to announce, indeed I am so proud to announce, that I have decided to follow in Donald's footsteps." The hush in the room was only broken by the sound of people taking deep breaths.

Denton continued, I have asked Ece to be my wife and she has accepted." Ece stood, placed a hand on his cheek, and softly kissed him.

The President was the first to stand and applaud. The place erupted into applause and cheers.

The dinner menu included a sumptuous choice of grilled steak, chicken or red snapper. After dinner the First Lady invited everyone to follow her out to the picnic tables.

At the rear of the picnic area was a stage decorated with white silk sheets, adorned with red roses. The guests wandered around adoring the ambience and then gradually seated themselves at the picnic tables. A large central table was reserved for the bride and groom, the President and First Lady, Anneliese, Mr William Webster, Denton and Ece.

Frank and Jerome wandered around, chatting to people, whilst surreptitiously maintaining surveillance.

Next came the first surprise of the evening. A band set up on the stage and a very special artist stepped up to the mike and began to sing. Everyone immediately recognised this lady…. It was the fabulous Shania Twain. Cheers and loud applause lingered throughout the last stanza of the song!

The open kitchen servers began to prepare the desserts. The dropdown exhibit tables were filled with a sensational selection. Banana Pudding, Pecan Pie, Sugar Dusted Churros, Crème Brulee, Chocolate Mousse and a grand chocolate cake. The speciality, being the national dessert, was a massive apple pie.

Guests were requested to make their selections, and the servers would deliver to their numbered tables. Anneliese asked the President and Eleanor if she could get them something. The reply was that they would prefer to wait a while. They had requested a Key Lime Pie for the President and Blueberries and Ice Cream for the First Lady. Apparently these would be brought out when the President made his request!

Chapter 54

Frank Junior, Adored by All

Anneliese's eyes were constantly searching around for Matthew, Frank Jr. and Lucia. Then at about 6.15pm she picked them out, crossing the lawn from the Main Lodge. She, with exhilarating excitement written all over her face said, "Please Mr President, excuse me. My husband and son have arrived." "Of course, my dear, "was the reply.

Anneliese rushed 50 yards across the lawn, picked Frank Jr up and hugged him as she kissed Matthew. Frank, always watching, arrived as they reached the President's table. Frank embraced Lucia as he whispered in her ear. "I will have to get back to work in a few minutes!" Lucia squeezed his hand and nodded.

Introductions were slow, courteous and generous. The last of the introductions was to the President and First Lady. Anneliese led Frank Jr by the hand, followed by Matthew, to the President. Frank Junior was nearly four and walking. The President, in a grandfatherly way, looked down into Frank Jr's eyes. "Hello, young man, you are a very handsome little guy!"

Little Frank Jr peered into the President's eyes and responded, "So are you Sir, I've seen you on the television."

Taking a deep breath, he looked up at Anneliese, then back at the President. As he released his grip on his mother's hand, he exclaimed in a louder voice, "And I love your place here, and your lovely girlfriend," as he turned to smile at Eleanor.

President Hayden chuckled. "Frank Jr, you couldn't have made us any happier. Please come and sit with us, "as he picked him up and sat Frank Jr between him and Eleanor. Clasping Frank Jr close to him, the President, in a soft voice, uttered "This is my wife, Eleanor. She was my girlfriend but we married a while ago." Frank Jr smiled at Eleanor then replied, "I understand; my Mum and Dad are married." Looking around, Frank Jr thought for a moment, then with sincerity, tenderly said, "My Dad thinks my Mum is a beautiful person, and I agree with him."

The President was lost for words. He issued a knowing smile to Anneliese and Matthew, then clutched Frank Jr to his chest. "Young man," said the President, "would you like some food? We have some wonderful desserts." "No thank you sir, we ate on the plane, but maybe later." "So is there anything you would like to do?" asked President Hayden.

"Yes, Sir," replied Frank Junior, "I would like to look around your home." The President ducked the inaccuracy. Turning to Matthew, the President asked, "Would you be happy driving Frank Junior around? Don't get lost because it's a large estate; about 180 acres, but you can see a few of the things you might wish to try tomorrow. There is a variety of leisure activities. Archery, badminton, and my favourite; the horsehoe pits. Also tennis, a cinema and a fabulous swimming pool!"

"I will get you a golf buggy and you can have a leisurely drive around." The President stood, took two or three steps, and a Marine appeared. The President explained, and in a couple of minutes a golf buggy arrived. Matthew departed with Frank Jr; giving the President the widest young smile he had seen in years.

Chapter 55

President Attacked, Ece Rescues

President Hayden, Anneliese and the First Lady all waved until the buggy was out of sight. The President turned to Anneliese saying, "He is a real little treasure! A real credit to both of you! And very advanced for his age!"

Putting his arm around Eleanor, with a gleeful expression, the President said, "My dear, is it time for you to try some of that Italian ice cream with your favourite blueberries?" "Oh yes, darling "Eleanor replied, "That beautiful boy has brought on my childish appetite." "Me too," said the President. "I'll have my Key Lime Pie, but Eleanor, we must save some ice cream and some of my pie for Frank Jr."

As Anneliese flexed her lips to speak, William Webster rose to his feet saying, "I will just go to the cookhouse and get it for you." Anneliese with great pride and pleasure shining in her eyes, now managed to speak. Tenderly clasping the President's hand, with a soft winsome tone, she uttered, "Thank you from the bottom of my heart for making us all so welcome today."

Anneliese swivelled to face Eleanor. "I am so grateful Mrs Hayden. You are a wonderful couple that will be in our thoughts forever." As Anneliese lent forward and kissed

Eleanor on both cheeks, Mr Webster arrived with the desserts.

William Webster placed plates in front of President Hayden and Eleanor. Standing a couple of feet behind the President, his stare became anxious. The President could not resist his favourite dessert, and with his fork and spoon, began to lift a large piece to his lips.

Shouting, then screaming, seemed to stop the world. As everyone, in just a second, played statues. Anneliese saw Frank sprinting across the lawn; screaming "don't eat that" The President had the spoon to his lips. Anneliese's reactions were acute. She smashed the plate out of the President's hands. The pie smothered Eleanor and as the edge of the plate hit the President in the mouth, his lip burst into a blood spout!

William Webster wasted no time. From behind, he grabbed the President's throat, and thrust a bright, shiny knife blade to the edge of his jugular vein.

Frank arrived, as everyone around either moved back or fell back. Frank began to try to talk Webster down. "William, don't do anything stupid. You have not done anything serious, but if you go any further it will raise the stakes!"

Anneliese, took over speaking. "William, you have been a fabulous CIA Director and if you stop this now, we can help you. I don't know what has caused this but, and I swear, I will speak for you and get you every possible help."

William Webster was beginning to weaken. His hand, holding the knife, was trembling like a palm tree in a force five hurricane. After two or three seconds of Webster staring around at people, like he thought they were from a different planet, Matthew and Frank Junior arrived back from their jaunt around the estate! Matthew, to please Frank Jr had been driving quite fast, and when only a few feet away from the small group of rubberneckers, hit the brakes and skidded four or five feet across the lawn, distracting all!

That was the signal Ece needed. Her Rosa Klebb, razor sharp shoes were back in action. Two jumping strides and she kicked the back of Webster's knee, just above the joint. He dropped, first to his knees, then fell face down on the lawn. Jerome appeared; standing over Webster, he reached into his inside pocket. Webster, now with a vicious demented stare, began attempting to roll onto his back, as his right leg kicked out at Jerome. The Mont Blanc pen was already hovering; only about two feet away from Webster's abdomen.

Jerome pressed the clip. The nerve agent dart sunk deep into Webster's stomach. In a second his brain shut down completely. His eyes rolled into the top of their sockets, and as every muscle seized, he dropped the knife!

Frank retrieved the razor sharp knife, then peered around at all the traumatised faces. The men he wanted were sprinting across the lawns. One of these Marines knelt beside Webster, pulled his lifeless arms together, and with two clicks, secured handcuffs.

Frank turned to the second Marine. "Go get a stretcher and get him out of here!"

Anneliese, Denton and Ece were now leading the President and First Lady across the lawn to the Main Lodge. The President was heard to say to Denton, "Please do everything to reassure our guests, and get them back into party mode!"

The President and Eleanor sat at a large coffee table in a pair of red leather armchairs. Brandy's were ordered, to quell the shock. After a few minutes and several deep breaths, the President asked, "So what do you think that was all about Anneliese?" As she drew breath to answer, the Marine Commander stepped into the picture.

Standing to attention in front of the President, he saluted, then with a concerned expression asked, "Are you ok, Mr President, Sir?" President Hayden, with a wry smile, replied, "I am fine thanks to you all! I was just about to ask Anneliese what that was all about. James, what do you think?" The Commander, with a polite soft tone looked toward Eleanor, then back to President Hayden. "Sir, all I know is that the CECD agent, Frank, had asked us to keep a sharp eye on you, your drinks, your food and anyone that went near. One of my most astute Marines was working as a server with the desserts in the cookhouse. Out of the corner of his eye he saw Mr Webster collecting your dessert. But then was sure he saw him pour a small phial of liquid into your pie. He told me, his heart was pounding as he was radioing Frank, because he knew Mr Webster was a Government VIP. He radioed Frank, and reported what he'd seen. He tried to say he'd got reservations. But Frank wasn't interested in the soft soap, and cut him off. That's as much as we know. But we have followed up and scraped together every piece of that Key Lime Pie and its now on its way to our laboratories in Washington!"

Eleanor laughed, as she spoke directly to the Commander. "Thank you, James, for your work today, and especially your young Marine. Tell him how grateful we are. He may have saved my husband's life with his vigilance! But one other thing." She giggled as she drew breath. "It's a shame, but you didn't get every piece of that pie!" She glanced down! "My favourite dress is still covered in it."

Everyone began to chuckle. Indeed, the Commander belly laughed. Then, as he saluted, he joked," Mam, I am sure that none of my Marines are competent with a lady's dress."

As the Commander retired, the next to arrive was Hana and Donald. Having paid their respects, they said how pleased they were that everyone was largely unharmed. They were closely followed by Ece and Denton. Moments behind, Lucia and last, but by no means least, Frank. Hana and Donald waved and exited, back to the dancing.

Chapter 56

Junior Stays with the President

The doors behind Frank closed slowly. The noise from the band playing on stage was deafening, confirming that the guests were back enjoying themselves. As the doors slowly eased together, Frank stood at the edge of the assembled company.

Looking around at the CECD agents and Denton, the President fingered his lips. "I'm sorry if my speech is distorted, but I need us all to get back to business! Denton, I have to get some leadership back into the CIA. Would you consider taking on the role, on a temporary basis, until I have had time to get the position organised?"

Denton, with a surprised expression, replied immediately, "Of course, Mr President, it would be an honour." "You are, therefore, appointed Acting CIA Director." President Hayden winked, and shook Denton's hand.

"Frank and Anneliese, I am begging you to stay on a few days more. Would you and the rest of the team spend time getting to the bottom of today's enigma?" Both Frank and Anneliese nodded and replied "A pleasure, Mr President."

President Hayden reached across, and grasped the First Lady's hand. "We both...."he looked at Eleanor...."We both thank you for your vigilance and bravery today. Ece, our little

Miss Twinkle Toes; you deserve a massive vote of thanks. I'm sorry Ece, but I have a question. Why did you wear those heavy weapon shoes today?" Ece, with a haunting smile, leaned forward, looking at her shoes. "Well, Mr President, it was nothing mysterious or mystical. I just had the thought that if it rained, your lawns may not be the best place for high heels!"

"Ece, I can't tell you how grateful we are that you were practical." President Hayden, continued. "Jerome! I cannot leave you out. Your achievement with that pen of yours rivalled the work of Tolstoy's "War and Peace", but with much greater speed!" Frank leaned across to pat Jerome on the back.

"One last thing, would you, Anneliese, explain to Hana and Donald that I would love them to stay with you and your team for the next few days. Right now, they have returned to their guests and are dancing and enjoying themselves. But we do really need them to help. After you have spoken to them, please ask them to come in and see Eleanor and me."

Anneliese graciously asked if they could all be excused. "You probably need to rest and relax for a few minutes." They all turned toward the entrance doors, which suddenly crashed open. A tiny face slowly appeared below the door handle. It was Frank Junior. "I'm sorry I clattered the door," as he wobbled in. Seeing Anneliese, he rushed to her. She clasped him between her knees, and gently lifted him into her arms.

Frank Junior, under the circumstances, didn't figure the importance of etiquette. He shouted, "Is Mr President ok? I want to see him! Dad wouldn't bring me in. He said the President needed time alone!" Frank Junior peered over Anneliese's shoulder. Matthew, with concern written all over his face, joined them. President Hayden shouted back. "Frank

Junior, come over and sit with us." Anneliese, Matthew and Frank Jr, walked across the oak floor to the President. Frank Jr. peered into Anneliese's face. "Can I stay with Mr President and his wife, please?" President Hayden was overjoyed.

Chapter 57

Anneliese Returns to Jackson

As the evening wore on, the bride, groom and guests continued to dance to the music artists, including several celebrities. The earlier disturbance became a distant memory. Frank Junior enamoured himself to the President and Eleanor. His childish conversation and humour saturated their hearts and minds. He made them feel young again!

All too soon, bedtime appeared. All guests had been allocated their own lodge. The Camp David grounds were peppered with luxurious country lodges. As time crept by, the wedding celebrations retreated and sleep beckoned. Marines, driving people to their lodges in golf buggies, headlights blazing, resembled the twinkling night sky.

Most guests assembled in the Main Lodge for breakfast. Anneliese, Matthew and Frank Junior, feasted on the sumptuous breakfast offerings. Frank and the rest of the CECD team, all seeming to be without hangovers, convened in close proximity. Next came the bride and groom, followed closely by Present Hayden and the First Lady.

Anneliese was in the middle of explaining to Frank Junior that she had some work to do for the President. Matthew said he would stay for most of the day to show Frank Junior archery and the swimming pool. Mr President had arranged to meet them for a game of horseshoes!

The breakfast was a relaxed affair. As the CECD team prepared to leave, President Hayden approached Anneliese.

He stood with Anneliese and gently held her hands. "Anneliese, dear, I know that leaving again must be hurting you, but we will make sure he has the best of times. The President moved to Frank Jr and Matthew. We will have the best fun today, and I will get you home this evening, and your Mum will only be helping me for one or two days.... I promise."

Frank Jr peered up into the President's eyes, with an innocent gaze. "Uncle Bruce, I'm sure we will have a good time today." Frank Jr took a breath and bent over to scratch his leg. "I've got a mosquito bite!" Then turning back to the President he said, "But please Uncle Bruce, tell us if you are getting tired. My mum always says I tire her out!"

Racked with emotion, Anneliese just about kept it all together. Kissing Frank Jr and Matthew, she said, "We have to go now, but I'll see you in a few days. And to give you something to look forward to, Daddy and I will take you on a visit to Toronto and we will go up the CN Tower and you can stand, with us, on the glass floor. Then we will go the next day to Niagara Falls and we will take a ride, under the Falls on the big boat, the Maid of the Mist."

Anneliese crouched again, and gave Frank Jr another cuddle. She straightened, turned and kissed Matthew. Then, with poise and dignity holding her together, with a wide confident stride, approached Frank at the door.

The President and Eleanor surrounded Frank Jr. "What would you like to do first, Frank?" Junior began hopping on the spot." First I would like to try horseshoes with you, Uncle

Bruce. Mrs Hayden could keep score, if she doesn't mind. Last I would like to go swimming. I'm learning to swim. With Dad helping, I think I will get it this time! And second, I'd like to have a go at archery." Frank Jr peered up at the President. "Don't know Sir, if I can do it, but I've seen films about Robin Hood and I'd like to become as good as him!" This would be a fantastic day of exploration for this little fella, and heart-warming enjoyment for the President and First Lady!

Chapter 58

To Establish Why Webster Attacked

It was a beautiful, warm, full moon night, as the team convened in the second floor conference room. Initially, coffee, strong hot coffee, was the elixir they all needed to combat their fatigue.

Anneliese was first to motivate herself into action. She stood, stretched and proudly scorched toward her favourite ally, the pure white, blank, flip chart. Standing, facing it, her tall, thin, but curvaceous figure brought it to life. The felt tip pen seemed to come alive, dragging her wrist slowly across the page. She wrote one simple word in capital letters. WILLIAM!

She turned away to face her team, but then as if by felt-tip magic, Anneliese, seemingly overcome by energy in the pen, swivelled and underlined the name....twice! Breathing deeply, she stood away, as if to admire her carefully chosen script.

By now, everyone was engrossed by this slow, meticulous performance. But this was not the end. She stepped back to the flip chart. Her arm slowly lifted as though it was being winched onto the page. Underneath William, she wrote, in a very slow and careful manner, another name. A name that did not mean anything to most in the room. Except one.... Jerome. She wrote the name ANYA.

Anneliese stood away, then turned to face her friends. Several seconds passed, then she seemed to come back in the room! With authority she said "So what do you think caused the atrocious behaviour of our director, Mr William Webster?" The faces around the room turned to one another with blank looks.

Anneliese thought this was time to explain her thinking. "I will ask you all to listen and be receptive to the idea that there are things that we humans do not fully understand yet."

"First you need to accept that we are all susceptible to good and evil forces. But before I go on, I want to tell you a story. There was a CECD agent that worked with me and was my best friend for years. She was fantastic at her job! I still consider her like my sister. However, in the midst of an operation, she tried to kill me. She was in the grips of an evil force that had violated her mind."

"Anya is no longer physically with us. But I know she is still with us as a force for good. I think William Webster was attacked by those same evil forces. He is a good man. He has done a myriad of good things in our world. There is absolutely no way he was involved with the terrorists. So the question is, what disturbed his mind to such an extent that he would try to take the life of President Hayden."

Everyone in the room seemed to be mentally absent. Donald, looking first at Hana, then around the room, was courageous enough to volunteer. "Anneliese, my knowledge of Mr Webster is miniscule. But he seemed a very sincere, likeable guy. My bottom line is this! The change in his character and personality was extreme. Just like the story you told about your friend, Anya. But changes so extreme can be brought on by many things. In my experience the big one is drugs. But I don't think there is any chance he was on drugs. I'm not sure where I'm going with this, so I'm going to call a halt. Before I do, however, the thing that keeps coming back to me is the assault on peoples' minds that Havana Syndrome inflicted. So maybe you should give me and Hana a chance to look at Mr Webster's computer and its history. In the meantime, perhaps Denton could research when he received it and how long he's been working with it."

Denton pondered Donald's thoughts, as he stood and shuffled toward Ece. He stroked his moustache, then stared into her eyes. "Would you care to help me with this? It may be worth checking!" With an uneasy expression, Denton turned to Anneliese, asking if they could go upstairs to review the paperwork. "Ok" replied Anneliese, "But concentrate on the work. No romantic interludes until the job is done." An intense knowing grin widened as she inhaled, then chuckled.

As they left the room, Anneliese asked Donald, "Do you have the names and serial numbers of the Marines that worked on disassembly. If so, Donald, I think we may need to talk to them. I think your idea may have merit, so we will need to determine events after you joined us in Istanbul." Donald nodded, then also made his way out to check the personnel list.

About 40 minutes passed. The rest of the team spent the time searching for other thoughts, other clues, but the flip chart remained totally blank.

Chapter 59

Webster's Computer – Havana Gas

Just as they were all having another coffee, Denton, Ece and then Donald reappeared. William Webster had been in the first allocation of the new Bietronics computers, over a year ago! Probably due to his CIA seniority. His computer had been recalled immediately after the capsules were found in the heat sinks. However, the CIA Director, jointly with the President, had insisted they had confidential top security information that needed to be erased, before their computer could be released. And that would take a while because they both maintained the communications were continuing to be accessed and worked on! However, the President was persuaded to release his computer very soon after.

William Webster's computer was not released, until later! Then Donald went away to Istanbul.

Now the team were back together, Anneliese took control again. She began to pace around the room, then started speaking as she moved. "I'm starting to feel there is mileage in Donald's idea. We need to get the Marines team leader here tomorrow morning. Denton, please do your utmost to organise that. We will start there, but we may need to move on down the line, and interview all the Marines that were on the disassembly assignments. But, Denton, just one other thing. Don't say why we need to talk to him. We want him to be off-balance if he has become involved in anything devious." Denton's face skewed. "If they were involved in any way, Anneliese, I'm confident it would have been unknowingly." Donald indicated his agreement! Then with a purposeful expression he first gazed at Hana. His attention slowly moved to Anneliese. His thoughtful handsome face transitioned into a smile, then he uttered, "The Director's computer is just sitting there above us." As he spoke, his eyes glanced to the ceiling. "If Hana and I could have half an hour, we could take it apart and take a look!"

Anneliese, with gleeful eyes, responded, "Well don't just sit there like two love birds, fly off your perch and get moving on it!"

They returned in 30 minutes. Donald's broad smile told the story. "Well, it's like this, you guys. We now have another serious health risk sitting up in the Director's office." Everyone leaned forward in their chairs with intense interest. Donald continued, "We took the computer apart, and sitting there in the heat sink was, guess what, a capsule; with one melted corner slowly emitting gas! That has been attacking William Webster, probably for months. All we need to establish now is how it was not made safe in the recall process."

"Fabulous," shouted a synchronised Anneliese and Denton! Anneliese, following a slight pause, said, "Denton, we will close this out tomorrow. But for now, we know Mr Webster was extremely Havana Syndrome sick." "I am going to begin preparing a report for President Hayden. We will talk with the lead Marine in the morning."

Anneliese was about to leave for her office when she glanced across the room. She had noticed Donald with his hands covering his face as he leaned forward with elbows on his knees. She stood completely still watching him, wondering what was on his mind. Hana leant across, putting her arm around his shoulder. Slowly his hands dropped from his eyes as he sat up, with straight back, in his chair. "I don't think it will help to talk to my Marine leader! This was all my fault. Thinking back, I'm sure it was my fault!"

Anneliese, followed by Denton, moved in front of Donald, who again, covered his face with his hands. Anneliese stretched her arm out, placing her hand alongside Hana's on his back. "Why Donald.... Why do you think it's your fault?"

Donald's muffled speech gradually cleared as his face lifted out of his cupped hands. "Just before I left to join the efforts in Istanbul, I was working in the hangar storage area. Some of the Marines were in the lower area, cleaning and checking computers about to be returned into service. Another Marine group in a separate adjacent sealed area had been dismantling, but had left to have their lunch outside in the sunshine. They were outside, taking off their safety overalls and breathing apparatus when Chuck arrived."

"The Marine "check and clean" group downed tools and joined their mates for lunch, outside in the sunshine. Chuck walked in past them and came straight to me. I was surprised to see him as Denton had been with us, only two days before, doing his review and audit. I said so to Chuck, but he just laughed and said Denton wanted him to see if the numbers were still increasing and wanted his view on how it was going."

"I gave him the up to date scores, and then he insisted I go have some lunch with the others, whilst he had a look around. Now comes the tough part! I left him alone in the hangar for about 20 minutes. He could have found Mr Webster's computer in the disassembly area. There were many there waiting for attention. If it was one of those, all he had to do was to move it into the finished stock area. Later, it would have been shipped back to Mr Webster's office, still with the capsule sitting in the heat sink untouched!"

Donald and Hana both stared at Anneliese, as she crouched in front of them. With softness in her voice, Anneliese uttered, "Donald, you probably have come up with the answer. But there is absolutely no way you should be blaming yourself. None of us suspected Chuck of malevolence. At that point in time, he was a respected member of our team."

"I'm going to get the report written, and will give your input as the final conclusion. We may be able to verify some of the facts tomorrow when we talk with the Marine!"

Chapter 60

Chuck Caused it!

Next day, Denton and Jerome met with Joey, the Marine leader. It was a relaxed meeting in the Coffee Shop. Denton treated them to coffee and a plate full of Tim Horton select donuts.

Joey, his cheeks bulging with chocolate donut, confirmed the date and time of Chuck's visit to the disassembly hangar.

Denton scratched his head. "Yes, I recall, that was around the time Chuck returned to file the Iranian's documents" As Joey devoured his fourth donut, and Denton and Jerome were about to shake his hand, Jerome asked one last question. "Joey, that was a really tough job you guys did in that hangar, wearing all that protective clothing and masks. Did you notice if Chuck wore any protective clothing?" "Ah, no he didn't; just wandered around checking things out." He stopped speaking, inhaled as he massaged his forehead, as if trying to liven his brain into action! "What was strange, now I think about it, was that as I walked back in from lunch, in the distance, Chuck was walking across the hangar. He was taking short fast steps as he carried a computer to the "finished stock" area. Thinking back now, before he began getting that close to any of the computer units, he should have dressed in protective gear. He knew the rules, and they were plastered on notices all around the walls! "They shook hands; Joey grabbed two more donuts as he left, saying, "Thanks for breakfast, you guys."

Denton peered at Jerome, then skewed his mouth. Jerome smiled in return. "Well, I think we now have conclusive evidence!" Denton put his hand on Jerome's shoulder and as he pushed him toward the stairs, said, "Jerome, your final question was a peach!"

When the team heard the news, the sighs of relief filled the conference room. Denton arranged for Anneliese to fly out of Langley later that evening for an audience with the President. Denton accompanied her.

Anneliese and Denton sauntered confidently into the Oval Office. They received generous greetings from President Hayden, then handed him the summary page that provided the final solution.

As the President read quickly down the bullet points, a grin developed and rapidly transitioned into a very wide smile. He slapped the one-pager on the desk as he attempted to suppress a loud belly laugh.

He failed, as his laughter boomed around the Oval Office. Anneliese and Denton joined the raucous chorus!

President Hayden slumped back in his majestic leather office chair, as he shouted, "I knew he was a good guy. He's always done his best for me and the country. I knew there was more to it!"

"Denton, would you please get me a large brandy from the drinks cabinet and whatever Anneliese and you would like. Let's do a toast to our good friend, William Webster."

As the euphoria ebbed away, but not totally, the President said, "gratitude is nowhere near sufficient, and recently I have praised you all so many times I feel as if its tarnishing. But with sincerity I say, you guys and your team will always be in our thoughts. So, please join me in a toast to my respect and love for you all!"

The President stood behind his desk, and explained that at 1pm tomorrow he had a slot after the news to update the country. Glancing at Anneliese, he stressed that his address would also be on UK television stations. "At last, I will be saying with complete honesty that we avoided disaster and everything will be back on stream soon."

"Now, Anneliese and Denton, I am aware that you have been living your lives with very little sleep, so for the moment we should call a halt and I will ensure our guys get you back to your beds in quick time!"

As they shook hands, Anneliese asked if she could make a request. "Of course, Anneliese." With a caring expression, Anneliese said, "We are all hoping we can get to visit Mr Webster in hospital before we leave. That's the easy part. But our whole team have asked us to appeal to you. And we do understand that politics may make it difficult. However, we are all sincerely requesting you to give Mr Webster his job back, if and when he recovers. We are begging you to consider our request!"

Chapter 61

The President's Address

In the morning, the Coffee Shop appeared the place to be. There was profuse excitement throughout the place. Constant banter, chatter and expressive exuberance, with everyone anticipating the President's upcoming speech. It almost seemed as though every CIA employee had crammed into the Coffee Shop and were spilling over into reception.

Anecdotes and colourful stories echoed all around. In their own building, the Secret Service had become the Conspicuous Intelligence Agency! The atmosphere and euphoria in that confined space, resembled VE day celebrations in the Mall, following the announcement of the end of World War II.

As time wore on, the crowd gradually gravitated to the bar. Celebrations continued, reaching a crescendo when the Bar Manager turned up the volume and people began to dance. The first couple was Denton and Ece, who seemed to be in seventh heaven. The CECD team were swamped with drinks and well-wishers. Mostly delivered by appreciative Marines and SEALs.

At 12.40pm the Bar Manager climbed on a table. A Marine blew on his bugle to get everyone's attention. As the room fell quiet, the Bar Manager, Santi, shouted that if everybody would care to move to the large Main Conference room, the President's address would be shown, at 1.00pm, on a gigantic Kenwood TV.

The stream of people down the hallway began. With obvious respect and politeness, the crowd waited as Marines, led by Frank, escorted Anneliese and the CECD team out first.

The room quietened as the TV came on and the lights were dimmed. After the usual adverts, the background music quietly and carefully evolved into a loud trumpet fanfare. President Hayden stood at the lectern. He looked, and probably felt, 10 years younger. The clouds had lifted and the sun was shining!

His opening words were "Our great country has survived an atrocious onslaught by evil forces. We have averted a disaster. This episode has woken me to how important the provision of health services is to humanity. And not just in the USA, throughout the world. We have always been the leader in the development of medical equipment and treatments. The terrorists saw this as our Achilles heel and attempted to decimate our medical manufacturing industry. They also attacked our Governments, both here and in the UK, exposing our personnel to a nerve gas causing Havana Syndrome."

"Our allies, especially in the UK also suffered, seriously suffered, from the brutal and ferocious attacks on our medical factories and facilities."

"We worked closely with our allies on this operation, and we have agreed that we will protect our health services, whatever the cost."

"I'm going to put my chips on the table, here in front of you all. Our, indeed your, health and well-being must always take priority over everything else. Children, older people like me, disabled people, people with degenerative diseases and those suffering the myriad of cancers must, and will be, our priority. We will protect and enhance every element of our health service."

"I have talked today with the Prime Minister of the United Kingdom. He is in total agreement. You, our citizens, our grandparents, mums, dads and children, deserve your elected representatives to put your health before everything."

"As I close now, I must mention one last thing. Our troops, Marines, SEALs, the CECD, the CIA and FBI, were tremendous in their defeat of the terrorists. But the most treasured and exclusive thing was the outstanding work by our allies. The UK in particular, the Czech Republic and Turkey."

"I would love to name them, and have our whole nation applaud them, but I can't and you know I can't. They have worked with us for some time now and will continue to do so. They have become my personal friends and as I told them recently, I now see they are human beings like us, with wives, husbands, grandparents and kids! But best of all, they work tirelessly for a better world for all of us!"

"Finally, I must pay tribute to two ladies that have put their hearts and souls into supporting me through these traumatic times. The first is my wife, Eleanor. The second must remain incognito. This young lady is a member of our courageous CIA team. During these extraordinarily difficult times, she risked her life to save mine, and several others! We call her by a pseudonym, Rosa Klebb, so let's have three cheers for Rosa!" The nation, and everyone in the room in Jackson cheered, then applauded. Finally, with his eyes welling up, the President softly uttered, "God Bless You All, and God bless this wonderful country of ours. God Bless the United States of America."

Denton pulled Ece close, saying, "Let's do it, let's get married!" With kaleidoscope eyes, she replied, "Oh yes, yes!"

Anneliese, Frank and Jerome huddled with them, enamoured with this young lady.

Chapter 62

The Team Visit Webster

Later that afternoon, Denton arranged for the team to visit the CIA Director General, Mr William Webster, in hospital.

Early evening they were all transported by helicopter to the Walter Reed National Military Centre, located in Bethesda, Maryland. William had spent the first week in the High Dependency Unit. An amalgam of secret drugs were used to treat him for the nerve gas he had ingested. Being a physically fit and determined character, he was making a rapid recovery. His physical injuries had received operative treatment and were almost healed.

As he was doing so well, they were all allowed in together. As they approached his room, Anneliese looked through the small glass viewing panel. She turned to everyone as they congregated at the door. "He's sitting up in bed and looks well"; the relief in her voice reduced everyone's tension. She slowly and quietly opened the door. One after the other, they began to shuffle in behind Anneliese. As they clustered around, a weary smile consumed his expression. Ece moved forward, placed a hand on the edge of his bed and leant forward, close to him.

"Sir," she began, "I'm so sorry I hurt you! Will you get better? It all happened so fast!" William, leaning on his elbow, moved forward to place two fingers on her lips. "Ece, you should not be saying sorry. I don't know what happened to me, but it is I that should be thanking you. So, please, accept my sincere gratitude. If you had not performed as an Agent should, I would be in much more trouble than I have already brought upon myself."

Looking at the faces around his bed, with sincerity in his voice, he said "I am so pleased, and grateful, to see you all. I am grateful because I thought you would all hate me. I'm really tired now but I will get myself well and then I hope to see you again."

They all began to exit the room. Denton held Anneliese's arm, saying "Stay, just for a few moments while I talk to the boss." Denton took Anneliese's hand and moved close to William's face.

He quietly and sympathetically explained to William that everything would be ok. He was sure President Hayden would reinstate him into his old positon. William, until then had been drifting off to sleep. His eyes opened wide. "Will that really be possible?" "Yes it will, "replied Denton. "Just work on getting yourself fit again and then we can get back to working together."

Anneliese interjected. "William, you are so respected by us all, so of course, it's possible. We will make sure you can get back to work with us" "Thank you so much. I can't explain how much that means to me." His eyes gradually closed, but the smile remained.

Having said their goodbyes, next afternoon, Anneliese and Frank sat waiting for take-off. Their minds were attempting to become accustomed to thoughts that were not searching for answers.

They were both fairly quiet as they rode out of Pearson airport onto the QE towards Oakville. The dim street lights, as they turned off into the Maple Grove area had a poignant feeling!

Matthew, Frank Junior and a new puppy, Tosh, were at the door to greet them. Anneliese and Frank were home! And life looked much more secure. It was now the best of times. It was the age of wisdom. It was the epoch of belief. It was the season of light. IT WAS THE SPRING OF HOPE!

As Anneliese and Frank walked up the path, Anneliese stared at Frank Junior as her mind flickered into pictures that imagined him as a grown-up. Before strong embraces and tears of joy, her thoughts wandered into the future. What would it look like for Frank Junior....what would he aspire to be?

Chapter 63

Anneliese and Family Return Home

As they settled into their happy tranquil, loving family life, Anneliese knew, in the back of her mind, that life would probably throw a spanner in the works, somewhere in the future. She must remain in readiness to tackle any strong turbulence because, she had heard evil, seen evil, and fought evil, all her life. The trick would be to ensure evil forces were constantly defeated.

Anneliese's pragmatic attitude, as always, led her to monitor and measure the deteriorating climate of evil around the world. Sure enough, the "spring of hope", did not last as long as Spring!

Frank Junior, at eight years of age, was a solid, tall and intelligent boy. As President Hayden had once remarked, his intellect was way beyond his years, and Matthew and Anneliese should be very proud of the way he was developing; polite, courteous and caring.

As the years passed by, their family, and Frank and Lucia, enjoyed every moment together, and were especially enamoured with the youth that Frank Junior was becoming.

Once eleven years old, his amazing results at primary school, led to him being offered a place at a prestigious high school in the local area, Oakville Trafalgar High School.

At the age of twelve, he was 5 feet, 9 inches tall, with the body of a man. He used the weight training gym in the basement of the house, every day. Matthew, his Dad, was also kept up to the mark and shared time, almost every day, working as a keen duo/trio with Frank Junior, and occasionally, Frank. The banter and competition between them had become addictive, increasing the adhesion in their already dedicated, triangular friendship.

Frank Junior, in high school, had superior results in most subjects. His specialisms were heading towards Mathematics, languages, History and Politics.

In parallel with academic subjects, he had begun to excel in the area of sports. He had become fixated with Ice Hockey and now, after a year, was representing his high school in the local league.

In the first instance, believing it would enhance his muscular development, swimming became another passion. Initially, he would go with his mates to a large outdoor swimming pool in Mississauga, just a few miles away. This would mostly be a weekend event, and as time went by, it wasn't just swimming that was the attraction. Girls gradually crept into the equation, and their small group of boy swimmers soon became a mixed group of eight.

All these pieces on Frank Junior's chess board worked fabulously well together. But the king was always Ice Hockey!

He was playing for the Milton Junior league team every week. During the winter months, they would sometimes play a match on the frozen Lake Ontario. But as his performance improved and he became a dominant forward player, he was invited to play for, first the Burlington City team and then, Oakville City. Throughout his development in this, at times, violent sport, he became an avid supporter of the local professional team, the Toronto Maple Leafs!

He, and a few of his mates, would go to every home game. Frank Jr. would use his photographic memory to record every move. He was using this to enhance every element of his play. This was providing fast payback!

There was a feature of the game that he found thrilling. All around the rink was a plastic glass enclosure. Players were sometimes bustled and hustled, crashing headlong into the enclosure. The players would, immediately, go on the offensive. Brutal clashes usually followed. Frank knew he was good at this. He would land blows that made his assailant withdraw. He was getting acknowledgement from all quarters, as a fearless opponent. Even when he was hit with a direct face punch, he would shrug it off and come back with ferocious blows to his opponent. He was making a spectacular name for himself!

Because he loved the game, he would, in his spare moments, read about the history of the sport. He was particularly intrigued by the game against Russia on 28 September, 1972. His mother's involvement with Russia, as a Secret Service Agent, during the Cold War, underlined his interest. It was a day in history for Canada. This was the final of the Canada – Soviet Union series. A player named Paul Henderson scored the winning goal for Canada in the final minute. All around the world, people had been glued to their TVs', willing Canada to win. And they did!

After hours of homework, he would devote many more hours, late into the night, watching videos of ice hockey matches. Particularly those that included players that had become his favourites; of course, Paul Henderson, but also Wayne Gretzky and Tim Horton.

Indeed, due to his passion for doughnuts, but even greater respect for Tim Horton, he would call into a Tim Horton's doughnut store on the way to school. Often he would see Mr Horton and had secured his autograph many times over.

Chapter 64

Frank Junior will be 15

Frank Junior was now close to his 15th birthday. Anneliese was away on business in London, helping the UK Prime Minister with foreign policy issues, as she did a few times each year. However, she had promised to return for his birthday!

About a week before his birthday, Matthew, his dad, received a phone call. After a ten minute chat, Matthew strode to Frank Jr's room and delivered an urgent loud knock on his bedroom door. With an excited pitch he shouted, "Frank Junior, may I come in. I've got some great news!"

With an expression that spelled delight, Matthew said, "Frank; that was my brother Alfie on the phone. He wanted to ask if my nephews, Mark and Mickey could come over for your birthday, and have a vacation with us for a few weeks?"

Frank Junior slapped his duvet and let out a raucous screech. "Oh, Dad, that would really be the best ever present for my birthday. But will they be ok travelling all this way on their own?"

Matthew got close and clutched Frank Junior to him. "Frank, I know it's been a while. Same as me, you probably picture them in short trousers. But Mark is now sixteen and Mickey eighteen. And according to Alfie, they are both very street wise! In fact he was telling me that both of them had followed in his footsteps, and excelled at Boxing."

Then they went a step further, or should I say a kick further. Mickey was first to take up kick boxing! He even went to be trained by professionals in the art of kick boxing, in Thailand. Mark took up the sport, and they were both very successful. So I'm absolutely certain they can look after themselves in a trip across the pond to us.

Matthew's eyes searched the ceiling as he inhaled a very deep breath. Returning to the look of pleasure in Frank Junior's eyes, he spoke once more. "Frank, having just explained how capable your cousins are, I am however, thinking of asking your Mum to travel back with them. I wouldn't forgive myself if anything happened to them, and as well as giving her two travelling companions, they would provide your Mum with some protection. You know I always worry about her, due to the nature of her work!"

Matthew turned toward the door, then stopped and swivelled to face Frank Junior once more. His pursed lips slowly and emotionally evacuated his thoughts. "It's been a long time since we have seen my family. Jobs, education, caring for and bringing up our own families. So this is extra special for all of us. And the best part is that it gives you and your Mum the chance to get to know my nephews. As children they meant so much to me, and now they are older I can re-kindle that feeling!"

Frank Junior, nearly 15, seemed to be on another growth spurt. Bodily, he was strong, powerful and athletic. His hand/eye coordination was at the top of the scale, which combined with his Mensa level intelligence, optimised both his competitive and combat abilities. However, his height was continuing to increase. He was already close to 6feet tall and sometimes he felt this was a minor negative. But, so far, it had not been an impediment in any shape or form. His real concern involved the future! If he grew much beyond 6feet, 2inches, it was unlikely he would be able to continue to be a strong ice hockey contender!

He wondered how tall his cousins would be. Mark, in particular, as he was only slightly older than Frank Jr.

It was a snowy East Coast night. From Toronto, all the way down to Chicago, and even New York, blizzards had come and gone through the last two days. As always, the main highways around Toronto were drivable and had been kept relatively clear by the local authorities. As Matthew and Frank Junior drove to Pearson Airport, most of the traffic seemed to be a constant battalion of snow ploughs and gritters, both in front and behind. Although most cars in the traffic were large rear wheel drive vehicles, Lincolns, Chryslers, Toyotas and Mazdas, they did not see a single accident.

They arrived at the airport with at least 30 minutes to spare. Parking in the multi-storey car park was always difficult. It had not been designed for the larger MPV's and off road vehicles. Every space needed the passengers to breathe in. All spaces were tight and opening the tailgate required care.

Matthew and Frank Jr. were in a Ford Expedition. The low roof in this antiquated multi-storey was always an obstacle. But not at this moment. They strolled into Pearson's Arrivals and waited alongside the multi-racial multitude. Everyone around appeared excited, probably meeting their families and loved ones. The noise level increased as passengers began to exit into arrivals. All around them, both prepared and rough DIY cards were being held up, with a myriad of different nationality names.

A few minutes passed by, then Matthew spied them! Mick, industrious Mick, was pushing the trolley full of cases. Anneliese, holding Mark's arm, was elegantly leading the way to the escape route, past the barriers.

In excitable fashion, with embraces, constant dialogue about the journey, and general chatter, they arrived at the car. Nobody knew how they had got there, so the chatter continued as Matthew opened the lift-gate to load the cases. Sure enough, with all the distractions, one thing had been forgotten. The low roof!

The lift-gate lid powered upwards, crashing into the ceiling. Pieces of plaster floated down around the car. Anneliese began to chuckle. A hysterical belly laugh followed, as Matthew stood, peering into the vehicle, with large pieces of white plaster covering his head and shoulders. White dust, all over him, imitated a bad dandruff day! The laughter was infectious. All of them were in absolute stitches for close to a minute.

The banter and sporadic laughter continued as they left the multi-storey behind. They were soon on the Queen Elizabeth highway, around Toronto, known affectionately as the QE. This road headed up towards Niagara, Ottawa and Montreal. But their journey to Oakville was only going to take about 20 minutes.

As the cheerful jocularity subsided, Mickey and Mark remarked that they were excited by all the snow. "Tomorrow, "Mark exclaimed, "can we build a massive snowman and pelt each other with snowballs? I saw snow like this when I was a kid, but we've not had this type of weather in the South of England for years!"

Chapter 65

Cousins Arrive from England

During the short drive to Oakville, the three lads, together in the rear seat, were excitedly getting to know one another again. Frank Junior had already taken note of his cousins' height. Mick was around 5ft 11 inches and Mark probably 6ft! Junior was somewhat relieved that Mark wasn't taller. It gave Junior some confidence that 6ft 2inches may be his maximum. At least, being hopeful, that was what he was trying to convince himself!

When home, they all enjoyed the family get-together, but tiredness eventually gained control. It was an early night for all, and sound sleep quickly consumed them.

The following morning, Mickey and Mark were still jet-lagged, so it was just a leisurely breakfast and then a look around the house and the street. Later Matthew drove the boys to the Misissauga shopping mall, whilst Anneliese caught up on her paperwork.

In the evening, the three lads made the basement their own clubhouse. All three did work together in the gym, then moved on to playing pool. Mick and Mark were talking with Junior about their boxing gym. Junior described his team work with the Oakville ice hockey Terrors and then attempted to describe the Maple Leafs team players and arena.

Out of the blue, Junior asked if they would like to go to a Maple Leafs game. His cousins were excited, asking if they had a gift shop, for presents for friends and family. Clearly wanting to return the favour, Mick asked, "Have you ever tried boxing? They call it the noble art! But once you get the taste for it, all you want is to nobble your opponent! If we can find a boxing club around here, we could go with you and see if you take to it!"

Enormous smiles all around as they agreed to viewing each other's sport. But the immediate attraction was Frank Junior's birthday party, the following day. His Mum and Dad were the organisers. The invitees would be a mixture of Frank Junior's friends and the older community. That was all Junior knew!

Chapter 66

Trip to a Sports Bar

13 March, 2008 had snuck up on them. Another casual breakfast, with stacks of pancakes, scrambled eggs and crispy bacon. Coffee was poured non-stop. Lucia had arrived early to help Anneliese and Matthew through the breakfast, and the whole day. She was superb at cooking and providing sustenance with naturally relaxed humour. Her hospitality trade had been learned from the bottom up. Firstly, in bars and restaurants in Tijuana, Mexico and subsequently as manager at the Wickenburg Inn; a semi-dude ranch hotel in Arizona.

It was a cold day with some snow still on the ground. About 10am busy mayhem began to emerge. First a group of contractors arrived to set up a canopied stage in the garden. People arrived and were coming and going everywhere. The party was due to begin at 4pm, and although a cold day in March, it was what Anneliese defined as a bright Canada day. The sky was electric blue and above the pine trees, could be mistaken for an artist's canvas. Just down the road, Lake Ontario glistened in the sunshine, as the Canada geese waddled along, searching every crevice for insects and bugs.

The boys decided to make an exit. As they strolled towards the lake, Mark stopped in his tracks. Mick and Frank Junior also stopped and turned to face him. With that, Mark exclaimed, "Wow, that's not a lake. Never seen anything that vast before. It's a sea! Where does it go?"

Frank Junior chuckled. "Mark, I'll show you on the map when we get home. But, essentially, it joins Canada and America. When it's really cold and freezes over, the trucks, including Dad's friend Brian, park their trucks on the ice and go ice fishing, under small tents. They sit there for hours, or scramble off if the temperature rises!"

The three lads trundled along the edge of the lake, until they reached a small café. They began talking, as they sipped coca-colas'. Mickey was tempted to have a beer, but resisted saying, "It's going to be a long day!"

As they sat, soaking up the winter sun, Mickey asked Junior, "Do you fancy trying to find a boxing club tomorrow?" Frank Junior sighed, then began to chuckle. With a confirming tone, Junior said, "Mick, we can do it soon. But tomorrow, after the party may be a bit too soon. Everyone is going to be hungover, you included. So let's wait, and see how it goes!" Mark lent across to Frank Junior, causing him to wobble on his bar stool. "I can see why you are doing so well at school. You have a level of common sense that is uncommon. You're right! We've only just arrived and we have two or perhaps three weeks." Mark eyeballed his brother. "Mick, there's no rush, let's just take it a day at a time!"

Back at the house, ladies were scurrying all around. Anneliese was directing operations as Frank arrived and joined them. Coffee and toast was endless.

The lads seemed to have no place to settle. Asylum was unobtainable as ladies cleaned, dusted and hoovered.

Matthew and Frank huddled together on the patio. It was a gloriously sunny Canada winter's day. Matthew poked his head into the family room, shouting "Come on lads, Frank has an idea to help us escape this mad house!"

They congregated on the front driveway. Frank with a relieved expression, uttered, "Let's get away for a couple of hours. Leave the ladies to cluck around the place whilst we relax in Donovan Baileys sports bar. Are we all up for it?"

Other than giggles and chuckles, there was no spoken response. Before Frank or Matthew could say another word, the lads were clambering into the rear seat of the Lincoln.

The Sports Bar was bigger than anything Mickey and Mark had ever seen. Two bars with exotic décor and, all around, attractive, friendly, waitresses.

Frank, Matthew and Mickey opted to commence with beers. Although Mark and Frank Junior appealed, they knew ID was essential. So their drinks were Coca-Cola. Frank and Matthew chose Michelob lights, but after listening to a whisper from Frank Junior, Mickey decided to join the Coca-Cola gang! The legal age for alcohol was 19!

Frank, beer in hand, ambled off and returned five minutes later. He had rented one of the 20 or so pool tables for two hours. Ushered by Matthew and Frank, they all sauntered in the direction of their pool table. All of them had played before, but this was not the English game. Frank attempted to explain the rules, which were slightly different. Giggles, humour, banter were all-consuming as they were about to begin. They tossed coins to establish who would play who. It was something of a shambles but nobody seemed to care.

Adjacent to the pool table was a large pedestal table. As play began, Matthew was seen talking to a blonde, blue eyed waitress. Frank Jr and Matthew were in play, about to finish. Frank Jr had won and Mark was up next. But he was distracted by the large TV screens surrounding them. He was engrossed with an Ice Hockey game. It was between two teams from the southern US states. The Florida Panthers and Tampa Bay Lightning. Mark put his arm around Frank Junior, asking, as he peered at the screen, "How do these teams practise Ice Hockey when they are in a really hot part of the USA?"

Frank Junior smiled with a mischievous look in his eyes. "Mark, this is the most inventive Continent in the world. We just ship them snow and ice in refrigerated trucks, straight to their training grounds!"

Mark thought for a second or two then placed his arm around Junior's neck and pulled his face close. "You fucker," he said, "You are pulling my dick!" Mark released his grip on Frank Junior who replied, "You're up Mark, careful there's no ice on the table! You are playing my Dad and he's good, so you had better concentrate." Mark, heading to the table, looked back. "Frank, think I need English balls to get through this! You guys on the North American Continent all claim to have big balls. But we won the World War, with only a bit of help from you guys!"

Matthew had ordered almost non-stop, chicken wings, wedges, fried langoustines', and garlic bread. At the end, 2pm, their appetites had been appeased. The waitresses clustered around, enticed by these young handsome lads. Frank Junior was the champion!

As they were striding towards the door, having embraced almost every waitress in the place, a very handsome black guy stood in front of them. His arms spread as they approached. Frank Junior, as they neared him, became excited. "It's Donovan Bailey!" As they got close, Donovan Bailey, with arms outstretched, clutched Frank Jr. "Hey, Frank, the girls told me it's your birthday. So I just wanted to say hello and give you my best wishes." Frank Junior took a step back and peered into Donovan's eyes. Frank turned and scribbled on a piece of paper. Handing it to Mr Donovan Bailey, Frank Junior with a pleading expression, asked "Donovan, we are having a party this afternoon and evening. I want to invite you and your partner to join us. It will be fun!" Donovan with a receptive look replied, "Frank, thank you so much! I would love to come. I have watched your progress through the junior ice hockey leagues and I am really impressed by your progress."

"But, we should talk tonight about basketball. You are growing at an outlandish rate, and I think, from now on, you may want to transition into basketball. I run a club, and I think it would be absolutely right for you. So let's talk later."

Frank and Matthew, ambled off to the car as Mickey and Mark were getting Donovan's autograph. Mickey picked out some t shirts, pictures, and other paraphernalia from the corner shop. Donovan Bailey was more than willing to wait around, as they brought all types of memorabilia to him for his signature.

Chapter 67

We can Handle Muggers!

Frank Junior, watching from the doorway of the shop, decided to slowly exit into the fresh air. Standing on the sidewalk, he stretched, inhaled then turned to view his Dad and Frank pacing across the car park.

This was the calm before the storm! As he watched them walking through the rows of cars, the doors of an "F" series pickup truck opened and four big hoody dudes stepped out. Initially, their movements were slow, until Matthew and Frank had passed, their truck.

Frank Junior became suspicious. His intuition said this didn't look right. He turned, and screamed at 80 decibels. Mick, Mark, Help, come quick!" Then he sprinted toward the group, who by now appeared to be arguing. His acceleration increased as he powered through the first 40 yards. He had another 60 yards to go. Mickey and Mark were about 30 yards behind!

As Junior closed in on the group, he could see that two of them were threatening with knives, arms outstretched, with Matthew and Frank backed up against a parked car. The other two were lifting their pockets.

One of the knife men swivelled to face Junior. Frank took the opportunity that distraction delivered. His powerful kick sent the knife over the row of cars. Frank was not going to stop there. With a screaming right hook, he dropped the guy. Frank Junior arrived, launching himself from ten feet away at the two pocket pilferers who had started to turn to face the onslaught. Frank Junior, screaming like a banshee, rained face blows, then kicks, on both of them. They were tough; took the punches, but returned a hail of kicks and blows to Junior's body. Junior hardly flinched, taking the first guy out with a tremendously powerful head butt. His nose, in shreds, spurted blood over everyone!

Matthew had the other pocket pilferer, his forearm tight across his throat, and a knee in his back; Mickey and Mark smashed their way onto the scene. Mickey, with astounding accuracy, kicked, swivelled and punched with amazing accuracy. It was so imaginative it could have been construed as artistic! The guy held by Matthew dropped to the floor!

Mark was carrying a pool cue he had grabbed as he left the Sports Bar. The muggers were out of action, totally defeated. Well almost! As they stood over them, exhausted, breathing heavily, checking each other for any serious wounds, one of the muggers rolled over, reaching into his jacket pocket.

Distant sirens were now heard. Getting closer all the time! The mugger ignored the noise, as he pulled a revolver out. With blood pouring from his mouth, he screamed, "You fuckers are dead meat!" Not another word left his lips. Mark sprang forward, kicking the gun into orbit. He followed with the pool cue, bringing it crunching down on the mugger's forehead. Mark wasn't finished. No one else would retaliate. With his mind dominated by aggressive hormones, he moved from one mugger to another, grabbing their hair as he pulverised their face. Frank pulled him off, sensing Mark was now in a mental frenzy.

The Canadian Mounties arrived. Three cars surrounded them, as Frank and Matthew were checking that they were all ok.

The Mountie sergeant, with gun drawn, shouted, "Lay on the floor with arms outstretched." Second to be searched was Frank. The sergeant looked at Frank's CECD identity card and asked him to stand. They gradually smiled at one another. This Mountie was Sergeant John, who had met them when they had arrived in Canada. They exchanged a few words; Frank explained what had occurred. Sergeant John had a few words with his men and they helped them all to their feet, just as an armoured police van arrived. The muggers were handcuffed, and dragged off to the van.

Matthew and Frank spoke to each of the youngsters. None of them felt they needed hospital treatment. Frank Junior's face was battered and bloodied, but nothing that would not repair itself in 24 hours.

As they were beginning to climb into the Lincoln, Sergeant John asked, "Is everyone ok? Are you sure?" Matthew Junior spoke. "Sir, we are all fine, and we want to get back to my birthday party!"

Sergeant John pushed his cap back and took a deep breath. "My God, he said, "you are little Frank Junior. I helped carry you out of the airport when you first arrived in Canada. Frank Junior, I am so pleased to see you again. Your family have a special place in my heart, and after today, you are amongst the people I most respect. Give my love to your Mum. She has been a Godsend to this world we are now living in."

Frank Junior, leant across the backseat. "Sergeant John, we are having a birthday party tonight, so if your shift will allow, please come. I know Mum would love to see you. She still talks about you leading us around, buying everything for the house we still live in. "Sergeant John nodded a thank you. "I will check with my family and maybe see you later."

They were just about to drive away as Sergeant John banged on the window. Matthew wound his window down, Sergeant John said, "just to let you know, you have done Ontario a big favour. Those guys today have tormented us throughout Ontario. They are responsible for at least fifty muggings. But now, thanks to you, we have them in custody."

Chapter 68

Home Battered and Bruised

Ten minutes later, the Lincoln squeezed into a space on the double driveway. The oversize grey entrance door opened. There stood Anneliese, hands on hips. Peering at the men with a distinctly supercharged frown. Her displeasure was obvious to each and every one of them.

Anneliese's eyes searched around each of them. As her vision cleared, Frank Junior, sitting with a timid expression and bloodied face, became her focus. Her eyes widened, and with a shocked expression she rushed to his door and pulled it open. "Junior, what the hell happened; are you ok?" Frank Jr spun to ease his legs out of the rear door. His jeans were ripped, along with his blood stained white polo shirt. Anneliese slowly helped him out of the car, and the rest of the group began to exit. Mickey and Mark started to chuckle. Frank and Matthew couldn't contain themselves, as the giggling became infectious.

With Frank Jr leaning on her, Anneliese, not appreciating the humour, shouted, "Matthew, and you Frank! You were supposed to take care of these lads." Glancing at Mickey and Mark, her anger grew. "Look at these two! Both of them battered and bruised. They look like they've been hit by an express train." Frank, now with his giggling under control, quickly spoke. "Anneliese, the truth is, they cared for us! They were magnificent. Matthew and I were being mugged by a knife wielding gang. These lads were more like trained SAS troopers than young teenagers."

"Let's get inside and we'll tell you the whole story." Matthew joined Anneliese helping Frank Junior hobble towards the door. Frank continued, "And this lad of yours, Frank Junior, was absolutely unbelievable. He is a totally fearless fighter. I've fought alongside many soldiers, but Junior is a natural when it comes to combat. And these two, Mick and Mark! Their boxing, and kick boxing, will give me treasured memories in my minds picture archive forever!"

Anneliese's expression was now changing, from anger into pride! Several guests were already in the house. There were gasps from them as the group entered the hallway. Matthew stood in front of the guests asking them to give the lads room. Anneliese left Frank and Matthew to explain, as she escorted the three teenagers upstairs, saying, "Lads, have a relaxing shower, clean your wounds, and change your clothes. Shout if you need help with anything."

She returned downstairs where Matthew, Frank and the guests were continuing to discuss, recount and deliberate over the whole episode! Gradually, the attraction of food, drink and music began to resurrect the party atmosphere. Anneliese and Matthew talked constantly about the conflict, whilst Matthew and Frank attempted to supply drinks. Frank, clearly enthralled by the young lads' performance reiterated, over and over, to all the guests, every detail of their fearless efforts in the conflict.

⸻◆⸻

Chapter 69

The Party Begins

All the guests, family and friends were happily mingling. Frank Junior, Mark and Mickey were gradually recovering. Legs, arms, shoulders were beginning to move without discomfort. Faces, with cuts and bruises, especially Junior's were becoming a distant memory, largely due to Mark sneaking drinks from the bar and sharing with Junior and Mickey.

The doorbell rang, which Matthew answered. Further pain relieving distractions were invited in. Six gorgeous young ladies, looking like cat walk models, elegantly entered. These beautiful young creatures were High School friends of Juniors', followed by two exotic females from the local church community. As they gravitated to Junior and his cousins, the doorbell rang once more.

This was a group of late-comers, contracted to set up a low, lego-type stage in the garden. Matthew led them directly into the garden, all the time wondering why they needed so many bodies. One of the last few guys stopped Matthew, explaining his four were a barber's quartet, hired by Anneliese, to get the party started.

The doorbell appeared to have developed a mind of its own. The ring was relentless. Every ten minutes or so; the warning bell was becoming an irritation. The next ring was a large group of guests; mostly neighbours and players and supporters of the Oakville Ice Hockey team.

Matthew decided he may now have time to sample a beer from the local beer store. As the bottle neared his lips, the phone rang. Matthew never usually swore, but as he headed to the hall, he was heard to say "Fuck me, will I ever get a beer?" Looking down the passage, he saw Anneliese had already answered the phone. She was holding the house phone to one ear, with a finger in her left ear, trying to suppress the party noise. Matthew, relieved, ambled back to his Red Dog beer.

A couple of minutes later, Anneliese scorched up to Frank Junior. With the girls crowded around, she bent to whisper in Junior's ear. Junior stood and, as he followed Anneliese out, said to his friends, "Please excuse me." He lifted the handset, and with a sparkle in his eyes said, "Hello, Uncle Bruce, how are you?" It was the President of the United States of America. His term of office had finished a while ago, but Anneliese had warned Junior that correct etiquette dictated that he should continue to be referred to as Mr President. However, Junior decided to continue with his childhood address.... Uncle Bruce!

There was a four minute conversation. Junior, his eyes smiling, and cheeks glowing, returned to his friends. He couldn't contain his wide smile, as this call had meant so much to him!

One of the girls, a very beautiful brunette named Hope, clutched his arm. She sensed his euphoria, "Junior, who was it? Who was on the phone? It's obviously been very special."

All the group closed in. Frank Junior pulled Hope close, and as a mischievous smile developed, whispered, "If I tell you, I will have to".... A long pause as he tenderly smiled into her eyes, he continued," I will have to ask you to dance with me later!"

Hope giggled and poked his cheek. Junior, screeched with bruised pain. Hope moved on to the arm of his chair. "Junior, oh I'm so sorry. I forgot. Yes, we should have a dance later, probably a slow one!"

The group, and especially, Mickey and Mark, were chuckling. Junior lent forward in the chair, still looking at Hope. "Ok, you want to know who was on the phone. It was my Uncle Bruce." Hope, with a quizzical expression asked, "Which part of your family is he from? Your Mum or Dad." "Well, neither" replied Junior. "Well, who is he then? You have never mentioned him before." Hope's questioning forced the issue.

Frank Junior gestured for them all to come close. "I will tell you," he whispered, "but only if you promise not to spread it around." The whole group eased closer, eyes enquiring and expectant. With baited breath, Junior whispered as he glanced around each of the group. "It was President Hayden; he's not President of the USA now, but he was when I was a kid, and I used to sit on his knee! He's a very special person to our family. And he said he is sending a present to me and it will arrive this evening!"

Mark, along with the rest, was gobsmacked. Jaws dropped, caverns appeared in every mouth. But Mark would always be first to express his feelings. His lips stuttered into action. "Junior," he blurted, "You are fucking kidding us. The American President phones you. You call him Uncle Bruce. When you were a kid, you sat on his lap. And now he's sending you a present. Fuck me, that's one hell of a story I will be able to tell forever.... And longer!"

Chuckling developed into strong belly laughs, both boys and girls were clutching their sides, requiring them to help one another to stay upright.

Frank, Anneliese and Matthew were enjoying the spectacle. But, once again, the tormenting doorbell gained their attention. Anneliese took a turn at the meet and greet. She opened the door to Donovan Bailey. Immediately behind him was Mountie Sergeant John and his wife, Isobel.

Following introductions, as they walked into the lounge, completely simultaneously, the barber's shop quartet began to sing. Initially just harmonising, and as Donovan strolled into the lounge, the room quietened. The barber shop quartet were now starting a song. Their fabulous harmony, with volume now at top level, took on the Sinatra song. The chorus of which immediately got the lads attention.

The words reached the boys ears. Frank and Matthew began to laugh at the chorus. "I get a kick out of you!" Frank ambled to the lads. He put his arms around Mickey and Mark. "Boys, that will always be remembered here as your theme tune. Tell your Mum and Dad that you will always be remembered whenever that song is played. And I hope those muggers put two and two together whenever they hear it. It's a spectacular song for two spectacular athletes like you!"

Chapter 70

Denton, Ece, Donald and Hana

The party atmosphere was buzzing, all around the house and garden. Music, singing, dancing and laughter almost drowned out the dreaded doorbell. But Anneliese heard it, and with wine glass in hand, answered the door to more visitors.

For a few seconds, she stood searching, with an enquiring gaze, at four faces under the porch light. Then her screams of delight were heard all around. It was her colleagues from the Istanbul Assignment; Denton and Ece, along with Donald and Hana. The immediate strong embraces previewed a gush of happy tears, first from Anneliese, then all three ladies. As emotions settled, Denton asked, "Well Anneliese, can we join the party and get a beer?"

They all joined the throng: gifts were piled on Frank Junior as embraces, hugs, cuddles, kisses and handshakes flooded the room. Denton moved to stand in front of Junior. His slow but loud dulcet tones echoed off the walls. "Frank Junior" he said. Taking a deep breath, Denton continued. "We were given this assignment today by your Uncle Bruce and Mrs Hayden. The President and his First Lady send their love and great hopes for your future!"

"Well, to be honest, we didn't need to be instructed to attend, we would have come anyway!"

The whole party, hearing Denton's words, became silent. Whispers and excited chatter spread like wildfire as the party got back in the swing!

It was now around 8.00pm. The party atmosphere was heading up the scale toward a crescendo!

Donovan Bailey took the chance to talk with Junior. As he stood to face Donovan, Hope, Junior's beautiful young friend, slid off the arm of his chair, into his armchair seat.

Donovan didn't need much effort to persuade Junior to try basketball at his club in Oakville. Junior was excited by the prospect and would have a first lesson in a week's time.

Mickey and Mark were now showing off their moves as they danced with two young ladies. Hope, a confident character, took Junior's hand and led him out to dance in their group.

The dastardly doorbell rang again! Matthew, with a grimace, placed his beer down and went to the door. Denton tapped Junior on the shoulder. "That's probably your birthday gift from President Hayden. You may wish to join your Dad and see this." Junior trundled to the hallway, with Hope tagging along behind.

Matthew, as he gripped the door handle, was bewildered by the bright lights shining through the door's glass panes. He slowly opened it. His first sighting was Jerome, standing on the doorstep. Jerome began to apologise, as Matthew's gaze moved to the astounding spectacle behind Jerome. Hordes of people, bright floodlights, camera flashes and honking car horns.

⚬—◄◆►—⚬

Chapter 71

Now the President's Gift

Matthew turned tail and ran back down the passage, screaming all the way, "John, Mountie John, I need your help!" In the meantime, Junior and Hope had stepped up to the door. Jerome asked, "Can we come in, just us at the front, and the guys with guitars."

Jerome stepped in beside Junior and they jointly ushered, first the lead singer, then the band, into the hall. Jerome, leaning on the wall, giggled, then spluttered "This is your present from President Hayden and the First Lady." An absolutely stunning young lady stood beside Jerome. This gorgeous lady stretched to shake hands with Junior as Jerome made the introductions. "This is Guapa and her band." The five guys behind Guapa all smiled and nodded. "Their official title is Guapa and her Guys. Pretty cute and simple, eh" uttered Jerome.

Hope went into a frenzy. Rushing down the passageway, she screamed, "Oh my God, Oh my God, it's Guapa!"

Matthew and Mountie John pushed past her, back to the hallway. Frank Junior escorted Guapa and the band through the lounge with the intention of taking them to the stage in the garden. But they had no chance! In the house, it was mayhem; the girls were screaming and even some of

Chapter 72

Junior Could be Professional

Bright sunlight, beaming in to the ground floor, woke most guests that had slept on the thick pile carpet floor. Anneliese, Lucia, Ece and Hana, formed the breakfast team. Lucia spent a few minutes preparing a plan, listing all the names; resulting in a schedule of 3 shifts, 6 people per shift.

Those up first would be served first! Lucia and the other three women began preparing scrambled eggs, pancakes, bacon, baked beans, fried tomatoes and toast. Coffee was already gurgling away in the coffee pot.

The teenage lads, and two of the girls, were last to rise and therefore, last to be served. All appeared gaunt and pasty, but as breakfast went on, they returned to the land of the living!

Breakfast was completed about 10.30am, and Lucia and Ece had all the washing up, via the dishwasher, finished by 11am.

From that point, guests began to leave. Nearly an hour of goodbyes, embraces and waving. Special affection for the CIA team, with promises to keep in touch, and arrangements to meet every so often.

The only visitor now remaining, other than Junior's cousins, was Jerome. With a sharp cough to clear his throat, he ventured, with an appealing smile, to ask Anneliese if he could stay for a while.

Anneliese knew that look! "How long is a while?" she asked, but with a receptive grin!" "Well, it's like this, "uttered Jerome. "I booked an extra week's vacation because I really want to spend some time with you guys. I've missed you so much. I promise I will help around the house, run errands, anything!" Matthew started to laugh out loud.

Anneliese also began to chuckle as she stepped forward and grasped Jerome, kissing his cheek. "You silly thing, of course you can stay. We would be upset if you left now! We've got a lot of catching up to do. And you will always be part of our family!"

The remainder of the day was a lazy, hazy, crazy day. With slow, carefully selected steps, they tidied and cleaned. By late afternoon, the clear-up was completed. Conversation gradually returned and reminiscing evolved.

As the week progressed, Jerome became a solid, respected member of the teens' team. He was accepted and respected by the lads, to the point where they wanted him with them, every minute of the day. His intellect, knowledge of the world, continuous humorous stories and banter with the lads, enamoured him to all of them. Every day they would journey out somewhere. Sometimes Frank would join them, because he enjoyed feeling young again, and absolutely loved being with Jerome.

One of the first excursions was to the Oakville Boxing Academy. They all accompanied Frank Junior. This was just a reception experience day. A trainer showed them around then one by one they were asked to demonstrate their boxing prowess. After punch-ball machines, a one-round bout with the trainer. Every one, except Frank, climbed into the ring!

On completion, the trainer got them all together. "I'm sorry Frank Junior, and the rest of you lads. You are much too good to start here as newcomers to the sport. You are all pretty special, and we couldn't teach you a lot." That deserved a celebration at Donavan Bailey's Sports Bar.

This occasion was short and sweet, some beers but mostly Coca-Cola. Donovan heard they were in, and came and found them. He pursued Frank Junior on the basketball theme and it was agreed Frank Jr. would attend, two days hence, Friday.

Once again, they all escorted Frank Jr. to the novice introduction at Donovan's Oakville Basketball Club. Donovan invited them all on the court, but explained that Junior would be given priority. Frank and Jerome chose to watch them from the coffee bar.

At the end of the session, which had lasted over an hour, Donovan called their group together. First he addressed Mick and Mark. "You guys are heading back to the UK soon but I hope you enjoyed your time with us. What I will tell you is that you both have natural ability. You, Mark, with your height, and a couple of years' hard graft, could be special."

He turned to Frank Junior. "Frank, you could turn out to be fantastic. I want you here! I have professionals that can work with you. And if you put the effort in, you could be really special. Frank Jr. scratched his cheek, thinking all the while. Peering straight into Donovan's eyes he said, "Donovan, can I explain? I am hoping to go to University in two years' time. Will I be wasting your time if I start novice training now?" Donovan inhaled, then puffed out his cheeks. "Junior, you appear special to me now! In two years' time, there's no telling how good you could be. There is only one thing I know! If you continually improve you could be exceptional. Your hand, eye coordination is superb. Athletically you are exceptional. Two year's is 730 days away. You have a massive amount of time at your disposal."

Mick put his hand on Frank Junior's shoulder. Frank Jr turned to Mick soliciting advice. "Junior give it a go. If it doesn't work, it's not the end of the world!"

Frank Jr appreciated the advice. Junior signed up and would spend the next two years in basketball training. As he was opening the office door to leave, Donovan exclaimed, "Frank, what University are you aiming to go to?" Junior swivelled. "Duke University, Sir!" Donovan Bailey giggled as he eyeballed Junior. "Well, that's great, because if you do well here, and I am 100% that you will, when you apply to Duke, we will give you a testimonial." Frank Junior, with an inquisitive expression asked, "What's that for, Sir?"

"Frank Junior, it's like this. If we say you are great at basketball, you may get offered a grant, bursary, or most probably, a sports scholarship. Duke is a dominant, renowned, Sports University, so you will have a great chance."

Chapter 73

Junior Refuses the Chance

The following several days were intensive bonding fun. Visits to a Toronto Maple Leafs game against Boston Bruins, a trip up the CN Tower, including a walk on the glass floor, and an unbelievable day at Niagara Falls, where they chuckled at the sex motels, advertising water bed exclusive treatments. They then experienced torrents of water with a ride on the Maid of the Mist, under the Falls.

The end came all too quickly. All of them had sincere brotherly feelings for one another. Even Matthew and Frank felt they were part of this strong relationship.

Mickey and Mark, on their flight back to the UK, were joined by Jerome. They all swore they would return soon, as they disappeared into departures.

Frank Junior dedicated one evening every week to basketball. Within a year, he was selected to join the Toronto Raptors junior academy. Donovan Bailey delivered the invitation. The glint in Donovan's eyes spoke volumes. This was a chance in a lifetime for this young lad! A youngster that had already convinced Donovan he could make it into the big time.

Frank Junior's reaction did not mirror Donovan's glee. Junior bent forward in his chair, as he clasped his hands tight together. His eyes slowly lifted and peered into Donovan's.

Junior's strained expression gave Donovan an unexpected response. After a deafening silence, Donovan spluttered, "Junior, you are not going to refuse this chance?"

Junior's lips twitched! "Donovan, I don't have a choice!" Donovan interrupted, "but you could make the big time, your ability, your attitude, your work-rate! It's what you have been working for!"

"Donovan, no, it's not! I have been playing basketball because I love it. You convinced me it was a sport for me, and you were correct. But it's not my future. It will continue to be a pleasure in my life, but it's not who I am. It's not my future. It's not my destiny!"

"I can't explain what drives me to think like this, or why I can't change my mind. I have to finish my education and concentrate on getting results that get me to where I must be. I know I can't give every ounce of me to both basketball and my education. I would be a complete hypocrite to believe I could even attempt it. You have been a fabulous friend and mentor. But please accept my decision!"

Donovan inhaled sharply and then slowly began to smile. "Junior, I am astounded by you. I have never met a youngster with such an intellect and clear vision of what his future looks like. I am proud to know you, and your family! I am often quoted as saying something that I always hoped would help youngsters like you find their future, their destiny! The quote went something like, "Follow your passion, be prepared to work hard and sacrifice, and don't ever let anyone limit your dreams." So, I once described exactly what you are doing. I cannot, therefore, argue with your dreams. All I can do is to tell you I have complete and utter respect for you!"

Donovan leaned forward in his chair and embraced Junior, patting his back. Both now were smiling. This genuine understanding was heaven sent!

The next year seemed to pass in the blink of an eye. Frank Jr enjoyed local basketball every week, as his friendship with Donovan grew and became stronger. To the point of perfection! Junior had read every article, book and detail about Donovan's life and unbelievable achievements. Consequently, his thinking was often influenced by what he knew of Donovan Bailey's trials, tribulations and bravery.

Chapter 74

All Hope, No Fears!
Destiny Beckons

Junior's high school results were historic. His application to Duke University, Durham was not only accepted, but also underpinned by a scholarship. Anneliese and Matthew's lives continued, as normal, but their minds were in a good place due to Frank Junior's achievements.

Frank Junior had continued to see Hope fairly regularly. Like all young men, occasionally testosterone kidnapped his brain. But he always found a way to resist the temptation, and so sex had never become an issue.

However, now he only had a month before he was due to start his life in a different part of the world, Duke University, North Carolina, USA.

Junior phoned Hope and asked her over for dinner. Anneliese had prepared an Italian menu. Trying to be romantically helpful, she had arranged that Junior and Hope would be alone in the house, while Anneliese and Matthew would be visiting an Oakville trendy Chinese restaurant.

The table was dressed, just as girls like; beautiful napkins standing in wine glasses, candles and a bottle of Chianti Classico, alongside a white Chardonnay.

Hope arrived, and as Anneliese let her in, they embraced as she explained they were having dinner in Oakville. Matthew, smartly dressed, came down the stairs and Hope passed them like ships in the night. Frank Junior, standing in the hallway, gave Hope a loving cuddle and led her into the kitchen. Junior's eyes and mind were overcome by Hope's captivating beauty. But dinner was ready, and Anneliese had prepared Junior on his obligations.

They sat and chatted through a fabulous Italian risotto. The wine gradually, and sensually, smoothed their nerves. Dinner was at an end. Both stared longingly into each other's eyes. But Hope was the one that decided to take the bull by the horns. Music leads to romance, and so it did on this occasion. Hope serenely stood, slowly moved round the table and gently clasped Junior's cheeks. As her lips drew close, Junior snatched a quick kiss, stood, and took Hope's hand. "Let's go on the patio, I am feeling like I'm catching fire, so need some fresh air." Slipping on jackets, the music softened, as they stepped through the patio doors.

Junior took both Hope's hands in his. As he paused, Hope felt the gentle music leading the way to romance.

It was a crisp, clear night sky; a magnificent glowing face smiled down from the man in the moon. They became silently lost in the wonderland of stars, twinkling and shining down on them.

Hope, in a soft, peaceful voice tenderly whispered. "You make me feel like I am hanging, suspended among glistening jewels." Lowering her eyes to meet Junior's, he could almost hear her heart pounding.

Junior eased through this silence, intent on finding a way to explain, without causing heartache! "Hope, for years now we have been much more than friends. But I've, deliberately, avoided leading you beyond that friendship rainbow. That's because" … Hope put her fingers to his lips to stop him. She finished his sentence. "That's because you respect and care for me!"

Junior inhaled, then said, "Yes, that's true. I treasure you more than anything, and always will. But the truth is, I always knew I would eventually head away from you. University is only the first step. I know the path life will take me on. I will, at times, sail through black holes into universes where I cannot take you."

Hope's tender expression hardened. "So what are you saying, Junior? Are you trying to find an easy way to dump me?"

"No, never, Hope darling!" he exclaimed. Pulling her close, he uttered, "Please believe me. My heart and soul will never leave you. I will never forsake you, wherever my destiny takes me!"

After a long breathless pause, Hope's weeping eyes looked into his. She gently whispered, "I understand. I can sense you are hurting too! Junior, you will be in my dreams every night, and in my thoughts every day".... They kissed and stepped back into the house.

Next milestone, Duke University! He would make his mark there. Then he would begin to press his footprints into a world that had always beckoned to him.

❖

311

Frank Junior follows in Anneliese's footsteps. Appointed to EAI, the Western World security organisation, he enters the lethal, shadowy world of a far-right UK Government.

Their slogan....... "it's your duty to die!!!"